Garner, dressed in the red serape and the sombrero he'd taken off the bandido whose throat he'd slit, staggered drunkenly back around the rock, making sure to keep his head low and his face turned away from the others.

There were just three men left. Besides the former owner of the serape and hat, one had passed out—and Garner made sure he stayed that way. Another, who had the bad fortune to surprise Garner while he was seeing to the second fellow's ropes, lay dead beside his compatriot.

Of the remaining three, two were faced off with Quincannon—one standing and presently yelling for something else to shoot at, and the other one sat on his heels behind the firing line, slouched against a rock.

Judging from the pile of amber and green and clear shards that lay at Quincannon's feet, there must have been a whole stockpile of cobwebbed empties in the ruins. But they'd shot and good-timed their way through those, plus the bottles they'd brought with them. Aside from the quart of tequila the rat-bag beside the horses was nursing, there was only one pint bottle left. Now or never.

He picked it up, then staggered back into Blue Feather's line of vision. He stopped and swayed.

Garner held the bottle out to the side and wiggled it, signaling to Blue Feather to come get it.

He set the bottle out to the side and, still bent at the waist, leaned farther over. He eased up his hanging serape and looked between the inverted V of his legs. Blue Feather lurched toward him, sloshing his bottle, shouting gleeful obscenities as he came.

Just a little closer, Garner thought as sweat trickled into his eyes. . . .

Turn to the back of this book for a special preview of
Gunning for Regret,
available from Berkley Books in March 2000!

DUST
RIDERS

WOLF MACKENNA

BERKLEY BOOKS, NEW YORK

THE DUST RIDERS

A Berkley Book / published by arrangement with
the author

PRINTING HISTORY
Berkley edition / October 2000

The Penguin Putnam Inc. World Wide Web site address is
http://www.penguinputnam.com

ISBN: 0-425-17698-3

BERKLEY®
Berkley Books are published by The Berkley Publishing Group,
a division of Penguin Putnam Inc.,
375 Hudson Street, New York, New York 10014.
BERKLEY and the "B" design
are trademarks belonging to Penguin Putnam Inc.

PRINTED IN THE UNITED STATES OF AMERICA

10 9 8 7 6 5 4 3 2 1

1

"The box," the bandit demanded. A filthy bandanna covered half of his dust-caked face. It puffed and billowed with every heavily accented word.

Elliot Quincannon swallowed hard, or tried to. His mouth felt like cotton, his knees trembled, and it was a good bet that all the water in his body was going to exit it, via his trouser leg, at any given moment. He was only twenty-three, he thought dismally, and that was far too young to die. Only twenty-three and practically engaged to a fine, upstanding young woman—oh, Miss Minion, dearest Miss Minion!—whom, he was rapidly becoming convinced, he'd never, ever see again.

Quincannon didn't come from the best family or the best address in Boston, far from it, but at least it was Boston, by God! Right up until a few minutes ago, he'd been a young man on the rise. He was only a legal clerk with Peabody & Strauss, but he'd had aspirations!

"I no ask you again, *hombre*. What you got in there?"

the highwayman growled before he ripped the small crate from Quincannon's white and trembling fingers.

All Quincannon could manage was a thin, "Oh, dear." He was going to die in the middle of the godforsaken Arizona desert at the hands—the filthy hands!—of this masked, illiterate, unwashed knuckle-dragger.

Even if they allowed him and his fellow passengers to live, even if they just took whatever was in the bloody box and rode off politely, he was as good as ruined. Malcolm Peabody of Peabody & Strauss was not a man you fooled with, no sir, and Malcolm Peabody had himself—in person!—instructed Quincannon to deliver that box. And the man for whom it was intended was *not* this grimy, gun-toting criminal. A foreign criminal at that!

Before Quincannon could try to swallow again, the Mexican had ripped the lid off the little crate. He stared into it. *"Mierda!"* he breathed.

One of his companions, a fellow Quincannon had heard called Pacito—such droll names, these Mexicans, Quincannon thought, despite himself—stepped over from Quincannon's fellow passengers, whom he had been relieving of everything but their fillings. Pacito's eyes grew wide. *"¡No me jodas!"* he whispered, shuffling closer with his fistful of loot. *"¿Diamantes, Ramon? ¿Esmeraldas?"*

"Sí, Pacito, sí. Y oro," murmured the first bandit, who seemed to be named Ramon. Or Esmeralda. Quincannon's Spanish was the next thing to nonexistent. The bandit clamped his pistol under his arm and reached into the box, stroking its contents. *"¡Chingar!"* he said softly. *"Mas oro."*

Neither one of the bandits looked anywhere but into the box. If it hadn't been for their pistol-toting companion, perched on horseback a few yards out, Quincannon could have easily swatted away at least one of their guns. That was, if he hadn't been dry-mouthed and about to piss his trousers, and if his feet hadn't been frozen to the ground in absolute, dumbfounded shock and horror that a thing like this could happen to a man like him.

And then the first bandit looked up, right into his eyes. Although the bandanna covered the lower half of his face, Quincannon had the sinking feeling that the man's mouth had stretched into a wide grin. Probably toothless.

"Gracias, señor," the man called Ramon—or Esmeralda—said almost cordially, his makeshift mask shivering. He pulled the pistol from his armpit and swung its muzzle directly into Quincannon's face. Quincannon's feet might have been frozen in place, but he leaned away, gulping madly to no avail.

"Maybe we no kill you now," the bandit said. "Maybe we just kill this one."

And before Quincannon had time to register what was happening, the bandit's gun had swung to the side and discharged. Right into poor Mr. Trimble's chest. The shot knocked Trimble back a few feet, into the side of the coach that the Wells Fargo clerk had promised him was the safest, bar none. He heard the thud as Trimble hit the ground.

Quincannon's bladder emptied.

The bandit cocked his head, regarding the corpse. "A man like that, with only one dollar and fourteen cents American? He is better off dead. But you? You are the prosperous man, *señor*. I let you go out of the kindness of my heart. Maybe another time you travel through, and I rob you again, no?"

And then his gaze shifted to Quincannon's sodden pants. *"Señor*, you have pissed yourself."

Pacito laughed and Quincannon, despite everything—despite the dead man on the ground behind him, despite the fact that these baboons were about to carry away his future and the goodwill of Mr. Malcolm Peabody in their saddlebags—felt heat rising up his neck. Peabody had trusted his parcel to a man who couldn't even hold his water. Quincannon wanted to die. But not badly enough to say so.

While Pacito continued to laugh beside him, the bandit holstered his pistol and reached into the crate, shaking it off, along with a flurry of excelsior.

He held his prize high in the air.

The third bandit, the stage driver, Mr. Hoskins, and Quincannon all gasped in the same moment, as if they had been rehearsing for weeks.

"Muchas gracias," the bandit chief said again, and then he and Pacito leaped onto their horses. The three bandits galloped off into the wasteland. A cloud of dust billowed in their wake.

"Good Christ!" said Mr. Hoskins, the first words he'd spoken since the bandits stopped their coach fifteen minutes earlier. Fifteen minutes? Such a short time to kill one man and ruin another.

Quincannon was vaguely aware that the driver had climbed down from the box, and that he and Hoskins were attempting to revive Trimble. But he couldn't tear his eyes away from the roil of dust, lessening into the distance with each second.

The Iberian Chalice. That was what had been in the box. That had been what Malcolm Peabody had entrusted him to carry across a continent. What could he have been thinking!

Behind him, the other two men were slowly rising from Trimble's body, dusting their knees. Quincannon could have told them he was dead. He heartily wished he could trade places with Trimble. It would be comforting to be lying there still and dead, or perhaps in the gentle arms of Jesus. A greater comfort still.

He imagined the Christ touching his forehead and saying, "There, there, Elliot. It wasn't your fault, not a bit. Now help yourself to the ambrosia and pearls, and I'll go put in a good word with My Father."

Trimble was the lucky one.

Hoskins was beside him. "What the hell was that thing, anyhow?" he asked. "Some kind of a rigged-out goblet?"

"Some kind," Quincannon answered dully. The bandits had disappeared into the low hills. He could no longer see their dust.

"Was them real diamonds on it?" said a gruffer voice. The stage driver.

Quincannon nodded.

"Never seen the like!"

Hoskins huffed, "What kind of a damn-fool idiot carries that sorta thing on a goddamned stagecoach? And with no guards? Good God, man, you don't even have a gun!"

It was true.

It was also true that Hoskins and the stage driver didn't have any guns, either, at least not anymore. The bandits had relieved the driver of his shotgun, and Hoskins of a hip gun, two derringers, and a boot blade. Judging by his mode of dress—dandified, with a brocade vest and string tie—and lack of a sample kit, and also the fact that he'd amused himself during the stage ride by playing one-handed poker on the empty seat beside him, Quincannon was fairly certain Mr. Hoskins was a professional gambler, and therefore not at all to be trusted.

Quincannon said, "I didn't know I was carrying it."

This was also true. He'd been under strict orders not to look in the crate. He was simply instructed to keep it on his person at all times, taking reasonable care with it, and to see it delivered, unharmed and intact, into the hands of one Mr. Antonio Vargas. Mr. Vargas would be meeting him in Tucson.

"Drat the luck," didn't quite cover it.

He looked out over the endless stretch of nothing that was the Arizona Territory. The dusty excuse for a town from which they'd come—just the stage stop and three other buildings, two of which had been little more than shacks—was roughly ten miles to the north. He could see absolutely no signs of human life, not even the relative comfort of the color green, only this low, brittle, sparse vegetation.

That, and rocks. Big rocks, little rocks, rocks the size of freight cars.

He hadn't realized what a comfort a little green would be in a situation like this. He longed for the sight of just one shade tree in full leaf. He would have hugged it.

But there was nothing, nothing. He croaked, "What do we do now?"

The stage driver spat on the road, such as it was, and said, "We wait. When them rascals chased our team off, they was headed straight for the next town. That'd be Rusty Bucket."

"How quaint," Quincannon muttered beneath his breath. Oh, to die in Rusty Bucket.

"Reckon they'll send somebody lookin' for us before too long," the driver went on, oblivious. "By cracky, son, that was some kinda beer mug you had! All gold and bejeweled! How much you reckon a thing like that's worth?"

"My life," Quincannon said miserably.

They moved the late Mr. Trimble's body, leaving it to rest in a pool of shade on the other side of the coach, and then there was nothing to do but wait. Mr. Hoskins and the driver, who introduced himself as Bumpy Stimson, perched inside the coach with the doors open, engaged in endless hands of five-card draw, playing for matches or sticks or whatever was handy.

Quincannon sat alone, his back against a coach wheel, intermittently shooing the flies from Trimble's still face with his handkerchief. Had Trimble been married? Had he had children?

Trimble had been a worried, fretful little man, but he looked somehow younger in death than he had in life. The lines around his eyes had eased. The tension that had showed in his forehead had gone. Trimble had no more problems.

Quincannon's, however, were just beginning. Now that they were out of immediate danger, now that his pants had dried and the bandits had gone, the full measure of this catastrophe came clear to him.

He was ruined at Peabody & Strauss, ruined! And once word got out, no one in Boston would hire him for the rest of his natural life. Not even if he finished his degree and passed the bar with flying colors. Not even if he passed it while simultaneously standing on his head and whistling "The Star-Spangled Banner" whilst juggling three axes.

And Miss Minion? She'd be a thing of the past, too. They were keeping company, although he hadn't asked for her hand as yet. But twice they'd lingered in front of the display window at O'Malley's Jewelry Salon.

He had hopes that soon he would be given permission to call her Gwendolyn. Perhaps, in time, she would break down and call him Elliot. Dear Miss Minion with her plain, pink face and her little gold-rimmed glasses, her quiet, humble ways and her small inheritance. His career was all she ever talked about.

His future.

He had none.

He felt the scandal gathering about his head like a swarm of angry black beetles, and for the first time he was actually glad that his parents were dead. If they'd been alive, the disgrace would have killed them.

And he was ashamed, deeply, personally ashamed. Not only had he let Malcolm Peabody down in the most horrid way possible, but he had acted like a spineless dolt. He hadn't said a single word of protest, not even, "Please, sir, don't take it."

He'd just stood there, practically as mute as a fence post, and let those ruffians rob him and wave their pistols around and actually kill Mr. Trimble, and his only rebellious act had been to wet his pants like an infant.

He cringed.

What on earth had Malcolm Peabody been thinking to send a lone, unguarded, unarmed employee roughly two thousand miles over dangerous terrain with the fabled Iberian Chalice? An employee who didn't even know what he was carrying!

The Chalice was priceless. Men had spent their entire lives in search of it, died for it. He'd overheard Peabody brag to a business associate that Lloyd's of London insured it for a million dollars, but Quincannon was certain that even that lofty sum wouldn't be sufficient recompense.

Of course, he had never actually seen the Chalice, not until today. Peabody had kept it in his vault at home, or perhaps somewhere else, somewhere even safer. No one knew. In any case, it was most certainly secreted in a location to which lowly legal clerks were never invited. But just that one glimpse of it, sparkling in the sun as the bandit raised it, had been enough.

The Chalice was centuries old, as old as the Crusades. Made of the purest gold and liberally studded with a cross of diamonds and emeralds on one side and another of rubies and pearls on the other, it had been a gift—more likely, a bribe—given to the Knights Templar by some forgotten mogul. It had been in Peabody's family for four generations, Peabody was fond of saying, and only the Lord knew who else's for generations before that, hidden away in dusty vaults, pulled out only on high occasions.

One of which, apparently, was the entrance of armed Mexican bandits upon the scene.

Quincannon pillowed his face in his hands. He felt tears pushing at his eyes, but he vowed he wouldn't cry. Oh, that would be the topper, wouldn't it? "Did you hear about that clerk, somebody-or-other Quincannon?" they'd say. "Lost Old Man Peabody's priceless relic, then wet his pants and bawled like a baby!"

And not just at Peabody & Strauss, not even just in Boston. That little nugget of news would make its way up and down the entire eastern seaboard.

He had to do something. He had to redeem himself somehow.

Slowly, he lifted his head. He *could* do something. He

could stop feeling sorry for himself, for one thing. He could act like a man. He could face up to it. He'd wire Peabody from the next pigsty of a town, and then he would go after the Chalice.

A western saddle wasn't so different from the sort he was accustomed to, after all, and he supposed any idiot could learn to shoot. Any idiot? Well, that was certainly him. The idea of actually leveling a firearm at another human gave him a qualm, but a quick glance over at the late Mr. Trimble steeled him anew.

Quincannon had a little more than two hundred dollars hidden in his shoes, money the bandits hadn't even dreamed of looking for. He might have been a coward and a wet-legged buffoon, but he was no fool, at least not where money was concerned.

He'd have to wire Peabody, of course.

His stomach turned over just thinking about it. What could you say to a man like Malcolm Peabody when you'd surely ruined him? But he would send the wire. If he was nothing else, Quincannon was honest to a fault. And then he would put the law on alert. Surely they would have some sort of constabulary in the next town, wouldn't they?

He'd outfit himself with a horse and whatever else was necessary. He supposed it would entail sleeping on the ground for a few nights, but he'd ride with the posse just the same. He would buy a pistol and learn to use it, or at least give a reasonable facsimile thereof.

He would get Peabody's Chalice back—and he would see those filthy bandits punished—if it killed him.

2

King Garner sat at the rear table of the Glad Times Saloon—chair rocked back on two legs, his back against the wall. He was a large man, over six-foot-two in his stockinged feet, six-four in his boots. Dark-haired, clean-shaven, broad-shouldered, and still lean of hip in his forties, there was a dangerous gleam to his dark blue eyes and the tilt of his stained Stetson.

"Two cards," he said leerily to the man to his right, Lemuel Pike. He never should have let Pike talk him into a game of cards.

Pike was a little weasel of an old man, as crazy as they came and twitchy to boot, but there was a craftiness underlying the crazy. Pike had latched onto him about two years back, and Garner had gotten used to having him around. He was company, and he was decent with a skillet. Garner freely admitted that anything was better than eating his own cooking.

Pike dealt him the pasteboards, then turned to the third man at the table. Brinks was his name, he'd said, and he appeared to be just another drifter, as were Garner and Pike.

"I'll stand pat," Brinks said.

"Three for me," cackled Pike, and took them. The sparse, grimy fringe on his sleeves shivered with the movement.

Garner glanced at his cards. Solid trash. *Never try to fill an inside straight, you horse's ass,* he told himself for the thousandth time. He'd never learn. He put his cards facedown on the table.

"Fold."

The bet went to Brinks, then Pike, then back to Brinks. "Call," Brinks said.

With a cackle, Pike spread his hand on the scarred table. A full house, deuces and sevens.

Brinks stared at the cards, his face darkening. "Cheat," he said, then put his own hand on the table. Three sevens. That made them just a tad too heavy on the sevens, especially since Garner knew there was another one in the hand full of nothing that he'd discarded.

"Hold on there, mister," he said, but Brinks was already shoving his chair back. Already pulling his gun.

Pike just sat there, grinning and blinking at him. As always.

Garner stood up. Before Brinks had a chance to fire, before Garner heard his chair topple and crash behind him, he had shot Brinks square through the wrist.

Brinks shrieked and his gun went flying. It put a dent in the bar front. "Dammit! Goddammit!" He cradled his bleeding wrist to his chest.

"Shut up," Garner hissed at Pike, who was laughing as he gathered the pot. It was all of four dollars. To the wounded Brinks, who was now doubled over and moaning, he said, "Hurts, doesn't it? Don't you know you shouldn't go wavin' guns around?"

Brinks snarled something at him. Blood was slowly pooling on the floor.

"Better get yourself to the doc's," Garner offered. He grabbed Pike's collar and pulled him to his feet, then leaned over and flipped Pike's winning hand facedown. "You badger's butt," he hissed at the smaller man, and pocketed the three offending cards. "Get goin'."

"C'mon, buddy," the bartender said. He'd come out onto the floor and was grudgingly helping Brinks toward the sidewalk. To Garner, said, "Ain't got no doc, sir, but we got a barber what's good at patching folks up." Then, to Brinks, he hissed, "What'd you want to go and draw for? Why'd you want to go and draw on a friend of King Garner's?"

Beneath the barkeep's arm, Brinks came to a sudden stop. He craned his head around, took a long look at Garner, and went dead white. "I'm s-sorry, Mr. Garner," he said. "It was a . . . a misunderstandin'. Hope you don't hold no hard feelin's."

Garner sighed. "Just get that wrist looked at."

"Pike, you've got to cut it out," Garner said, not for the last time and certainly not for the first. "You're no good at it, for one thing. What are you gonna do if someday I'm not there to haul your backside out of trouble?"

Pike leaned against the fence. They had walked down to the livery, and were standing in front of the corral. It was dusk, and the sky had turned pink and purple and gunmetal gray.

"Ain't no good sayin' 'what-ifs,' King. You was there today. And ain't no use tellin' me to quit. It's like a whatyacall. A compulsive. I gets in a game, and I just got to do it!"

Pike probably had fifteen or twenty years on him, and every single second of it showed on his craggy face. Once a card cheat, always a card cheat, that's what Garner's daddy used to say. That was, right up until the day they hanged him for stealing a mangy horse. It had been quite literally mangy, with large, hairless, scabby sores and maggots burrowing into its backside and every kind of vermin known to God and man on its mud and manure-caked

hide. The only reason his daddy had got caught was that
the damned plug had up and died while he was leading it
away.

Lemuel Pike sort of reminded him of his daddy. A good
campfire cook and pretty fair company, but bad luck, anyway you looked at it.

Garner never knew when to let go.

He reached into his pocket and pulled out the three
cards he'd taken from the table. He handed them to Pike
and, sighing, said, "Next time, at least try to match up the
decks."

Pike hesitated, the cards halfway to his pocket. "What
you mean?"

"Those are green on the back. The deck we were playin'
with was red. Beats me how you've lived this long."

Pike looked at the cards for a moment, then stuck them
in his pocket, shrugging. "Green, red, what's the difference? A feller can't help it if he's color-blind, King."

"And stop stockpiling sevens and sixes. Jesus! If you've
got to cheat, at least think big. Jacks or queens or somethin'!"

"Aw, ever'body does queens. That the stage?" Pike
asked, effectively changing the subject.

Garner followed Pike's gaze to the approaching roil of
dust and squinted into the gathering darkness. "Wonder if
anybody's still alive," he said flatly.

Every man in town had heard about the team, minus
the coach and its passengers, having pounded into the livery earlier that afternoon. Old Man Crowley over at the
Wells Fargo office had started a pool, and Garner had wa-
gered a dollar on a total massacre.

The stage, accompanied by four riders, rolled past Garner and Pike and came to a halt halfway up the street.

"Can you see? Is anybody still alive?" Pike asked. Pike
had laid two bits that they'd killed all the passengers, but
let the driver live. Pike was the eternal optimist.

Garner stood up. "Too dark to see." He started ambling

up the road. Pike followed on his heels like a slab-sided pup.

"Why don't we go down to Tucson, King?" Pike said.

"You know why." Garner saw the driver jump down. He was out of luck so far as the pool went, but maybe Pike was still in the running.

"Aw, King, you ain't never gonna find that dang horse'a yours!" Pike insisted. "I liked ol' Red, too, but it's been nigh on six months! You can get another one! Hell, Sanchez and his outfit is prob'ly somewhere in Sonora by now. Whatcha say to Tucson? Or we might maybe head up to Flag, now that the summer wets are comin'. I know a woman in Flag."

"You lose your quarter, Pike," said Garner, who was only half listening. The coach's door had opened and two men climbed out. No, scratch that, two live men and one who was well past a state of decline.

The body was borne across the street to the undertaker's, its backside banging the road with every step the bearers took. For a minute Garner's attention was captured by this spectacle, and he felt just a little indignant on the corpse's behalf. But then he became aware of raised and angry voices over by the coach.

"Well, where is the next town?" a young voice demanded. "That is to say, where's the nearest law?"

That he was far too young was the first thing Garner noticed. Maybe not in years, but in attitude: at least, the attitude he was currently exhibiting. He had short, sandy hair and was skinny and tall, maybe six feet, and he was dressed in a dusty back-east suit, topped off by a silly little bowler hat: a big-city scarecrow.

One of the men who'd ridden out to retrieve the coach said something that Garner didn't quite catch, and the boy suddenly took off his bowler and threw it down to the ground. "No!" he barked. "I will not accept that answer!"

"Tad's fulla piss an' vinegar, ain't he?" Pike muttered.

"Much more'a that horseshit and he'll be full of lead," Garner replied.

They were all the way up to the coach by then, and while the young man continued to rant and rave, Garner tapped one of the bystanders on the shoulder. When he turned around, Garner recognized him as the other live occupant of the coach. "What happened?"

The fellow, who appeared too slick to be either a townie or a rancher, said, "Got held up. Mex bandits. Cleaned me out of a hundred and twenty-some dollars. My stake money."

He didn't seem too upset. Right off, Garner pegged him for a gambler, probably one with plenty of extra cash sewn into the lining of his jacket, maybe his vest. He said, "Catch any names?"

The gambler studied on this for ten or fifteen seconds. "A little cockroach named Pacito. And there was a nasty bastard called Ramon," he said finally.

Garner stiffened. "This Ramon. Was he riding a big sorrel horse, two white socks behind and a bald face?"

The gambler cocked his head. "I believe you're right."

Beside Garner, Pike swept off his hat and slapped his thigh in disgust. A billow of dust rose up. "Aw, crud!" he wailed. "Here we go again!"

Garner paid him little mind. He said, "Name's Garner. What's yours?"

"Hoskins. Frank Hoskins." He reached into his pocket, pulled out a pack of ready-made cigarettes, and tipped it toward Garner.

"No thanks," he replied, and they both jumped back a foot to accommodate the sprawling body of Hoskins's loudmouthed companion, who had just got himself punched in the jaw and laid out flat. Garner looked down at the dazed boy, who was trying to shake his head. "Friend of yours?"

"Hey, cut that out!" shouted Pike, who had already bent over the lad. "Can't you see he ain't equipped?" Pike always was a sucker for the underdog, and if ever there was an underdog, this boy was it.

Hoskins struck a match. "Nope," he said around the cigarette he was lighting. "Just on the stage. Name's Elliot Quincannon, or so he says, and he's gotta be a couple cards short of a deck. What kind of a lamebrained fool would carry a thing like that around with him?"

"Like what?"

"Like that gold cup he had on him," Hoskins replied wearily, as if he'd heard that cup discussed so much his ears were blue. "Those Mex boys made off with it in a heartbeat."

Pike had the boy sitting up by then, and most of the men had wandered away or gone inside the stage office. Hoskins tipped his hat. "Reckon I'll be off before he starts yammerin' again."

He made his way down toward the saloon, and had gone half a block before he stopped and turned around. "You say your name was Garner?" he called.

Garner nodded.

"Would that be King Garner?"

Warily, Garner said, "Yeah."

But Hoskins only shook his head and grinned. "I'll be double damned," he said, and then went on his way.

"That's the way, boy," Pike said. He'd managed to get Quincannon up to his feet, and currently had him braced against the overhang's post. "You're gonna be all right. Just keep that lip a'yours buttoned in the future."

"What kind of a town is this?" Quincannon moaned dismally, to no one in particular. "No sheriff, no telegraph?" Gingerly, he felt his jaw and winced. "What am I going to do?"

Garner was damned if he knew. And frankly, he didn't much care. He said, "C'mon, Pike. I want to backtrack the stage and get on their trail."

"Backtrack whose trail?" They suddenly had Quincannon's attention, although neither of them paid him any mind.

"Oh, sure, King, that's right," Pike said, making no attempt to move from beneath Quincannon's arm. "You just go an' find 'em inside this black bitch of a night. Ain't no tracker that good, not even you."

"Whose trail?" said Quincannon, a little more urgently. "Am I correct in assuming that you gentlemen are going after those brigands who robbed the stage?"

"Aw, hell," Garner muttered. Pike was right. The sun was nearly down, and the moon was little more than a sliver. Nobody'd be finding anybody until first light.

"Gentlemen?" said Quincannon indignantly. "Are you listening to me?"

"Well, gimme a hand, King!" growled Pike. "This here boy's heavier than he looks!"

"No," Garner said for the seventh or eighth time. He'd lost count. Quincannon was desperate, but nothing could convince him to haul the kid along, not even the promised reward, which, during the course of the conversation, had blossomed from fifty dollars to a thousand. Now, where would a kid like that lay his hands on a thousand dollars?

"Look at you!" he boomed. "You're so green you're practically sproutin' willow twigs out your ears! Son, you wouldn't last five minutes on the trail."

Quincannon opened his mouth again in one last desperate attempt, but before he could get any sound out, Garner said, "And don't go tellin' me one more time how you can ride—sort of—and you can learn to shoot—you think. I don't want to hear it."

With that, he shoved back his chair and went upstairs, leaving Pike to deal with the boy.

In his room, he peeled off his gunbelt and hung it on the headboard, the butt end of one Colt dangling within easy grabbing distance. He tossed his hat atop the bedpost. With a satisfying crunch, he ground his heel down on a black widow that had the bad fortune to crawl from under the chifforobe's bottom, and then he stretched out on the bed's thin coverlet, fully clothed. He wanted to make as early a start as possible in the morning.

But after fifteen minutes, sleep hadn't come. He sat up and lit the lamp, then rolled himself a smoke and leaned back against the headboard. And for one blessed moment, he was not in that crumbling hotel room above the Glad Times Saloon. He was sitting on the front porch of a little ranch, staring out over acres and acres of prime grazing land that was dotted with horses. Beautiful horses. Fat, shiny mares and gamboling foals.

But it only lasted a moment, and he sighed, cursing the darkness that kept him from Sanchez, kept him from Red.

He was so damn close, and that bastard still had his horse. At least the sonofabitch knew a decent mount when he rode one. At least he hadn't traded him or shot him or sold him off. And they were out there right now, probably crowing over the gold thingamajig they'd taken off the kid. And his horse, his Red, was tied to their picket line.

The years had mellowed Garner. He wasn't the hothead he'd been at twenty, or the harsh dealer of justice he'd been at thirty. He was edging forty-five these days, and he just wanted to be left alone. But then that goddamned Ramon Sanchez had made off with Red. And with him, he had made off with Garner's future.

Red wasn't just any horse. He was fifteen hands of half-English Thoroughbred and half good Texas cow pony, and at the quarter mile he could leave any other equine in the territory choking on his dust.

He had cow sense, too, and Garner had brought him along slow on the mavericks they ran across on the plain. No rope-'em-and-throw-'em breaking for Red, no sir, not this horse. Just bring him along slow, ease him into it. And Garner had eased him into quite a horse.

Red reined like a dream. He was easy-gaited, a treat to

the eye, a good horse to rope off, and steady to shoot off, too. Most studs were real knotheads whether there happened to be a mare around or not, but Red was calm, a real "using" horse of the first water. He knew when a mare was ready and willing, and didn't make much fuss until the time was right. Of course, then it was Katie bar the door.

Once, down in Tucson, he'd mounted a nice little Appaloosa mare right out on the main street. Garner chuckled, remembering. At the time her rider hadn't much appreciated it, although he probably did now. Probably had himself a real nice two-year-old colt or filly out of it.

But Red was older now, and more settled. Garner had planned to find himself a patch of good grazing land up north, planned to parlay that red stallion into a whole line of fast, smart, good-looking horses.

But then along came Sanchez. The sonofabitch had swiped Red out of a livery corral down in Tombstone while Garner had been in jail for having the gall to wear his gun in town. Garner had been on his trail ever since. It didn't help, though, that Sanchez had the advantage of a four-day lead. The next time he saw that upstart marshal, Virgil Earp, he was going to nail him to a barn door. You would have thought he'd understand about a man's gun, and especially a man's horse!

He heard the door creak, and found his Colt. He relaxed, though, when he saw the decidedly female silhouette framed in the doorway.

"Don't shoot, sugar," Lola said, her voice teasing.

He let the pistol slid back into its holster. She came in and closed the door behind her.

Rusty Bucket wasn't much of a town at all. No sheriff and no telegraph, as that pip-squeak Quincannon had pointed out a number of times. But it sure as hell had the best-looking whore for thirty miles in any direction. A fairly talented one, too, as he'd discovered the previous night.

"Want some company?" she purred, drawing nearer to the bed.

"Sure," he said, after a slight hesitation, and stubbed out his smoke. What the hell. He wasn't going anywhere until dawn.

3

Elliot Quincannon woke at sunrise, just in time to watch Garner and Pike ride out of town without him. He had expected as much. Mr. Garner had made it perfectly clear that he didn't want a thing to do with greenhorns in general or Quincannon in particular.

This made absolutely no sense to Quincannon. They were both tracking the same miscreants, weren't they? And his Chalice—well, Malcolm Peabody's Chalice—was certainly a theft of far greater magnitude than Garner's stupid horse!

But when Elliot Quincannon made his mind up to do something, it got done, by God! Garner was going to take him along whether he liked it or not.

He rose and dressed hurriedly, then wrote out a letter, to be delivered to the nearest marshal's office, and a telegram which he took to the stage office, with instructions that it be carried to the nearest railhead and wired to Malcolm Peabody immediately.

He then took himself to the livery, where he woke the stable attendant. He purchased the gentlest horse they had— guaranteed personally by the stableman—plus a saddle and blanket and a bridle and halter for the grand sum of forty-three dollars.

The man at the livery, doubtless feeling a little guilty, pressed a pair of hobbles on him as an afterthought. When Quincannon held them up as if they might bite him, the stableman said, "Those is for when you camp at night. So your horse don't run off."

On the rare occasions when he had ridden, someone else had always led the horse away and done something or other with it, and frankly, he didn't see how this little leather contraption could hold a fifteen-hundred-pound animal who had other ideas.

Still, he did the polite thing and thanked the stableman.

Next, he led his new horse up the street to the general store and banged on the door until the sleepy owner woke up and let him in. He purchased clothing better suited to cantering across the open range: sturdy denim trousers, two cotton shirts, two neckerchiefs, and a hat. He stared in the store's wavy mirror, and decided he looked utterly ridiculous.

Still, there were boots to buy, and socks. The store owner, still in his nightshirt and robe, insisted he'd need a long duster, despite the warm weather. "Never know when they's gonna be a downpour, son," he'd said, and pulled a stiff, white garment from the stock and added it to Quincannon's growing pile.

Next came a cheap, nickel-plated watch to replace the good silver one the bandits had stolen. He chose a pretty pearl-handled pocketknife from the display case. A canteen, saddlebags, foodstuffs, matches, ammunition, a used Colt pistol and holster, two thin blankets, and a rope rounded out his purchases.

"What do I need a rope for?" he asked. He was dizzy from all the things this man said he had to have. The scoundrel was clearly taking advantage of him!

Quincannon's skepticism must have showed, because the storekeeper said, "Fine, you don't need it. But if you has to haul your horse out of a wash or drag a pal up over a cliff, don't come cryin' to me."

Quincannon took the rope.

"You want canvas water bags? Didn't say how far you was goin'."

Quincannon thought on this. "I believe the canteen will be sufficient."

The man shrugged and added up the bill.

His pistol heavy on his hip, his saddlebags packed—with a bit of help from the storekeeper—and ready to ride, Quincannon clambered gracelessly up onto his horse, a rather unkempt-looking strawberry roan mare with a roached mane. He checked his watch, and saw with satisfaction that it was just seven.

He would go to the place where the bandits had stopped the coach, then follow their tracks across the desert. They should be easy to follow, for not only would there be the imprints of the three highwaymen, but of Pike and Garner's horses as well. He would catch up with them, and they would have to let him accompany them. It was that simple.

"Let's go, Rosie!" he announced to the elderly mare beneath him.

There was no response.

"Walk on!" he commanded, bringing home the point with a squeeze of his knees. Nothing. In exasperation, he kicked her. Her only reply was a long, soft snort.

"Swat her," suggested the storekeeper, who was leaning in the doorway, eating peaches from a tin.

Quincannon gave the mare's neck a smart slap with the reins. Nothing.

"Aw, Jesus," said the man, obviously disgusted. He set down his peaches and walked out, licking his fingers. "Not like that. Like this."

He raised one hand over the mare's freckled rump and brought it down with a resounding *crack*!

Quincannon didn't regain his seat—or his left stirrup—until he was nearly a mile up the road.

Garner rose from his squat and dusted cold ashes from his hands. "Sure didn't make much distance before they camped for the night." A campfire had been kicked out. Three horses had been picketed nearby.

"Aw, they probably knowed there weren't no law for miles an' miles," Pike pronounced from atop his horse. He took a swallow from his canteen, then gazed up at the sun. "I'm gettin' mighty hungry."

Garner glanced up, too. "You're always hungry. And it isn't noon yet."

Pike twisted his mouth. "Don't you go gettin' that look with me, King. Old Millie needs her a rest, and I do, too." Having said his piece, he dismounted.

"Fine," said Garner, who knew better than to try to change Pike's mind when it came to food. And he was right. The horses could use a rest. "But just jerky. And no more than a few minutes," he added. "Those boys aren't far off. I can smell 'em."

"Aw, you're just smelling the beans what got kicked into their fire," Pike said. His sweat-stained back was turned toward Garner. He dribbled part of the contents of a water bag into his hat, then carefully offered it to his chestnut mare. "Now, don't you go spillin' none'a that, Millie," he muttered.

Garner followed suit. He watered his gelding, a well-muscled copper bay he called Faro. He had to admit that Faro was a damn fine mount, although he fell far short of Red. He hadn't yet met a horse that came close.

Garner took a drink for himself, all the while staring at the horizon. Today, maybe tomorrow, he'd have Red back if the Good Lord was willing. It was about time the Lord willed something in his favor. Not that he had any favors coming.

He found a piece of jerky and began to chew on it. He

grimaced. "You got goat meat again," he said in disgust. "How many times I got to tell you, I don't like goat meat?"

Behind him, Pike said, "Was all they had what was jerked. You don't like 'er, you can take 'er back."

Garner growled, but he kept eating.

They had kept up an easy jog for most of the morning, having stopped twice before to give the horses a breather, and had made fair time. The way he saw it, Ramon Sanchez and his buddies were probably five, maybe six hours ahead. They'd have no reason to suspect anyone was following them. Like Pike had said, there was no law in these parts.

That was a good thing, as far as Garner was concerned. He was going to see to it that Red was the last horse—or anything else—those mangy coyotes ever stole. He didn't need or want any tin badge interfering with his little necktie party.

He'd been the law, once. For seven long years he'd lived behind a badge. Before that, he'd been a hotheaded fast-draw artist, with more notches on the butt of his Colt than he cared to remember.

Then one day, the citizenry of Medicine Rock, Arizona, had talked him into pinning on a star when they grew weary of Greeley Fox and his boys riding in and ripping up the place every six months. He'd taken it, not because he was overly inclined toward law and order, but because he had an old grudge against Greeley Fox. But by the time he'd taken care of Greeley, he'd got to liking the power of that little piece of tin. People did what you told them to, by God.

But the years had gone by, and folks of Medicine Rock forgot what it had been like when Greeley Fox was around to give them grief. They wanted a new sheriff, a shiny politician in a pressed suit and a sharp-creased hat and polished boots. Garner knew when it was time to quit. He had.

Eight months later, he'd had a good belly laugh when the word finally trickled down to Bisbee that the Farley

brothers had ridden into Medicine Rock and shot the place
up. Robbed the bank to boot. And one of their bullets had
landed square in the skull of that fancy new sheriff. Probably ruined his suit, too.

But old habits were hard to break. Once he'd finished
laughing, he'd got on his horse and tracked down the Farley brothers, and packed the bodies into Medicine Rock
over the backs of their mounts. They were pretty ripe by
the time he brought them in, but he didn't much care.

He'd led those horses right up to the front of the jail.
He'd tossed the reins over the rail and the money bags at
the feet of the blustering, red-faced mayor and two city
councilmen. And then he'd turned his horse around and
jogged straight out of town without ever once speaking a
word.

He supposed that this one incident, more than his wild
years, more than Greeley Fox, more than anything, had made
his reputation. Sometimes he wished that after he'd laughed,
he'd just gone and had a whore instead. They had some
good ones in Bisbee. There was this little redheaded gal in
particular, who had a mole in the shape of the state of—

"King!" hissed Pike, breaking into his thoughts like a
sledgehammer. So much for the redheaded gal.

"Yeah."

"King, there's a rider comin' in. Looks sorta wobblety."

He turned and followed Pike's gaze back along their
trail. There was a horse coming, all right. A rider in a too-
big hat clung to the horn, and he was swaying in the saddle like a falling-down drunk. His mount appeared to be
in distress, too. It was stumbling every third or fourth step,
and its head hung so low that it was practically on the
ground.

"Want I should pick him off?" Pike offered hopefully.
"Could be them bandidos, tryin' to trick us."

"Just hold on," Garner said. He continued to watch the
rider.

Not two minutes later, the horse came to a stop less that

fifty yards out. The rider sat motionless for a moment, then slowly toppled from the saddle. He crumpled to the ground on the roan's off side, with his foot still stuck through the stirrup.

"He's caught up," announced Pike, who had been watching, too. He shook his head thoughtfully. "Wrong side. That ain't good."

The boy had landed on the horse's right, not the usual side for mounting and dismounting. Any horse was liable to kick his brains out, dragging on the stirrup like that.

Any horse except this one, it seemed. It looked more likely to fall on him. Still, if it spooked or just started ambling, the rider could be in a fix.

"Swing out and walk up to the left," Garner said. "I'll go to the right."

"I could shoot that plug from here, King."

"You're sure gun-happy this morning," Garner replied dryly. "'Sides, it might go down on that fella." He was already walking, the brittle vegetation scraping at his britches and boots.

Pike sighed. "Reckon you got a point."

As it happened, the horse did not move an inch. Pike knelt to the rider directly and freed his boot from the stirrup. Garner saw to the horse. She was old and tired, and so parched that her tongue was beginning to swell and the corners of her lips were cracking.

He checked for water bags and found none. He checked the canteen. It was dry. There was still a price tag on it. All of a sudden he had a very bad feeling.

"King?" said Pike from the other side of the roan. "King, you ain't gonna believe—"

He didn't need to look. "It's that idiot, Quincannon," he said with a groan.

"By gum! How'd you know that?" When Garner didn't answer, Pike continued, "Well, yessiree Bob, it's him, all right, and he's fixin' to dry up an' blow away. Got one lip split and another on the way. Hand me down some water."

But Garner was already making a direct path back to
their horses. Of all the fool moves! What was wrong with
this idiot, Quincannon, anyway? Had his mama dropped
him on his head? If she hadn't, Garner was going to, that
was for damn sure!

He reached Faro and Millie, pulled down one of Faro's
water bags, and started back. None of this was that poor
old nag's fault. Quincannon might want to go and kill himself on the desert, but he didn't have any right to take the
mare down with him.

He came to a halt in front of the roan and poured a few
fingers of water into his hat. He offered it to her and she
drank greedily, nipping at the bowl of his inverted Stetson
when she'd drained it.

"Not yet, old gal," he murmured, stroking her neck.
"Wait a bit. There's plenty."

Pike was standing a few feet away, arms crossed. "If'n
it wouldn't be a whole lot of bother, you s'pose I could
have some for the boy?"

"Five minutes ago you wanted to shoot him *and* his
horse."

"That was five minutes ago. You seen to one, King.
Now let me see to the other."

Garner scowled at him, but he tossed over the water
bag.

Quincannon came slowly to consciousness beneath a very
low—and very unstable—ceiling. He blinked, and realized
it was a blanket flapping the wind, an ugly brown blanket
that someone had set up on sticks to shield him from the
sun. Another blink, and it all rushed back in on him: the
Iberian Chalice, Garner and Pike, and the reason he'd ridden out here on this fool's errand.

"I must have been mad," he croaked, and slowly sat
halfway up, bracing himself on one elbow. His eyelids felt
like there was sand grating beneath them.

"Don't know about mad," said a voice from behind him,

"but it sure as hell was a blamed-fool stunt." He twisted his head to find Pike, who handed him a full canteen. "You'd best drink some more. And don't go smilin' just yet. I put some salve on it, but that lip a'yourn is split pretty deep."

Quincannon took the canteen and gingerly lifted it to his mouth. To think that warm water could taste so sweet! He had downed half the canteen before Pike wrested it from him, muttering, "Goldang it! I already put near a quarter bag down your throat!"

But Quincannon was still desperately thirsty. He grabbed for the canteen again. Pike slapped his hand away. "You just whoa up there, boy! Don't want you takin' sick and pukin' it back up."

He watched as Pike set the canteen out of reach. He put his fingers to his throbbing lip. It stung when he touched it.

Pike snapped, "Don't mess with that," and he took his fingers away.

"Where's Mr. Garner?" he asked, and was surprised when his voice still came out in a rasp.

"Nursemaidin' that mare a'yours," Pike said. He rose and began to take down the blanket. It fell over Quincannon's head in a brown flutter, but Pike didn't seem to care. He just snatched it up again and rolled it into a tight little bundle.

"What the hell was you thinkin', boy, ridin' all this way with just one canteen of water?"

"Is my horse all right?" Quincannon asked weakly, bypassing the canteen question. Actually, he'd been in such a rush to get after Garner and Pike that he'd completely forgotten to fill it. He thought it best he didn't admit to it, though. Like allowing somebody to slap his horse on the rear, or carrying packages for people when he didn't know the contents, it was a mistake he wouldn't make again.

He tried to stand, but lay back down again. The desert

seemed to be swimming, and his knees felt like half-melted aspic. He certainly hadn't expected this when he set off.

"Don't you worry. Your mare'll be fine." Pike tucked the bedroll under one arm and grinned. "A lot finer than you, once King sees you're fit enough take a dressin'-down."

"Pardon me?"

"You can take another swig," Pike said, tipping his head toward the canteen. "Just a couple'a swallers this time, or you'll get sick. Mind me now."

Quincannon started crawling toward the water, since it seemed that Pike wasn't going to go fetch it for him. What was wrong with these people? Couldn't they see that he was ill? If he were back in Boston, the Widow Rudge at the boardinghouse would have brought him all the water he wanted, and a cool cloth for his head. But if he were back in Boston, he wouldn't be sick, now, would he?

He had just unscrewed the lid and taken one gratifying gulp when Pike said, "Best steel yourself, boy. Here he comes."

A shadow fell over him, and he looked up into the dark face of King Garner. He supposed that Garner, under ordinary circumstances, was a man whom dear Miss Minion would have called handsome. That was, if he were cleaned up and stuck in a suit and vest, and if he were smiling. He was not smiling at this given moment.

"Cork that water," he said curtly.

"It's a screwtop," Quincannon croaked.

"Pike!" Garner shouted, and Quincannon jumped. Pike appeared at his elbow and grabbed the canteen, then scurried back a few yards. "Can you stand up?" Garner growled.

Quincannon tried, and this time, after a few falters, managed to gain his feet.

As he stood there, hatless and weaving beneath the blistering sun, Garner said, "You feel all right?"

This gesture of common decency was more than Quincannon had hoped for, all things considered. He gave his shirt a tug, ran his fingers through his hair to comb it as best he could, and rasped, "Yes, and thank you, Mr. Garner. I believe I am much recovered."

"Good," said Garner. And then he brought up his fist and punched Quincannon square in the jaw.

A shocked Quincannon landed flat on his backside, his head ringing. He raised a hand to his jaw and worked it around carefully. It wasn't broken, but it was the same place that cretin in town had hit him the day before, and it hurt like the devil.

"Give him some water and send him on his way," Garner said to Pike, and turned on his heel.

"Stop right there, Mr. Garner!" Quincannon shouted, although it came out as a rough bark. "I won't be sent back to town!"

Garner turned toward him, his face twisted into a scowl. "Well, you sure as hell aren't comin' with us. I already lost over an hour trackin' those boys on account of you, so you just get on your horse and get your butt headed for Rusty Bucket. If I find that damn jug you're so crazy about, I'll send it back to you." He walked away.

"I won't go back to town!" Quincannon tried to shout, but this time it came out as a dry whisper. "I won't be turned back!"

"Here, boy." Quincannon looked up, and found Pike standing a few feet away, holding Rosie's reins. He tossed them down. "Take it easy on the mare. I gave you one'a our water bags and it's only partway full, but that oughta be plenty. You be sure to stop every hour or so and see to her."

When Quincannon only stared at him—he hadn't the slightest idea what the old man was talking about—Pike plucked Quincannon's brand-new Stetson from the saddle horn and turned it upside down.

"Fill this about three or four fingers deep. She was awful dried out and she'll want more, but you got to make that water last till you get back to town."

"From my hat?" Quincannon croaked, incredulous. Didn't horses drink out of buckets? Well, come to think of it, he hadn't bought a bucket. An obvious oversight.

"Crimminy," muttered Pike in disgust. "Back-easters!" He tossed the hat into Quincannon's lap and marched off to where King Garner was already mounting his horse. Quincannon watched as Pike mounted, too, and the pair of them set off without a backward glance.

Rosie snorted and bumped him with her nose. "I know, I know," he muttered. "Three or four inches, every hour or so." With difficulty, he climbed to his feet. Leaning on the saddle, he stuck two fingers into his pocket and plucked out his new watch. Twelve-thirty. He didn't suppose it mattered, but he liked to keep track of these things.

Next, he dug through his saddlebags until he found the provisions the storekeeper had packed away for him. He removed a piece of jerky and bit into it, taking care not to jar his lip. The dried meat was tough and it was stringy, but he found it had a rather interesting flavor. Seasoned beef? Mutton, perhaps.

Chewing, he picked up his hat, settled it on his head, patted Rosie on her neck, and then clambered into the saddle. Immediately, he wished he hadn't. He sucked in air through his teeth, as if that act could cool his burning backside. He'd thought he was just sore from Garner knocking him on his rump, but good Lord, he must have blisters on his blisters!

Well, it was going to smart no matter which direction he traveled in. And even if he had to endure another "dressing-down" by King Garner, even if it meant he would run out of water and perish from thirst, there was no way he was going back to Rusty Bucket. The Iberian Chalice was his responsibility!

He unscrewed his canteen, took a careful swallow, and watched until their dust dwindled down to just a puff in the distance. And then he chewed the last bite of his jerky, took another single swig of water, and applied what horsemanship he'd discovered earlier that morning, by the time-honored hit-or-miss method.

"Get along, Rosie," he said, and clucked his tongue.

The mare started, at a soft jog, along Garner and Pike's trail. Hanging on to the saddlehorn, standing in his stirrups to ease the fire in his backside, Quincannon followed the puff of dust.

4

"**Dang it!**" **Pike** exclaimed. "That fool kid's followin' us!"

Garner continued to look straight ahead at the trail the Mexicans had broken through the brush. "Spotted him three hours ago."

Pike twisted in his saddle and threw Garner a murderous look. "Why in tarnation didn't you say somethin'?"

Garner shrugged. "Kept figurin' he'd give up."

"Well, he didn't," Pike said, exasperated. "And we can't send him back to town now. It's too dang far to stretch the water!"

Pike was right, of course. They'd taken plenty of water for two careful riders, but they hadn't counted on splitting it out with a third who was damn near reckless with the stuff. They were beginning to ride up into a forest of rock, where scattered boulders and low brush had given way to yellow and reddish stone that thrust from the rising desert floor like an old dog's molars. It was the sort of country that made Garner's skin crawl.

"King? What you thinkin'?"

"Let's get on up into these crags."

"But what about that kid?"

"Just ride."

• • •

Quincannon pulled up his mare and tried to find a more comfortable position in the saddle. He could feel every thread in the seat of his britches, and they were all on fire. It seemed obvious to him that these western saddles had been designed by a sadist, and any person who could sit in one all day had to be either masochistic or numb from the waist down.

He was neither. He was a man who liked his comforts. Not that they had to be extravagant, mind you. They couldn't be, not on his salary. But he'd taken great pride in purchasing the rather modest leather armchair in which he relaxed at night. Now, there was comfort! He liked to close his eyes, inhale the good leather scent of it, and imagine that he was not in his cramped, third-story room at the Widow Rudge's, but in a library or a study. His study.

He pictured the study of his dreams, in some future time when he had completed his law degree and had been made a full partner in the firm of Peabody & Strauss. Peabody, Strauss & Quincannon, it would be, then. His study would be filled with gleaming, gold-stamped, leather-bound books from floor to ceiling, and he would have read them all. Perhaps Malcolm Peabody himself would come over on the occasional Sunday afternoon. They would have a glass of port and discuss important pending cases, and he would be very wise indeed.

"Ah, Quincannon!" Malcolm Peabody would say in amazement after he'd made a point. "Such insight!"

And Quincannon would simply tip his head in acknowledgment.

It was a very nice dream. When he was having it, his one regret was that he didn't smoke a pipe. It would have added so to the picture.

Well, he supposed he could always start.

Right now, however, he was in dire straits, and he knew it. He'd followed Garner and Pike's dust up into some hellish-looking rocks, and now it seemed he had lost their trail.

He supposed he was a dolt. He supposed any ten-year-old child could have tracked them. Any ten-year-old child who had been raised out here in this godforsaken wilderness, that was.

His water was nearly gone—only enough for two more "three or four fingers' full"—and the last time he'd checked his watch, it was five-fifteen. It would be dark in a couple of hours.

If he'd done what King Garner had told him to do, he'd be practically back to town by now. There'd be a restaurant dinner waiting. Not that Rusty Bucket's restaurant had anything nearing adequate cuisine, but it was certainly better than what he could stir up from the provisions in his pack. There'd be that lovely bug-ridden bed, too.

More than anything, he wanted to get off Rosie—for good, if possible—and lie down. Preferably on his stomach. With a cool cloth on his jaw and his smarting lip.

But now he couldn't go back. There wasn't enough water. He could only go forward and hope for the best. He ran his tongue carefully over his cracked lip, and clucked to Rosie.

Three minutes later, he found the imprint of a horseshoe, left in a miraculously soft patch on the rocky ground. He congratulated himself. "Who says I'm not a tracker?" he muttered, and forgetting himself, smiled.

Immediately, he winced and sucked at his lip. But he urged Rosie on.

A scant five minutes after that, he rounded a bend in the rocky forest, and ran headlong into Garner and Pike.

He gasped.

Garner, lounging in the shade, growled, "It's about damn time. What'd you do, stop to shoot marbles?"

Quincannon blinked. "I . . . I beg your pardon?"

"Well, you're here now. Get off that mare and let Pike check her over."

As badly as Quincannon wanted to climb down off the mare, he hesitated. "Mr. Garner, do you plan to strike me again?"

Garner paused long enough to make Quincannon nearly nervous enough to take his chances on the desert. But at last, grudgingly, the big man said, "Not right now."

Slowly, Quincannon dismounted and walked a few stiff paces from the horse, into the deep, purple shade of the rocks. Every step was torture.

Garner lit the cigarette he'd been rolling, and shook out the match. "You can sit if you've a mind."

Sitting down was the last thing Quincannon wanted to do, and he shook his head. "No, thank you, sir. I'll stand." At least the shade felt wonderful.

One corner of Garner's mouth quirked up into a fleeting smile. "How's the mare, Pike?" he asked, somber again.

Pike led the mare into the shade, then looked in her mouth and nodded approvingly. He felt the water bag, then held the canteen next to his ear and shook it. "He done just fine with her, and himself, too, King. Good on you, boy. You're learnin'." He cocked his head and scowled. "By Christ! That backside a'yourn must be smartin' something fearful!"

It was, but Quincannon had his pride. He said, "I'll be all right, thank you."

"He's busted some blisters, King," Pike said. His gnarled face contorted with sympathetic pain.

"Let's see," said Garner, and when Quincannon simply stood there, he said sharply, "Turn around, boy!"

Quincannon turned.

He heard Garner sigh. "Aw, hell. He'd have to be bleedin', too. Break out the doctor bag, Pike. And you shuck out of those britches, Quincannon."

Quincannon whirled around, or at least gave a fair imitation of it. "I beg your pardon?"

Garner looked at him as if he were simple. He said, "You've got blood blisters on your ass, Quincannon, and they've broke. They've got your britches stuck to your butt, in case you haven't noticed. Now, unless you're aimin' to hold us up while you get blood poisoning and die—which I'm here to tell you is a long and painful process—get shed of those pants and let Pike slap some unguent on you."

Quincannon felt the flush rising up his neck. "I assure you, Mr. Garner, I shall be—"

"Do it," snapped Garner, and his face suddenly looked so frightening that Quincannon obeyed.

Despite the embarrassment of being pantsless in the wasteland in the company of two strangers, one of whom was smearing some vile but soothing concoction over his backside and upper legs, Quincannon felt oddly safe. Perhaps, he thought idly, it was that horrid-tasting medicine that Pike had forced him to drink. Perhaps it was just that he was no longer on Rosie.

Dear Rosie. Garner had stripped her of her saddle and bridle, and she currently stood hobbled nearby, lipping grain from a feedbag. He hadn't bought a feedbag, had he? Oh, well. At least he could see how the hobbles worked. Very clever!

"You're done," said Pike, and stood up. "You got extra smallclothes?"

"What?"

Pike shook his head. "Knew I shouldn't have give you that extra swallow'a laudanum. Well, I reckon you can fit into King's spare long johns."

"But it's summer!" Quincannon protested. His tongue was beginning to feel uncommonly thick. Numb, as well.

He watched as Pike walked off, then turned his attention to Garner. He had vacated his previous position, and was standing with his back turned, staring up at the sky.

"I appreciate your having relented on your previous decision, Mr. Garner," he said carefully. "How soon will we be off again?"

"It's not a permanent relent," said Garner, still staring upward.

Suddenly Pike was back and threw a clean, but very gray, set of long johns down to him. "Put 'em on, boy," he said. "You're embarrassin' me."

As Quincannon slowly worked his way into the garment—everything seemed to be going very slowly, come to think of it—he said, "Did you hear me, Mr. Garner? I asked you if—"

"I heard you. And don't put the top half of it on, you idiot. It's hotter than blazes! Just let it hang down. It'll give you some extra cushion in the saddle."

Gratefully, Quincannon rebuttoned his shirt. Or tried to, anyway. "I shall be ready in a moment."

Garner said, "We aren't goin' anywhere today."

"But it's still light!"

The big man closed his eyes for a moment as if arguing with himself. When he opened them, he said, "You see that?" He pointed up toward the rocks behind them, and into the sky above.

"Smoke?" Quincannon said. A thin line curled upward, across the pale blue sky.

"Want to take a guess as to who's makin' it?"

Quincannon thought for a moment, then gasped. "The bandits!"

Pike's cackle rose from the deep shade beside the horses. "Oh, he's a smart one, ain't he, King?"

Quincannon couldn't contain his excitement. He grabbed his britches and began to pull them on over the thick leggings. Why, this was splendid! He'd retrieve the Iberian Chalice and be back in Rusty Bucket tomorrow, and headed for Tucson the following day! He'd hand over the prize to Mr. Antonio Vargas with Malcolm Peabody's best regards, apologize for the brief delay, and then he'd wash his hands of the entire, grisly matter and get back to Boston by the nearest conveyance. And he'd gladly forget that any of this ever happened.

He said, "Then, by all means, let's go now and—"

"Just hold your horses, boy," said Garner, cutting him off. "We're not going to do a damn thing."

"Why not?" Quincannon demanded. He buttoned his pants lopsidedly and fumbled with his belt buckle. Whatever Pike had smeared on him was indeed a miracle cure, because he could barely feel any discomfort at all. In fact, he could scarcely feel his fingers or his toes, and Pike hadn't touched them.

"Because Sanchez knows this country as good as I do. Maybe better. Because those three have met up with two more, so there's five of 'em up there now. Because—"

"Wait a moment." Quincannon gave up on his belt buckle, and simply tied the ends together in a granny knot. "How, pray tell, do you know that there are five?" He felt that somehow, Pike's ministrations had made him brave and invincible as well as having healed his behind. He gave his belt a last tug. He was ready to take on the world.

Pike said, "'Cause I snuck up there whilst we was waiting for you to lollygag your way up to us, that's why. They's two of 'em on guard, and they's in one'a them places that's like . . . what'd you call it, King?"

"Strategic," Garner said. He seemed bored with the conversation. Quincannon, however, found it fascinating. "Only one way in and one way out," Garner went on, "and each pass can be covered, up top, by one man. And each man can cover the other." He stopped and frowned. "Kid, you keep movin' around like that, and that laudanum Pike fed you is gonna hit you like a ton'a bricks."

"It certainly is not. I say let's ride! Why, the three of us, combined with stealth and surprise and a certain degree of keen bravado, can surely . . ."

The rocks began to spin, and the ground commenced to wobble beneath his feet. "Can surely . . ." he said again, and then he entirely forgot what he had been saying.

"Excuse me," he whispered to Garner, who seemed not at all discomfited by the pitching earth or the swimming sky. "By any chance, do you suffer earthquakes in Arizona?"

Garner and Pike watched without comment as Quincannon wilted to the ground, unconscious.

"Too much'a that snake oil," said Garner after a moment.

"Well, I reckon the pup's had a tough day," Pike commented.

Slowly, Garner stood up. "Help me haul him back on his blanket. Belly side down. And get that damn knot out of his belt."

They drank water and ate hardtack and jerky, and Garner missed both his coffee and Pike's good cooking, but it couldn't be helped. Tonight there'd be no fire for them. The boy stayed out cold, and Pike took the first watch, promising to wake Garner at two. There was no need, though.

The screaming woke him.

5

Before he was all the way awake, Garner was on his feet with his gun in his hand. The cry sounded again, the anguished scream of a man, long and drawn out and distant, but piercing just the same. It gave him what his daddy used to call the collywobbles.

"It's them, up there," came Pike's voice, a whisper. Garner looked for him, searching the darkness, and finally saw the dull glint of Pike's old Winchester back in the rocks. "You reckon they found that thing'a the kid's?" Pike hissed. "That cup deal? You reckon they's fightin' over it?"

"Sounds past the fighting stage," Garner muttered.

He had holstered his pistol, but drew it again when a shot split the night. As it echoed through the rocks, someone fired again, twice and fast, and then it was still.

They waited in silence for a long time, listening for any sound that might betray creeping bodies and stealthy feet, but there was nothing, only Pike's muttered, "Goddamn scorpions!" and the crunch of his boot. At last, Garner allowed himself to ease off a tad. And then he remembered the boy.

"Pike!" he whispered into the darkness. "Where's the kid?"

"Ain't you seen him?"

"Can't see my hand in front of my face."

"You always was blind as a bat come dark, King."

Garner ground his teeth. "There's no moon, goddammit."

"Ain't no excuse," Pike whispered. There was a soft crunch and a glint of dull metal as he moved to Garner's right. After a moment he hissed, "Aw, he's sleepin' like a baby! Ain't moved an inch, and missed all the hoorah. You want I should wake him up?"

Garner shook his head. "Christ, no!" he said. "Time to switch the watch?"

"I reckon. Maybe I oughta climb up there again and have a look-see."

"No, get some shut-eye."

"You sure?"

"Whatever those boys up there were doin', it was strictly to each other."

"Well, you'll wake me if'n you gets scalped, won't you?"

"You ought to go on the stage, Pike."

There came soft scuffling sounds as Pike got comfortable—the old coot could curl up and be happy on a bed of horseshoe nails—and then, "'Night, King."

Garner grunted in reply.

Quincannon was in the middle of a lovely dream. it was fall and there was a nip in the air, and he and Miss Minion were strolling on the Boston Common. She had just consented to be his bride.

"Oh, Mr. Quincannon!" she said, worrying her gloves and blushing profusely. "That would be very nice." And then she had allowed him to brush a kiss over her cheek. "Now come with me, Mr. Quincannon," she said. "We must tend to your bottom."

He didn't know whether he was awakened by the shock of that dreamed utterance or the toe of Garner's boot digging into his shoulder. But in either case, he came fully awake rather suddenly, and was immediately disappointed to find himself still on the desert, and flat on the ground on his belly.

"I'm awake," he said to Garner's figure, still dim and looming in the early-morning light. "And I would appreciate it, sir, if you could refrain from kicking me."

Somewhere out of sight, Pike mimicked, " 'Please don't slug me, please don't go kickin' me.' Why, the boy ain't no fun at all, King. Get us a new one!"

Quincannon decided to ignore him. He climbed slowly to his knees, and his head started to pound, doubtless the aftermath of Pike's medicine. When he made it to his feet, he discovered that his backside hurt like the blazes—although considerably less than it had yesterday—and his muscles were so stiff and sore that he could barely walk.

He asked, "What time is it?" From what he could see through the massive fingers of rock, there was only a rosy glow on the eastern horizon. The shadows were still long and deep, and the air held a residual chill.

"Time to move on," Garner said, and handed him Rosie's reins. She was already saddled and bridled and ready to go.

"Oh, God," he whimpered, and involuntarily took a step back.

Muttering, "Jesus," Garner bent over and snatched up Quincannon's blanket. He folded it quickly, but didn't roll it. Instead, he put it on Rosie's saddle. "Well, go on, boy," he said gruffly. "There's no engraved invitation."

Quincannon gulped, but stepped up to the saddle, and finally, painfully, managed to make it up. And actually, the blanket, combined with the trailing top of Garner's long johns—which he doubled under him to augment the padding—was a comfort. He wished he'd taken time to empty his bladder before climbing up, though.

He was about to attempt a dismount when Garner, already atop his bay, called, "Let's move." He and Pike started out through the rocks, and Quincannon had no choice but to follow.

By the time Garner called a halt, Quincannon was in agony. No man had ever suffered so much for his honor, he thought as he fairly leaped from Rosie's back and availed himself of the closest rock. Much relieved, he buttoned his trousers and went to join the others. They had walked ahead, leading their horses into a rather large, boat-shaped clearing in the stone. And Garner, he suddenly realized, was bending over a dead man.

There were three bodies altogether, and dried blood spattered the rocks. The men had all been shot, but the third one had been tied to a rock and disemboweled. His intestines were roped out over the ground, and covered in grit and dirt. All three men had been scalped. Flies buzzed thickly over them, their sound seeming to amplify the stench and horror of it, and Quincannon quickly added nausea to his list of complaints. He retched, but nothing came up.

When he lifted his head, Pike was watching him. "Dry heaves," he said, unaffected by the gore. "Take a slug outta your canteen. It'll settle your stomach."

Garner stood up. "So much for Ramon Sanchez."

Quincannon opened his mouth to say something, but suddenly felt sick again. He threw up the water he'd just swallowed.

Pike asked the question that had been on his mind, if not on his lips. "That Sanchez?" he said, pointing to the disemboweled body.

"What's left of him," replied Garner. He walked to the other two bodies, nudging each with his boot as if to make certain they were dead.

"They ain't moved since I took a gander this mornin', King," carped Pike. "You think it was Lazlo?"

"Who else? And I was just checkin'."

"Who is Lazlo? And what about my Chalice?" Quincannon managed to get out before his stomach cramped, and he doubled over again.

"Do you see it?" Garner barked, then muttered, "Don't see my goddamn horse, either, do you?" With that, he marched to his gelding, effortlessly swung up into the saddle, and jogged through the clearing and out the other end.

Pike shrugged his shoulders, then swung a leg over his mare. "Reckon that means we're goin' again. Come on, boy."

Still queasy, Quincannon managed to flounder stiffly into the saddle. He averted his eyes when he rode past the bodies. "Mr. Pike?" he called. "Mr. Pike, what about the departed? That is, shouldn't we bury them and say some words?"

Pike didn't turn around to answer him. "Ain't no time to bury 'em. And if'n you want words said over 'em, I got two. 'Good riddance.' "

Garner led them through the rocks and out the other side, and the land gradually spread into a broad plain, with rolling hills to the west and hazy mountains in the distant east, and an island of deceptively low, dark rocks far to the south. The trail they were following—two riders leading three horses—went south. He had expected as much.

Quincannon was doing some better, he noted. Not good enough to ride any farther with them than Black Tanks, but good enough to get himself to the next town, once they stocked up on water again. The outlaws had to be short on water, too, because they were making a beeline for the tanks.

He had briefly considered trying to outpace them. He could get to Black Tanks before they did by arcing out to the east and then cutting back west before he reached the hill called Jaguar Hump. He could wait in the rocks that surrounded Black Tanks, and pick them off. It would be easy. He'd done it before and caught the Farley brothers. Laid himself flat on a ledge and picked them off, one by one. They'd returned fire, but it hadn't done them any good.

But he'd have to hold to a hard gallop to get there. Pike

could keep up, but the kid surely couldn't. He was having trouble at a slow jog, even though he didn't complain. Stoic little bastard.

And besides, they didn't have enough water to be pushing the horses like that, thanks to Quincannon's little stunt. Old Faro was practically half camel, but even Faro couldn't make it to the tanks at a gallop on just a third of a water bag. No, less than that. Quincannon's bag was empty, and they'd have to share with him.

He reined in Faro, and Pike and Quincannon rode up beside him. Quincannon looked like he could use a week in the hospital. He was sunburned despite that big hat of his, and there was a purple bruise spreading over his jaw. Garner almost felt sorry for him, then thought better of it.

"Water the horses," he said, and swung out of the saddle.

"And feed us," Pike said as he dismounted. "Weary as I'm gettin' of that jerky, it'd taste powerful good about now. Didn't take the time to eat no breakfast."

Quincannon half fell off his horse, then leaned against her, hugging the saddle, his head down.

"You all right, boy?" Garner asked.

"Splendid," came the muttered reply. "Never been better."

Garner grunted, and got busy helping Pike with the horses. If a man didn't ask for help, you had no call to give it to him. Sometimes, not even then.

"Lazlo's headin' for Black Tanks, you reckon?" Pike asked. Yesterday afternoon, when he'd made the trip up the hill, Pike had made a tentative identification of the two newcomers. One of them, he was pretty sure, was Cherry Lazlo, a scalp-happy sonofabitch if there ever was one, and the other man was either Tom Smithy or Mink Scraggs. Both Smithy and Scraggs were light-haired and of a similar height and build, and known to travel with Lazlo. Lazlo himself, a big man with setter-red, waist-length hair and a belt strung with scalps, was unmistakable.

Garner nodded. "Where else would they be goin'?"

"Lazlo?" said Quincannon, holding his hat for Rosie while she drank. Pain etched his face, but he was trying to hide it. You had to give him something for that. "Just who is this Lazlo fellow, and what are these Black Tanks?"

"Lazlo's one character you don't want to meet up with if'n you can help it, an' if'n you want to keep your hair," said Pike.

"Is he an Indian?"

"Hell, no," Pike said. "Irish or French or Polish or somethin'."

"But he scalped those men back there!"

"What we've mostly got around here is Apache," Garner said. He pulled a piece of hardtack from his bags. "And most of them are on corralled on the reservations. Apache don't take scalps. They do every other rotten thing in the book and a few other tricks that aren't in it, but they don't lift hair."

"But—"

"Lazlo learned his trade workin' for the U.S. government," Garner went on. "Used to be, they paid a bounty for scalps. I hear he made a good livin' at it." He bit a brittle chunk off of his hardtack.

"Until somebody noticed that quite a bit of that hair he was bringin' in was the wrong color," Pike said, picking up where Garner left off. "Hand me some'a that trail biscuit, King."

Quincannon paled beneath his sunburn, and Pike added, "Reckon he'd be real took with that sand-colored mop a'yourn. Now, me?" he said, lifting his hat to expose a thinning pate. "I don't reckon I'd be worth the energy. Want some biscuit?"

Quincannon took it, but Garner noticed that he didn't eat, but only turned the hardtack over and over in his long, sunburned fingers, staring at it. "You'd best chew on that whether you want to or not, boy," he said gruffly. "Get somethin' in your belly."

"What are the Black Tanks?" Quincannon asked. Mouse-like, he nibbled the hardtack's edge.

"Quit takin' them girlie bites," said Pike, who was already into his second ration. Pike could bitch and moan about dry rations, but when push came to shove, he'd eat just about anything.

"Water hole," said Garner. "Tanks."

Quincannon's features took on that "don't try to make a fool out of me!" look, an expression that Garner was fast becoming acquainted with. "Excuse me? Someone built water tanks clear out here? Is there a farm nearby?"

Pike laughed, and Garner said, "Out here, we call 'em ranches, Quincannon. And no, there's not a settler for miles. It's from a Spanish word, *tanque*. Means a pond or a reservoir. Out here, it's just a hollowed-out place in the rock." Quincannon started to open his mouth again, and quickly, Garner said, "No, nobody hollowed 'em. They're just there."

"Full'a bugs, too!" Pike added happily.

Garner passed out jerky and rationed the water, and then they set off again. Normally, after a stop, he would have gone the next ten or twenty minutes on foot, leading the horses. But he'd forgone that since they'd picked up Quincannon. He doubted the boy could make it a dozen feet on his own.

He had planned to send Quincannon east, to Mesa Verde, once they took on water at Black Tanks. But now he wasn't so sure. Sending him off on his own to find his way to a town that was little more than a piss-hole on the map might be the next thing to killing him. And riding him over to Mesa Verde would lose Garner at least two days of tracking. In two days, Lazlo and the red stud would be long gone.

He mulled this over for several hours, and by the time the ground had grown dark with black, cindery rocks, by the time they started climbing over the pitted volcanic stone

that marked this region, he still hadn't come to any satis-
factory conclusion.

"Wait here," he said to Pike. Alone, he rode ahead to
reconnoiter the water hole.

He took a circuitous path up into the rock, then ground-
tied Faro when he could go no farther on horseback. He
pulled a spyglass from his pack, then scrambled up the rest
of the way on foot and knees and belly, coming out high
above it to rest on the perch from which he'd shot the Farley brothers. The rock still showed the scars of the Far-
leys' bullets, and unconsciously, he touched the place on
his head where a shard had clipped him.

Lazlo and his friend were long gone. He twisted, bringing out the spyglass, and searched the southern horizon.

He smiled. Lazlo and his buddy had gotten cocky. They'd
lingered at the tanks. Beneath a rapidly clouding sky, Garner could just make out a dust trail moving away to the
southeast, just past the dappled flank of Jaguar Hump.

He collapsed the spyglass and slid down the rock,
reached his horse, and picked his way back to the others.
"They're gone," he said.

"You look like the cat what swallered the canary bird,"
commented Pike as they started out.

"Maybe," he said.

"Well, bugs or no," Pike rattled on, "I'm gonna get me
all the way wet in that tank. I got grit in all my creases."

Even Quincannon brightened at the prospect of water.
He was probably thinking about easing his backside down
into it.

Garner couldn't say he blamed him.

They rode up into the rock formation by a much easier
route than Garner had taken earlier, although the horses'
shod hooves skidded and slipped on the stone footing. When
they rounded the last turn and the tank was before them,
Garner got off his horse and smacked it on the rump. Faro
made a beeline for the nearest pool, with Garner close behind.

But when the horse reached the water, he dipped his head, but didn't drink. Pike and Quincannon were dismounting when Garner shouted, "Wait!"

He reached Quincannon's horse just in time to grab her bridle. With a sharp *clank,* he pulled her nose up from the water.

There were two tanks eroded into the black stone, the largest roughly circular, and about fifteen feet across and perhaps four feet deep in the center. The smaller was oval, perhaps five feet across and eight or nine feet wide. They were both a good deal fuller than usual for this time of year, and glistened bright with reflected sky.

However, on the surface of both pools, water bugs, tiny shrimp, and frogs the size of his thumbnail floated, lifeless.

"Son of a *bitch*!" he spat.

"Aw, Jesus, King!" Pike wailed. "What'd he want'a go and do that for?"

"What?" Quincannon asked. "What is it?" He was swaying on his feet, and looked like he might go down at any moment.

"Lazlo," said Garner, and his voice was full of venom. "Lazlo poisoned the water."

6

They moved on, but not far. They rode over and down the rock—which, Quincannon thought, seemed like a huge black and barren island, afloat on the sea of the desert floor—and down into the shade of its southern-eastern slope. Quincannon busied himself rubbing more of Pike's ointment on his backside while Pike unsaddled the horses. Garner started checking their water supply, carefully consolidating the last dregs from the bags and canteens.

The news wasn't good.

"We've got half of this left," Garner said grimly, and held up a canteen. Unconsciously, Quincannon licked his lips. "And that's for all of us," Garner continued. "We'll wait here till sundown, and then we'll head for Mesa Verde. It's a long haul, but we can make it so long as nobody's horse goes steppin' in a badger's burrow."

Now, according to Pike, Mesa Verde was a twenty-mile ride. It struck Quincannon that they likely didn't have enough water for one man to reach civilization, let alone three. It also occurred to him that Garner, for reasons known only to him, was painting an uncharacteristically sunny picture.

Also, it had been growing steadily darker since about three in the afternoon. The sky was blue-white one minute, and the next time Quincannon looked up, it was the color of gunmetal. Now, at five o'clock, clouds had lowered, and the heavens had taken on a sickly, yellowish tinge that bathed the desert in a strange, muted light. He could no longer see the sun, only a faint and shapeless lemon glow through the congested clouds.

To the east, the sky lit for a moment with lightning, and Quincannon's heart lifted.

Pike saw it, too. "Aw, swell." He slid down next to Quincannon, who was stretched out on his blanket, backside up and newly balmed. "Just what we was in need of. A dust storm. How's your butt, boy?"

At any other time in any other place, that little remark might have called for its utterer's social ostracism, but at this particular moment, Quincannon found it oddly comforting.

He said, "Much better, thank you, Mr. Pike. A dust storm, did you say?" He struggled back into his borrowed long johns and britches.

The whole of the desert seemed to be taking on an eerie glow, as if it had been painted with a translucent coat of phosphorescent yellow ocher. The wind had come up, too. The brush began to crackle softly with it. A sagebrush lazily tumbled past them, its movement finally halted by a large prickly pear about one hundred yards to the southwest.

Pike scratched beneath his hat. "They's pretty common this time'a year." He turned toward Garner, who was standing away from the rocks, arms folded, staring toward the south. "Hey, King, you recamember that duster we had last July down to Galvin City?" he asked in obvious delight.

Garner didn't reply, so Pike turned back to Quincannon and said, "Took the roof right off'n the Bent Nail Saloon, she did! Set 'er down clear acrost the street, smack-dab in Old Lady Hamilton's hog pen! Lifted one'a them hogs straight up in the air and set him down in the horse trough out front of the marshal's office, too." He shook his head pensively and scratched at his ear. "We never did find the goats."

He misunderstood Quincannon's look of abject horror, and added, "Oh, that hog were killed instant. We had us a big ol' barbecue. You'd best tie your hat down. Here, boy, I'll show you. And where's your neckerchief?"

Quincannon allowed Pike to help him with his bandanna and hat, even allowed Pike to practically strangle him with the cord, but he knew the truth of their situation. They couldn't make it to Mesa Verde: not if it was twenty miles away, not even if it was five. A dust storm was coming, and coming fast—a storm that could send hogs flying and rip buildings asunder! What would become of them with no shelter, no aid, no one to help them?

The wind picked up. The gale threw biting bits of twigs and weeds and grit into Quincannon's face. The sky had grown so dark that he could barely see Garner's silhouette.

Lightning crashed on the horizon again, lighting the sky a deep, dirty yellow. This time, Quincannon heard a rumble of thunder.

"But won't it rain?" he asked Pike, nearly pleading. "Didn't you hear the thunder?"

Pike raised his brows. "Back where you come from, does it al'ays give out water when it thunders?"

"Every time," said Quincannon, confident in the superiority of Boston. Something stung his cheek, and he picked a bit of stickery twig from it. His fingers came away bloody.

"Well, here, it don't," said Pike. They were both shouting over the whistle of the wind, now. "Too early for rain. Why, I seen dry lightning and heard them clappers for three, sometimes four weeks without so much as a blessed drop hittin' me. One year, I believe we went five."

"Weeks?" wailed Quincannon.

"Here she comes," Pike shouted over the wind, which was suddenly a roar.

It hit Quincannon like a solid wall of pressure and sound,

rolling him from his blanket and smashing his back into a boulder. It whined and keened relentlessly, painfully in his ears, and he briefly imagined that the air was fill of tiny, armed men being hurled to their doom.

He closed his eyes, covering his face as well as he could while the storm pelted him with a ceaseless battery of gravel and dirt and broken brush. He supposed Malcolm Peabody had his wire by now, and was cursing the day Elliot Quincannon had been born. He wished he'd had time to write a letter to Miss Minion, one they would find on his body, if ever it were found. "Marry another," he would have said, "I bless your union with Mr. Peters from the second floor."

Pike grabbed his wrist and dragged him up into the rocks, nearly breaking his shoulder in the process, and momentarily erasing thoughts of letters and Miss Minion. When Pike let go, Quincannon found himself partially out of the wind, with a boulder at his back that somewhat shielded his shoulders and head.

"What the hell was you doin'?" Pike shouted over the howl. "Get back to shelter!"

Pike had a strange idea of shelter, but Quincannon shouted back, "Where is Mr. Garner?"

"Out there!" yelled Pike, and then added, "He can take care'a hisself."

The wind picked up speed, if that were possible. He had never weathered a hurricane or a cyclone, but he didn't imagine either could be much worse than this. It was as if the Lord were throwing a tantrum, and had chosen an unpopulated place to do it. Quincannon beat back the urge to stand up and shout, "There's somebody down here, dammit!"

His back and legs were mercilessly pelted by a never-ending onslaught of pebbles and detritus that stung him, newly offending his sore backside. They were leaving bruises, he was sure. Tomorrow, if he was still alive, he would be as dappled as a firehouse dog.

Several times, gusts nearly lifted him from the ground.

He was certain that Pike's restraining arm was the only thing saving him from being blown straight to California and on to the Pacific Ocean. Despite the bandanna, dust and grit clogged his nose. When he opened his mouth to breathe, he sucked in what seemed like half the desert.

At some point, Quincannon slitted his eyes open for a moment. He saw a sagebrush, impossibly tangled with a long arm of cactus, sailing directly for him. He shut his eyes as it impacted on the rock face above him. He didn't try to look again. His eyes were full of grit, and he couldn't see past his toes, anyway. They watered, and he felt the dust caking to mud in his tear tracks before it dried and blew away.

The thunder moved closer, and the lightning with it. More times than he could count, the insides of his eyelids were suddenly illuminated to a bright orange, followed by a deep, rumbling crack that made his dust-clogged ears ache and throb. Those cracks were becoming less rumbling and more sharp all the time. He wondered if there was iron in the black rock, iron that would draw the lightning and sear them all to the stone.

Every few minutes, he felt Pike put a hand on his arm or shoulder and give it a squeeze. Whether Pike did this to comfort him or just to make sure he was still there was of no matter. He was grateful for the human contact.

As the wind continued to screech around him, mercilessly scouring the desert, the rocks, uprooting vegetation— and intent on carrying him, he was certain, to his doom—he began to pray.

Garner had taken shelter with the horses. With his back against an upthrust of black rock, he sat cross-legged and hunched: his face covered by the crook of his arm, his hand death-gripped about the tangle of reins.

The horses had been crazed at first, and for a moment he'd thought he was going to lose that nag of Quincannon's. They were calmer now, though, although still antsy, standing with their hindquarters square into the merciless pelt of wind. Their heads were lowered, their eyes were closed, and their nostrils were narrowed to slits, although Rosie's legs still shifted nervously. Every now and again she tossed her head, pulling on the reins.

She was a rental horse if ever he'd seen one, and had likely been one for most of her life. She wasn't trail-wise, had no sense of whether water was good or bad, and she sure as hell wasn't storm-wise. She had no trust in humans to get her out of her troubles. She wanted to go home to her nice, safe barn, and she wanted to do it yesterday.

Faro and Millie, on the other hand, had been through dust storms before and had rarely known a stable. They would stand and take the blinding dust and pelting stones and screeching wind for however long it took to go away. Horses, once they learned what was what, were smarter than most folks gave them credit for.

Too bad these particular horses were going to die.

A half canteen to get three horses and three riders twenty miles! Pike had seen through him, even though he hadn't let on. Pike might be a cantankerous old geezer and a piss-poor card cheat, but he was nobody's fool. Pike knew they might have made it to Mesa Verde—horseless and crawling and half-dead—if it had been just the two of them.

But it wasn't just him and Pike, was it? No, he had to go and get soft. He had to let the kid tag along, when he should have ridden back and slugged him again just to drive home the point, and sent him back to Rusty Bucket with his tail between his legs. Right now, Quincannon would have been cooling his heels back at the Glad Times Saloon, cussing him and cussing Pike and feeling lower than a well digger's boot. But he would have been alive and well, and not facing a slow death.

The howling wind picked up new speed. Suddenly it shifted direction, gusting down with incredible force and bringing with it a shower of pebbles and a pad of spiny prickly pear. It hit Faro in the neck. Startled, the horse half reared, pulling Garner along with him and panicking the already storm-spooked horses.

Rosie broke free, ripping the reins from his hands with enough force that he felt the stab and burn as the skin peeled from them. Cursing, he let her go. She disappeared into the roar. He couldn't catch her without losing the other two as well. Hell, he couldn't see three feet past his nose!

He pulled away the prickly pear and spoke to Faro as best he could, tried to soothe him. He got a mouthful of grit for his trouble and Millie stepped down hard on his foot, but at last the horses settled.

He hunkered down again, his back hard against the rock. With his hat pulled low over his eyes, bandanna securely over his nose and mouth, he waited. He lost track of time, lost track of everything except the ceaseless pelt of gravel and the unrelenting roar of the wind.

Beside him, Quincannon felt Pike stir. His lips to Quincannon's ear, he shouted, "Smell that, boy?"

Quincannon shook his head. He had long since ceased to breathe through his nose, and at present was trying to strain the grit from the air with his teeth. He didn't know how Pike managed.

The sky lit up again, and this time the thunderclap sounded right on top of it. For an instant Quincannon could see the land before him, could see Rosie in the distance, could see a wet line moving swiftly across the desert.

"Rosie?" he croaked.

"Glory, we is saved!" Pike shouted just as it began to pour.

Water sheeted down at a hard angle, instantly drenching him and sluicing dirt, made mire, from his face and clothing. Pulling down his bandanna, he turned his head into it and opened his mouth, and was half drowned for his trouble.

Pike dragged him to his feet. "Hurry up!" he shouted, and wrenched Quincannon from their meager shelter. Pike dragged his aching body into the blast of the torrent. "Move, boy!"

The sky fairly hurled rain, fat drops that hurt his face and arms. Another burst of lightning and another deafening thunderclap, and he saw Garner, frantically trying to hold their horses and dig through their saddle packs at the same time.

Then they were upon him, and he shouted, "Hold 'em, Pike! Get your mare, Quincannon!"

"What?" he shouted back. It was too much, too fast.

Garner was swiftly ripping empty water bags from his pack, hurriedly shaking them open. He glanced up and yelled, "Catch her, dammit, or this time I'll really hit you!"

Quincannon limped out through the sheeting rain.

He located Rosie standing head down and dejected in the torrent, and crept nearer to her with each new burst of lightning. He seemed to remember that you were supposed to speak softly or coo or some such thing, but considering all the storm noise, he didn't suppose it mattered. When he got within five feet, she made a show of spooking, but it was only a show. The poor thing was exhausted.

He had her in two shakes. He turned his back into the pelt of rain and rubbed her sodden face. His hand came away muddy. "There, there," he said to her over the storm. "I was frightened, too."

By the time he slowly led her back to the rocks, falling twice into holes deep enough to fill his boots and yank his aching muscles, the wind died as suddenly as it had come. The rain was falling straight down instead of sheeting at an angle, and had eased from a harsh torrent into a soft, cool gush. He looked up into thinning thunderheads. A clear, starry sky broke through in the east. Lightning flashed to the west. The worst of the storm had passed.

The rain was still falling, though. It pattered on his hat and poured in sheets from the black rocks. The air was filled with the after-scent of rain, and the desert had turned chilly.

As he rubbed the gooseflesh from his arms, he could make out Garner, filling the last of the canvas water bags from the thick stream that ran off an angled ledge overhead. Pike had stripped to his underwear and was rinsing out his shirt and trousers beneath a similar rocky downspout. He was singing "Camptown Ladies"—although he mangled the lyrics badly, Quincannon noticed—at the top of his lungs.

Quincannon grinned. "We is saved," Pike had said. The man was a latter-day prophet. Quincannon raised his head and opened his mouth, and let the sweet water course over his tongue and down his throat. They would all sleep well tonight, if somewhat damply, and tomorrow they would be off again, on the bandits' trail.

He felt rugged. He felt . . . well, manly! He had survived the most hideous piece of weather ever to befall a traveler. He had partially survived saddle sores and burst blisters. Another few days and he would have survived them completely. He'd seen three scalped bodies, and one that had been . . . Well, he'd rather not think about that.

He'd nearly quenched his thirst at a poisoned water hole, flirted twice with imminent death from dehydration, been punched in the face two times, and by God, it couldn't possibly get any worse than it had already been!

As the rain ran in thick, cool drizzles from the brim of his hat, he confidently assured himself that from now on, finding that chalice would be a cakewalk. Malcolm Peabody would give him a hero's welcome, Miss Minion would be his, and Mr. Peters, on the second floor, could just go and find himself another girl!

Lame and faltering but triumphant just the same, he led Rosie up to the others. Grinning, he called to Pike, "I thought you said it wasn't going to rain!"

Pike was now deep into a chorus of "Marching Through Georgia"—calling out the "hurrah, hurrah!" part with extra gusto—and didn't hear him, but Garner did. He snatched

away Rosie's dripping reins and said, "You can thank your
lucky stars he was wrong this time. She all right?"

"I think so," Quincannon replied somewhat meekly. He
hadn't thought to check. He didn't think she was bleeding
or anything. Besides, why did he allow this man to intim-
idate him so?

By that time, the rain had all but gone its way, leaving
nothing but the last few, fat drops. They fell from the sky
and quickly disappeared into the puddled, gravelly mire of
the desert floor. Pike, looking disgusted and swearing softly,
had stopped singing. He climbed back into his sodden
clothes.

The horses took advantage of the muddy hollow that
had been his bathtub, and drank deeply.

Garner quickly went over the mare. Once he was satisfied that all was well, he said, "Wring out your blanket if
you can find it, and grab yourself some jerky. Find a place
to bed down that isn't runnin' with water, and try to get
some sleep. Come morning, you're heading for Mesa
Verde."

"But why are we going to Mesa Verde?" Quincannon
asked, perplexed. "It seems to me that with those brigands
so close at hand, it would lose us valuable time to—"

"*You're* goin'," Garner broke in. "Alone."

7

"King," Pike said softly, "you can't send him packin'. Not after all this." His cross-legged shape was shadowy and vague, the only light being from the stars and Garner's cigarette.

"Don't you get after me, too," Garner replied gruffly. He was cold and he was wet, and he was wishing he could wrap himself around that damp cigarette, just for the meager heat it provided. He kept his matches in a tin box and had thus saved them from a soaking, but the desert wasn't going to provide any dry kindling tonight.

"He goes up against Lazlo," he continued, "and he'll get himself killed. Likely scalped, to boot. You know that as well as I do. I'm tryin' to save him from himself. I told him about six times that if I found that gold jug of his I'd send it to him, but the damn fool just keeps comin'.'"

They'd been arguing the point, one way or another, for the past two hours. And before that, Garner and the boy had shouted themselves hoarse. Finally, his teeth chattering with cold, Quincannon had stomped off and found himself a place to sleep.

Pike snugged his wet blanket around him. In the chilly

air, steam rose in faint wisps where the blanket pressed against his bony frame.

"Well, I done said it before, but I'll say it again. That's a boy with a purpose, King. You seen it in him, too. He might be raw and he might step on his own pecker half the time, but he's gonna go out there after Lazlo whether we's with him or not, and you know it. And he's a nice boy. Calls ever'body 'mister' and says 'please' and such. I ain't been called 'mister' in a coon's age! Makes me feel sort'a grand."

Garner didn't say anything.

"If'n he's with the two of us, he stands a chance."

Garner still didn't speak, just studied the glowing ember of his smoke. After a moment he said, "We take him along, then we're all as good as dead. Can't fight Lazlo and baby-sit at the same time."

"Then forget about that red horse a'yourn," Pike said. "Forget about Lazlo! Let's all go to town—and, for once, stay there longer than it takes to take a piss—an' get some whorin' in. I could use me some time with a woman."

"No. And there was a woman in the last town."

"And all her time was took up with you, weren't it? This time I want'a go to a two-whore town." He paused. "What if I was to learn the boy to shoot and spy and be crafty and such?"

Garner snorted, but he grinned despite himself. "Hell, Pike, that's the blind leadin' the blind! You can't teach a lifetime of sneakin' in two days or two years. And besides, you couldn't hit the side of a barn with a handful of beans!"

Pike drew himself up. "I could if it was close. And you ain't one to talk. You can't see a damn thing past sunset."

"I can see you good enough, you old billy goat," Garner replied.

"All right, then. You see so good, you learn him."

"No."

"Fine. I'll do it. But he's comin' along with us."

"No."

"Goldarn it, King!" Pike half shouted. "What makes you think you're gonna be able to nose up a trail once it comes light, anyhow? Best as I can tell, that storm 'bout picked up the whole county and blew 'er down on t'other side'a the Colorado River. Only reason we're still here is 'cause we was hangin' on to this rock!"

Exaggeration aside, Pike had a point. All traces of Lazlo's trail—and the red stud's—had been blown away with the first good gust of wind. Garner had a general idea where that horse was going, though, and a general idea was more than he'd had in the last month.

He wished Pike would just shut up and let him get on with it. The old man was tough, but every once in a while he slipped into a strange sensibility that Garner couldn't quite wrap his brain around. There lurked in Pike something of the knights of old, something that believed in valor and purity, and in chivalry, although he likely didn't know the word. Garner knew that Pike had taken Quincannon under his wing because he saw the boy as something fine, something better than they were.

He was probably right. Quincannon was educated. He seemed to be right-minded. He was probably good to his mother. He said "please" and "thank you" and, like as not, knew which fork to use at a fancy dinner. As if any of that mattered a tinker's damn out here.

Garner had gone clear through the sixth grade. Pike had once told him, in a liquor-induced haze, that he'd quit halfway through his second year to help his old man on the farm, back in Virginia. But this boy had gone all the way through school and on to college.

Under normal circumstances, Garner wasn't much impressed by a man's scholastic achievements. They didn't matter a damn in the Territory. Hadn't that scum, Pen Bloodworthy, been a college man? They made a big deal about it at the trial, as he recalled. Bloodworthy had killed fourteen men in his time, and had gone to the noose cursing them all in Latin. Or maybe it was Greek.

Jackson Woodrow had been a college man, too, he thought with a shudder. That madman had chopped and sliced his way through the west for better than ten years.

He supposed, all things considered, that an education was a good thing to have if you were going into a trade that called for it—but not a single one of those trades included being scalped by Lazlo. That night in Rusty Bucket, Garner hadn't been paying much attention to anything the kid spouted, except to say no to it.

He took another drag on his smoke and said, "The kid. Didn't he say he was studyin' something or other?"

Pike rose up out of his sulk long enough to say, "He's readin' the law. I knowed you wasn't payin' no attention! Why has I always got to repeat everything after the fact?"

"I thought he said that gold jug belonged to his boss. What is he? The boss of the law school?"

"Tarnation, King! He said he goes to that law college at nights. Days, he works for a lawyer, Mr. Malcolm Peabody, who's some big muckety-muck back to Boston. Said he's nigh on halfway finished with his schoolin'. He's a smart pup."

Garner snorted. "Couldn't prove it by me. Besides, if you think he's so smart, why you want to go and get him killed? Seems to me your best bet's to bang him over the head, crate him up, and ship him off to Boston, where it's safe."

"A boy like that?" Pike huffed. "Why, he'd be on the first train comin' right back, riggin' hisself out with guns and horses and the like, and gettin' lost on the desert whilst seekin' out mayhem."

Sighing, Pike shook his head. "Can't you see it, King? Sometimes a feller's just got to do a thing. This boy's got his mind set, like I has been tryin' to tell you. He's stubborn, like somebody else I could mention, but I won't. And he's smart as a whip. He can learn what needs to be done, and he'll do it. But no, you just go right ahead and do what you want to. You always does. Just chase after that red

stud a'yours, and the hell with everybody else. I'm goin'
to sleep."

With a little squishing, Pike stretched out on the ground
and pulled his hat low. He was snoring inside of three minutes.

Garner rolled himself another smoke. Cold and wet and
angry at everybody and everything, he sat staring out over
the desert for a good, long time.

"I said, wake up, boy."

Quincannon jolted awake. Pike bent over him, a grin
stretching his lined and stubbly face. The sun had crept
over the horizon, bringing with it what promised to be a
hot and muggy day.

"Get hoppin', an' don't ask no questions."

"What?"

"I told you," Pike whispered, "don't ask no questions.
Just ride right along with us like you ain't never had no
doubts." Tossing Quincannon a conspiratorial wink, he
hopped down off the ledge and went to join Garner near
the horses.

Quincannon put his curiosity on the back burner for a
moment, and concentrated on the pain of getting up. Holding his breath, he carefully rolled over onto his back. He
blew the air out in relief, and smiled up into the dawn sky.
He was still sore, all right, but the demons that had in-
vaded his muscles had been reduced to pint-sized hobgob-
lins, and his blisters had all but healed. He noticed that
Pike had brought him the jar of salve, and he shucked his
trousers and gave his backside another quick coating, just
in case.

After he'd emptied his bladder and rolled up his blanket, he slithered down the rock, the top half of Garner's
union suit still flapping from his waist like a gray flag.
And Pike needn't have called out instructions, for Garner
didn't give him a chance to say a word.

"Tack your horse up, Quincannon," Garner said curtly

as he busied himself with saddling his bay. "Decided to ride you down to Mormon Wells. But that's only because Pike, here, was about to have a baby, thinkin' about you going to Mesa Verde all on your own."

Over Millie's back, Pike grinned at him.

"Yes, sir," said Quincannon, and got busy saddling Rosie.

He had never actually saddled a horse. Back in Boston, the hostlers at the rental stable had always done that for him. And out here, the man in Rusty Bucket—and then either Garner or Pike—had seen to tacking up Rosie. But it couldn't be that difficult, could it?

He watched Pike, and followed his lead by first picking up the saddle blanket. It wasn't sodden by any means, but it was still more than damp. It stank, and he held it by his fingers. He watched Pike shake his out, and did the same, then watched Pike slide his blanket into place. This action he also aped.

Next came the saddle. It took him three tries where it had only taken Pike one, but eventually he got the saddle where it should be, and without a stirrup tucked beneath it.

The girth was harder. He couldn't see what Pike was doing with his, and he couldn't quite figure out just how he was supposed to fasten the saddle on Rosie with all that latigo strap on one end and just a big ring on the other, and he finally had to ask for help.

Saying, "How old are you, kid?" Garner came to assist him. He would have much preferred Pike.

"T-twenty-three," he stammered, surprised at the question.

Garner made several deft loops through the ring with the latigo, tugged the cinch twice, kneed poor Rosie in the side, then tugged it again and neatly tied it off. "Christ," he muttered, and walked off.

"You didn't need to kick her," he said quietly, patting her neck.

"Oh, she were holdin' her breath," Pike announced hap-

pily. He threw one of Quincannon's sleeping blankets up
into the saddle and smoothed it, then handed over his canteen, saddlebags, and bedroll. "If King hadn't showed her
some knee, both you an' that saddle would'a been hangin'
from her belly 'bout two shakes after you climbed on."

He had better luck with Rosie's bridle. He worked the
bit into her mouth and got all the straps buckled in the
right places—not too tight and not too loose—and after
Pike gave his approval, he at last struggled up into his
blanket-padded saddle. Pike passed out hardtack and jerky,
and they ate breakfast as they rode.

Garner ranged out ahead. Quincannon hung back with
Pike. He was grateful that Garner had relented—at least
temporarily—and didn't think it wise to press the point by
reminding him of his presence.

"How did Mr. Garner come by his nickname?" he asked
when he got a chance. They had been riding for about two
hours, and Pike was in an expansive mood. He'd been talking at length about his early days in Virginia. Quincannon
was certain that it would have been fascinating if he'd had
the slightest interest in sharecropping or tobacco, which he
didn't.

"His what?" asked Pike.

"His nickname," said Quincannon. "You know. King."

"Ain't his nickname," replied Pike. He shooed an enormous fly off Millie's neck. "He's got a big brother name
of Monarch, and a sister called Queenie. Well, used to,
anyhow. I guess Monarch got killed real young, that were
back in the Mexican War. And Queenie, she got hitched
and moved back east to Missouri. Took with fever in seventy or seventy-one, round about, and died." Quite suddenly he broke out in a grin. "I reckon their folks had pretty
high hopes to saddle those kids with monikers like that,
don't you?"

"I suppose," said Quincannon. It had never struck him
that Garner was someone who would have actually had a

family. It seemed incongruous, somehow. He changed the subject. "Where, exactly, is Mormon Wells?"

"'Bout thirty miles south. The storm wiped out them varmints' trail, but King figures they'll be headed south anyhow. See that hill?"

Quincannon nodded. He couldn't help but see it. They'd been skirting the edge of the mound, dappled with brush, for the past half hour. Like Black Tanks before it, it rose, a singleton on the desert floor.

But Black Tanks had been a monumental mass of solid stone, eroded into valleys and hard peaks that stabbed the sky. This hill, on the other hand, looked as if it had been formed by giants, giants who had swept the desert floor and piled their rubble here. It was low and long and clay-colored and ugly: part boulders, part loose gravel, with nothing but dust and a few desert shrubs to hold it together.

"Well, this here's Jaguar Hump," Pike continued. "'Course, from this side, it's just an ugly ol' hill. You can tell better from the other side why it got its name. Looks kinda like an old jaguar cat, all hunched up and sleepin'. Big sucker, ain't it?"

Quincannon nodded. It wasn't so high, but the sides looked treacherous, and he'd been greatly relieved when Garner had elected to go around it instead of over.

"Me an' King, we figure Lazlo and his buddy disappeared themselves behind it yesterday afternoon," Pike went on. "Likely weathered the torrent here, too. If'n them sons-abitches didn't drown, they's headed straight south, at least for the time bein'. Maybe to Indian Haunt, maybe all the way to Mexico. Hard to tell. King reckons they'll put into Mormon Wells for vittles and fresh water. It's on the way."

Quincannon sat up a little straighter in his saddle. If Lazlo was going to this Mormon Wells place, they could trap him there!

"Shouldn't we be trotting or something?" he asked. "A brisk canter, perhaps?" Suddenly the horses' plodding walk seemed far too slow.

Pike grinned. "Oh, we'll be pickin' up some speed after we get shed of the Jaguar."

About ten minutes later, when they were about to round the base of what Pike referred to as the "jaguar's butt," Garner called a halt.

Before Quincannon could say, "Why are we stopping?" he had his answer. Garner ground-tied his horse, yanked his spyglass from his saddlebags, and began to climb the hill. Obviously, he was going to reconnoiter the land ahead.

Pike dismounted. "Best give your mare a rest, boy," he said, and proceeded to offer water to his chestnut.

Quincannon followed suit. As Millie and Rosie drank, he watched Garner climb high and higher up the hill, sometimes moving easily, sometimes losing ground in tiny avalanches of loose stone, sometimes climbing to rocks and moving hand over hand. He braced himself against a small outcrop high above, and then Quincannon saw him pull out his spyglass, saw him appear to sight down on something, then saw him fold the glass and put it away.

And then Garner slipped around a big boulder and disappeared from sight.

"Where's he going?" he asked Pike.

Pike looked up. "Likely found an easier place to skitter down on t'other side." He had finished watering Millie and moved on to Faro by that time. When the horse finished drinking, Pike wiped an arm across his forehead, then sat down on the ground. Quincannon's muscles had mended, but not so well that he was at all certain they'd bend clear down to the ground and get him right back up again. He stood.

"You fond'a cards, boy?" Pike asked.

Quincannon was looking up, searching the rocks for a sign of Garner's return. That, and wishing the weather wasn't so hot and sticky. His armpits were chafing and he was boiling in those long johns of Garner's. Sweat soaked his hair and ran ceaselessly into his eyes. "I play a little bridge now and then," he said. "Why?"

He flicked his gaze down to Pike's face in time to catch him rolling his eyes. "*Bridge?* What's the world comin' to?"

"Mr. Pike?" he asked tentatively. "I should like to learn to shoot. I was wondering when—that is, *if*—you might be so kind as to—"

"Here's King," said Pike, and stood up.

Garner came walking around the butt of the hill, and he looked pleased. Or, at least, Quincannon thought he did. Quincannon took a step forward, then stopped himself. He was actually beginning to feel better, and he was in no mood to be the recipient of another tongue-lashing from Garner, just because he'd called attention to himself.

Still, Garner appeared happy, or at least smug. Perhaps those miscreants had killed each other! Perhaps there had been a fight, or perhaps the storm had killed them. Quincannon knew it had nearly killed *him*, and he'd had more appropriate shelter in the black rocks than these men, who had only had the crumbling face of Jaguar Hump for protection.

But, "You water him?" was the only thing Garner asked when he walked up to Pike.

Pike nodded, and Garner stepped up on his mount. It amazed Quincannon every time, the dexterity with which these men got off and on their horses. He'd never master it.

He floundered up on Rosie once again, and trotted to catch Garner and Pike, who were already rounding the butt of the Hump.

"Mr. Pike?" he called once he bounced and flopped within talking distance. Wretched gait! Wretched saddle! "Mr. Pike! What did he see?"

"Quit tryin' to post the damn trot, boy!" Pike said as Quincannon trotted past. "You're gonna kill yourself. Them stirrups is longer than on back-east saddles, and for good reason. Ride with 'er, not against 'er. And slow down, for the love'a Mike!"

He tried. It helped, but not much. That was, until he managed to slow Rosie to a jog.

Pike rode up beside him, and they settled into an almost comfortable pace. "Some better," he said with a grunt.

"What did Mr. Garner see from the hill?" Quincannon asked again. Garner was far out in front, and the desert before them was empty, save for a few birds, the scrub, and an occasional storm-damaged cactus.

"Reckon that's it up ahead," Pike said, and pointed.

8

At first, all Quincannon could see was a few circling birds. Big birds. Then he noticed quite a few more on the ground.

As he rode closer, he saw that they seemed to be squabbling over something or other, squawking and flapping their wings. Garner stopped his horse about twenty feet away and walked up, but the birds didn't startle and rise, as Quincannon had expected. Instead, Garner had to walk into their midst, shouting and waving his arms before they took to the air. He chucked a rock out into the brush, and a coyote crept from its cover and retreated, slinking farther out on the desert.

By then, Quincannon and Pike had ridden even with Garner's horse. They dismounted, and walked over to join Garner.

Pike did, anyway. Quincannon stopped halfway and doubled over, willing himself not to vomit. And when he could stand up again, he turned his back.

Pike and Garner joined him in a few minutes. Muttering, "Damn buzzards," Garner walked past, to the horses.

"C'mon, boy," Pike said, and started him moving.

"I'm fine, just fine," he said, shaking off Pike's hand,

even though he wanted nothing more, at that particular moment, than the childish comfort of sobbing into someone's
arms. He had seen that it was a man the birds had been
eating. He had seen what was left of his face, had seen
the bloody place where his scalp should have been, had
seen the dark stain on his tattered shirt where a knife or
bullet had ended his life.

He hated it here, hated the west in general and Arizona
Territory in particular. What was wrong with these people,
these people who killed brutally and without conscience,
who discarded the bodies of their victims like so much
trash, who left them to the vultures and the coyotes?

Somehow he reached Rosie, and he put a hand on her
saddle to steady himself. The birds had come down again,
come out of the skies to bicker over the corpse, to tear at
its empty eye sockets. He looked away. "Who . . . who was
it?"

"Well, it weren't Cherry Lazlo," Pike said matter-of-
factly.

Garner, stepping up on his horse, said, "Mink Scraggs.
That'll make it a mite easier."

"You sure, King? I still say it could'a been Tom Smithy."

"Scraggs. Didn't you see that mouth organ stickin' out
of his pocket?"

"Nope," Pike replied, "can't say as I did. But if you
seen it, I reckon that's good enough for me."

Suddenly Garner turned and snapped, "Christ on a
crutch, Quincannon!" and he froze, halfway into the saddle. "I'm gettin' sick of watchin' you flail around, and I
bet that mare is even sicker of it! Get back down."

Shocked and blinking, Quincannon obeyed.

"Take your damn foot out of the stirrup."

He did.

"Gather your reins in your left hand. No, not that tight,
you idiot, you're gonna break her jaw! And try to get 'em
halfway even."

Quincannon fixed his reins.

"Grab a fistful of mane with your rein hand, or grab hold of the horn. Now put your foot in the stirrup. Don't go kickin' her in the belly, dammit! Pay attention! How the hell did you live to be twenty-three goddamn years old without learnin' anything about horses? Right hand on the cantle."

"The back'a the saddle," Pike stage-whispered.

"Shut up, Pike!" roared Garner.

"But you grab the horn in your right hand, Mr. Garner," Quincannon said meekly. "I watched!"

"Do what I'm telling you!" Garner barked. "I said the cantle, you idiot, not the skirt. Now step up. Let go of the cantle when you've got your balance, and swing your right leg over her. One motion."

It was magic. Just like that, he was in the saddle.

"My goodness!" he said, so surprised that for a moment he forgot about the squabbling birds, forgot about the body. This mounting-up business was all momentum, and starting in the right position! He'd mastered it!

But Garner growled, "Get off and do it again. And this time, don't drop into her saddle like a sack of beans."

He did, taking care with the toe of his boot and his reins, and it was easier the second time.

"Better," Garner said grudgingly.

Pike laughed. "Reckon you're gonna turn him into a real hand after all, King!"

"Not in a million years," Garner muttered, and urged his horse south.

Quincannon didn't remember the body again until they were well past it. With a start, he turned in his saddle, but all he could see, low in the brush, was a roiling mass of wings and the glint of flashing beaks.

Garner led them south, staying well out ahead. He was in no mood for small talk. He'd taken pity on the kid and distracted him back there, but in the process he'd taught him how to mount up without looking like an idiot. That was bad. He wanted Quincannon feeling as helpless as possible, because helpless people finally gave up. They went home and left the real work to their betters.

Lazlo was headed south, all right. His trail picked up about seven miles from the body. The face of the land had gradually changed from flat desert to low, tawny hills, and in these, at the base of a crumbling bluff, Lazlo had apparently weathered the storm. Pike had made his arms into wings and crowed like a rooster when Garner found the place, and declared Garner the jim-crack tracker of all time. The boy had been speechless.

But Garner had simply grunted. It was blind luck, that was all.

They investigated the shallow cave where Lazlo had stashed the horses for the worst of it. It was good shelter, and the ground bore the imprints of many hooves.

From there on out, the trail was as clear in the miry dirt and gravel as if Cherry Lazlo had painted a black line in his wake. One man, leading four horses. And likely wearing a belt full of scalps. It was a miracle Lazlo himself hadn't fallen prey to scalp hunters, for that red mop of his would be a prize.

Garner considered taking it himself. There had been a time not too many years before when he would have scalped the bastard without a second thought. He would have flashed it in the bars and cantinas of a dozen dusty little towns, and he knew he'd never have to buy himself a drink.

After all, Lazlo was the worst kind of scum. He'd gutted Ramon Sanchez solely for the sheer pleasure of hearing him scream. Not that Sanchez was any treat, either, but he hadn't deserved what Lazlo gave him. And there was no reason to poison those water holes back at the tanks. Lazlo couldn't know anybody was following. Just sheer meanness, that was Lazlo's reason for being.

Garner was more certain than ever that he'd head for Mormon Wells, if only to sell off the extra horses. He hoped one of them would be Red.

Despite the sultry weather and a threatening sky, he pushed Pike and Quincannon into a lope, off and on, for the rest of the afternoon. Quincannon surprised him by falling off only twice. He got right back on, though, once he caught his mare.

They rode into Mormon Wells well past dark, with their hats flattened by the wind and a real ripsnorter of a storm under way.

"This is quite nearly a real town!" he heard Quincannon shout to Pike as they rode down the main street. "Do you think there's a telegrapher's office?"

Weather vanes spun sickly on rooftops. Lanterns swung wild beneath overhangs. Merchants' signs flapped and creaked, and dried road apples bounced along the ground. Three tumbleweeds, caught up in each other, went sailing across the road right in front of Garner, spooking Faro before they flew over a hitching rail and plastered themselves against the door of a café. Through the big front window, Garner made out two men, checkered napkins stuck in their collars, staring at the door and scratching their heads.

They stopped at the nearest livery, and found it shut tight against the coming storm. Holding down the brim of his hat and fighting the wind, Garner dismounted and banged his fist on the door. It opened a crack, after quite a bit of rattling, on the thin shoulder of a girl. Garner blinked.

"You coming in or not, mister?" she shouted. "I can't hold this door for more than a sec—"

The wind gusted and slammed the door shut. He heard her cuss, and smiled.

He shouted, "Push!" at the same time as he yanked hard. The door, which was wide and high enough to admit a good-sized buggy, swung out suddenly, then caught in the wind like a sail and flew back on its hinges. With a resounding *bang,* it smacked the side of the barn. He slapped his horse on the rear to send it inside, and Quincannon and Pike rode in after it.

The girl was outside now, tugging on the barn door, trying to pull it against the wind, but she wasn't making any
progress. Wild yellow hair lashing her face in tangled whips,
she shouted, "Don't bother to help me or anything, you
weasel's butt!"

Garner took her by the shoulder and fairly shoved her
inside, then heaved back on the door. It didn't want to give,
but neither did he, and finally, it budged. He pushed it out
until it caught the wind again, and he let it bang shut. With
some difficulty—and a little help from Pike, inside—he got
it open far enough to squeeze himself inside the barn.

He stood weaving for a moment, waiting for his balance to return. It was a little like a sailor who had been
long at sea, he supposed, standing on still ground for the
first time. In his case, he'd been leaning into that bitch of
a wind so long that without it, he nearly toppled over.

It was relatively quiet inside. The wind still howled and
the boards of the barn still banged, but when it wasn't trying
to shove your face down in the dirt—and when it wasn't
whistling past your ears, full bore—the storm didn't seem like
such an untamed, howling thing.

Recovered for the most part, he slapped his shirt and
pants with his hat in an attempt to shake free the topmost
layer of windblown grit. "She's comin' up a corker," he
announced, happier to be out of it than he would admit.

Nobody answered, and when he looked up, Quincannon
was still standing in the straw-strewn middle of the barn,
limply holding Rosie's reins, and staring at that girl with
his mouth hanging open. The girl, who was trying to run
a mane comb through her snarled hair—with little luck—
was paying attention to nothing but her own problems. She
was dressed in britches and what must have been her
daddy's shirt, for the buttons were about to pop.

"Quincannon!" he said sharply. He grabbed Faro's reins
and led him past the boy.

"Yes, sir?" Quincannon said without tearing his eyes
away from that girl. Or maybe it was the buttons.

"Put your eyes back in your head and see to your horse. You'll have plenty of time to look later."

"What? Oh." The boy colored, muttered, "Yessir," and led Rosie toward the empty stall beside the one Pike had commandeered for Millie.

"God damn it to hell!" yelped the girl. Then she seemed to think better of it, and looked up, adding, "Beg your pardon, gents. But I only just got this mop straightened out from when Mick Mullberger brought his mare in." She picked up a tangled strand, held it in front of her face, and scowled. "Every year about this time, I am keenly tempted to take a pair of horse clippers to it."

"Oh, no, don't do that, miss!" Quincannon said in abject horror, and then he blushed all over again.

Pike had his back turned, but Garner saw his shoulders shaking.

"That's right, miss. Be a shame to chop off all that pretty yellow hair," Garner said, and tipped his hat. He led Faro into a stall and got busy with the girth. "You happen to see a fella, a fella that might have rode into town late this afternoon? Would have been leading a string of four horses. One's a big red stud."

The girl looked up from her comb. "No. You might try Balder's or Cree's, though."

"And we'd be at . . . ?"

"Boudreau's, smack-dab in Mormon Wells, which is a queer sort of name seeing as how the last Mormons moved on before I was even a glint in Daddy's eye. And in case you're really lost—and wasn't that a buzzard of a blow last night?—Mormon Wells is in the Arizona Territory," she replied. With a grimace, she yanked the comb through another section of hair.

Thanks," Garner said with a grin. "We had the Territory part just about figured out." He couldn't tell what she looked like under all that storm dirt and tangled hair, but he was getting a kick out of her, all right.

"I'm Lisa Boudreau," she went on. "*Miss* Lisa Boudreau,

more's the pity. And I wouldn't be down here in this hel-
lacious weather, 'cept Darby—that's my brother—busted
up his leg, and Daddy's down with the grippe. You want
these horses grained?" She aimed a finger at Quincannon.
"And what's his problem? He's a pretty one, all right, but
he looks kinda tetched in the head."

Pike's silent chuckle broke out into a belly laugh, and
Quincannon quickly turned his back. Garner couldn't see
his face, but he would have bet good money that it was
bright red again.

"I reckon he's just admirin' your beauty, miss," Garner
said, and after waiting on a gust of wind that gave the
boards of the place a good rattling, he added, "As are we
all." He slung Faro's bridle over his shoulder and hefted
the saddle.

The girl sniffed. "Sure. Tell me another one. That'll be
forty cents a head, grained and groomed up right. Twenty-
five if you just want the use of the stall. Payable in ad-
vance. And you can put your tack over there." She tipped
her head toward the shadowed end of the barn, where saddles hung from ropes, and bridles and harness depended
from pegs. "It'll be safe. There's somebody here all the
time."

"We'll take the deluxe accommodations, miss," Garner
said, and shelled out a dollar-twenty.

They hung up their tack and gathered their saddlebags
and packs. Miss Lisa Boudreau let them out the back way
so that the alley would provide some shelter from the in-
creasing wind, and they set off for the hotel.

When they pushed into the lobby and sagged against
the wall, Pike, able to talk at last, said, "What was wrong
with you back there, boy? You was took with her! You
coulda said your name! You coulda at least said howdy!"

Horror claimed Quincannon's features. "Taken with her,
Mr. Pike? Taken with her? I should say not! I'll have you
know that I am very nearly an engaged man. And besides,
I have nothing on my mind at present except the retrieval

of Mr. Malcolm Peabody's Chalice. It was just . . ." His voice fell to a whisper. "She was wearing trousers! I've never in my life seen a decent woman wearing trousers. Not even an indecent one! Her limbs were . . . separated!"

Shaking his head, Garner muttered, "Christ Almighty," and pushed them both toward the desk.

"Just how many 'limbs' did she have, there, boy?" Pike cackled as they crossed the lobby. "Were it three or seven? He was starin' at her long enough to take a solid tally, weren't he, King? How many legs does that sweetie a'yours got, boy?"

Flustered, Quincannon hissed, "Mr. Pike! Keep your voice down!"

But Pike wasn't one for decorum. As loud as he could—and much to Quincannon's dismay—he said, "An' you looked so purty, too, what with all them smallclothes hanging out the back'a your britches."

Quincannon gasped, then grabbed at the top half of Garner's long johns that dangled from his waist like an apron put on backward. He closed his eyes.

Pike was enjoying this a little too much for his own good, but Garner didn't have the heart—or the inclination—to stop him. He just signaled the clerk for the register, and quickly skimmed it, without luck, for Cherry Lazlo's mark. He signed his name, plus Pike's and Quincannon's, and flipped it back around.

"K-King Garner?" the clerk asked after he'd peered at it. He gulped, and ran a finger under his collar. "*The* King Garner?"

"Three beds, however they fall," Garner said wearily. "Just someplace that doesn't leak wind." He hoped they'd put him on a separate floor from these two.

"Hey, King?" Pike asked, laughing. "You reckon this here's a three-whore town? We got us a boy in dire need of edification!"

The clerk held out a single key with trembling fingers,

stepping soundly on Garner's hopes for a separate room. He figured if he asked for two, the man might bolt.

"Just get your butt up the stairs, Pike," he said with a sigh. "You, too, fancy pants."

9

Garner and Pike had no more than tossed their packs into the room when Garner announced that he was going down to Cree's Livery—and Balder's—to inquire about Lazlo and the red stallion. Pike went along, but Quincannon stayed. Garner said that Lazlo wouldn't have hung around in town, and even if they uncovered a clue to his whereabouts, they couldn't do anything about it tonight.

Alone, Quincannon went through his saddlebags, digging out his shaving kit and his only change of clothing. The continuing dust storms had managed to dirty them, but after a good shaking out, he deemed them serviceable.

He threw his filthy britches on the floor, along with his shirt and his borrowed underwear, which was now stiff and sickly brown with dried salve and blood and pus. Then he set to the business of trying to take a sponge bath in the bureau's shallow basin. If Pike and Garner wanted to go tramping around in this god-awful wind, getting stung by flying nettles and grimier by the second, that was their business. He, however, intended to bring a touch of civilization to his person, and the sooner the better.

He washed as best he could, then shaved in the poorly

silvered mirror affixed to the bureau's top. Feeling almost spry, he put on his fresh clothes and strapped on his as-yet-unfired gun. After several days of wearing it, he had felt almost lopsided without it. The returned weight of it felt good. He'd have to ask Pike again about lessons. He had no wish to end up like Sanchez, or that Mink person. Lord, his poor face!

He felt his stomach turn over, and sat down on the edge of the bed.

The room was small, just enough room for a bed and a cot and a dresser. The wallpaper, which upon closer investigation seemed to have once been a pattern of wild roses, was filthy and peeling. But the frayed quilts seemed to be clean enough, and when he flipped one of them back, the linen beneath wasn't peppered with bedbugs fleeing the light. It was a step up from Rusty Bucket.

Having, for the most part, pushed the image of those ravenous buzzards from his mind, he picked up his saddlebags again and rummaged through until he found the small, silver frame he was looking for.

Grit had worked its way into every crevice, nook, and cranny of his belongings, and the little picture was no exception. He rubbed his thumb across the surface, leaving a track that exposed Miss Minion's face. He thought it best to look at it again, considering what a fool he'd made of himself over that blond girl at the stable.

Yes, Miss Minion's hair was certainly neat and tidy. Not a strand out of place. The sign of an organized mind in a woman. Not like that girl. Lisa, that was it. Lisa Boudreau. Miss Minion would have the sense not to venture into gale-force winds! Also, Miss Minion had the sense not to have such a French-sounding name. Smutty postcards of ladies in their underwear, that was all the French were good for!

Ladies wearing men's britches.

She'd really been quite pretty.

He forced himself to stare at Miss Minion's plain face. No, it wasn't plain at all! It was kind. Of course, you

couldn't really tell from this photograph. She'd taken her
glasses off, so that her eyes looked a little weak. That
wasn't her fault, was it? And people always scowled a
little when posing for the camera, didn't they? Of course
they did!

That scowl line between her eyebrows was awfully deep,
though, wasn't it?

Annoyed, he stuck the photograph away. He had more
important things to do than compare Miss Minion with a
girl he barely knew, a girl he'd only said a few words to.
What were they? "Don't cut your hair," or some similar
nonsense. Gad. He hoped she wasn't present when they
picked up the horses in the morning.

The storm had lessened considerably. At least, wind-
borne detritus had stopped battering the windows, and the
panes had ceased their rattling. He checked his watch, and
saw that he had fifteen minutes before he was to rendezvous
with Garner and Pike at the café next door.

On a scrap of paper spread over his knee, he wrote out
what he hoped was an optimistic telegram, apprising Mr.
Malcolm Peabody of his progress to date. Confidently, he
stuck it in his pocket, picked up his dirty clothes, folded
them neatly on a chair, and left, locking the door behind
him.

He picked a table well back from the front window. After
all, you never could tell about this Arizona weather, and
he had no desire to be perforated by flying glass should
the wind happen to come up again and hurl a brick through
the panes.

But after more than a half hour of watching the lightning and counting the seconds between the flashes and the
booming thunder, of more wind and no rain to speak of,
Quincannon finally ordered a meal from the chalkboard
menu.

The Sanderson Café offered a meager choice: beefsteak,
biscuits, and gravy; beef stew, biscuits, and gravy; and roast

beef, biscuits, and gravy. At the bottom, APPLE PIE 5¢, WITH
GOOD WISCONSIN CHEESE 8¢ had been chalked in as an afterthought. He ordered the roast beef.

It appeared in good time, and even though he was reasonably certain that he could have resoled his boots with
the beef, he devoured it. As much as he had enjoyed those
first few bites of jerky on the trail, it had gotten old in a
hurry, and anything freshly cooked was a treat. He mopped
up the last drops of gravy with a surprisingly light biscuit—the last of six—and ordered apple pie. With some of
that "good Wisconsin cheese."

He had nearly finished when Pike and Garner walked
in, and it was a good thing Pike got there first and held
the door, because Garner didn't break his stride until he
had reached Quincannon's table.

"I went ahead," Quincannon said apologetically around
a mouthful of pie, and swallowed.

"Give me your money," Garner demanded.

Quincannon's jaw dropped.

"Hurry up, boy!" Garner said through clenched teeth.
"How much you got?"

"I beg your pardon?"

Wild-eyed, Garner lunged forward. Quincannon scrambled from his chair just in time to avoid, he assumed, being
held upside down and having the coins shaken from his
pockets.

"Now, why don't you ask him nice, King?" urged Pike,
who had a grip on the back of Garner's shirt and was holding on for dear life.

"If you fellas are gonna fight, take it outside," the waiter
shouted from across the room. "I ain't foolin'." He bran-
dished a club to underscore the point, and Quincannon,
who was already on the floor, pressed his back tight into
the corner.

"We was just funnin' a mite, mister," Pike replied, then
whispered, "King? You hear me, King? He's a good boy.
He'll do it if'n you ask him nice."

Looking straight into Quincannon's eyes, Garner shook off Pike's restraining hands. "Get up," he said.

Quincannon flicked his gaze to Pike, who smiled at him and nodded a little too enthusiastically. Discretion being the better part of valor, Quincannon stayed put.

"C'mon, boy!" Pike hissed, jabbing a thumb back toward the club-carrying waiter. "You're gonna get us tossed out before we've et, and I wanta sink my choppers into some meat what ain't decimated."

"Desiccated," Quincannon said automatically.

Garner held down his hand. "Just get up," he said, only a tad more kindly. When Quincannon hesitated, he added, through gritted teeth, "Get up, goddammit, or I'll pound you into somethin' they can serve with gravy and spuds."

Quincannon got to his feet. He did not, however, take advantage of Garner's hand. He dusted himself off, signaled to the waiter that all was well, and setting his chair upright again, slouched into it.

"If you don't have the funds to pay for your meal," he said, "all you had to do was ask in a civil manner."

Pike, who had snagged Quincannon's last bite of apple pie, muttered, "They's right about this cheese. It's real good!"

"It's not the meal, dammit," Garner said. He'd sat down, and leerily, Quincannon leaned away from him. "How much cash you got on you, Quincannon?"

"I should say that I have roughly thirty-one dollars and forty cents remaining."

Garner swore under his breath and turned away to stare angrily at the wall.

"Ain't enough," said Pike, and twisted toward the menu, then the waiter. "Two steaks, and burn 'em," he called before he turned back.

He leaned toward Quincannon. "That sonofabitch Lazlo sold King's horse to the fella over to Cree's Livery. He's cut up some and he's got a stone bruise on the right front, but he's more sound than crippled. He'll heal up in no time.

Trouble is, Buster Cree wants two hundred for him, as is."
He shook his head. "Said he paid a hundred an' fifty, and
he deserves a profit. Buster Cree ain't a fella to dicker with
you none, 'specially after he gets slugged in the belly."

Pike slid a disapproving glance toward Garner. "You're
lucky he didn't up it to three. I don't know why you didn't
tell him who you was, King! Hell, most folks'd hand over
their mothers t'you if they knew who you was and you
said you wanted her!"

"Ah!" said Quincannon, who had a one-track mind.
"This Lazlo," he whispered, leaning forward eagerly, "is
he still in town, Mr. Pike? What about my Chalice?"

"Gone," said Garner. "Sold the horses and rode out late
this afternoon, before the blow . . . And I didn't hit him that
hard."

"But what about the Chalice?" Quincannon asked.
"Could he have sold it here in Mormon Wells? Is there a
jeweler in town? A goldsmith?"

His questions fell on deaf ears.

"I reckon we could come up with that money somehow,
King," Pike said. "I could get up a game of cards."

"No," barked Garner. "And while I'm thinkin' about it,
hand over those pasteboards."

"But, King!"

"Now."

Pike dug three playing cards from various places on his
person and slid them onto the table, and when Garner said,
"All of 'em," he produced three more. Garner stuck them
in his pocket and grumbled, "Last thing we need is you
gettin' plugged over a two-dollar pot."

"You ain't no fun anymore, King," Pike muttered.

Their conversation had afforded Quincannon time to
think. These men, rough though they might be, were his
best chance of finding the Chalice. He was aware that they
had already saved his life in countless ways, even if it was
grudgingly.

Now that Garner has reclaimed his horse—at least, he

seemed about to—he was more than likely going to end
the chase, and Quincannon couldn't have that. He had to
keep these men at his side if he was to recover Malcolm
Peabody's Chalice, and along with it, the life he'd known.
And maybe, just maybe, he could persuade them.

Picking his words carefully, he said, "If you had the funds
to buy back your horse, Mr. Garner, what would you do?"

Garner, who had resumed his former position and was
staring a new hole in the wall, said, "That's a damn-fool
question. I don't have any money."

"If you did."

Garner scowled. "I'd head north with him. Got my eye
on some land up under the Mogollon Rim. And I'll get the
money. Don't you worry."

"How do you propose to purchase this land?"

Garner turned and stared at him.

Quincannon sat up a little straighter and said, "That's what
I thought, Mr. Garner." It came out a tad smug, though he
didn't mean it to. "Gentlemen, I have a proposition for you."

"The judgment horn itself wouldn't wake that boy," Pike
said. They were back at the hotel, and Quincannon had immediately lain down on the cot and dozed off, fully clothed.
In a loud voice, Pike said, "Fire! Injuns!"

The boy didn't move.

Garner grunted. He'd picked up a newspaper downstairs,
but his arms were too short to read it. Maybe Pike was
right. First his night vision, now this. He'd be blind as a
bat inside two years. But at least he had Red back. Almost.
For the first time in months, his stomach wasn't sour.

Pike nudged the boy with the toe of his boot, and evoked
no more response than a little grumble. He said, "We ain't
gonna kite out on him, is we?"

"Fast as I can," Garner replied. "Don't know about you."
He folded the newspaper back to the front page. At least
he could read the headlines. RICH NEW SHAFT IN DAISY MINE
was the lead story. He supposed he wasn't missing much.

"Aw, you don't mean that. After the boy said as how he'd send for the money from his boss?"

"Can and do." He tossed the paper to the floor and leaned back against the headboard, arms splayed wide along its top.

"After you said as how you would?"

"Never said so, not right out."

"Well, you surely gave out the appearance of agreein'."

Garner didn't say anything. He'd found his horse. He was moving north as soon as Red was paid for and healed up.

Pike shook his head in disgust. Quietly, he said, "You beat ever'thing, King. We was with him when he sent that telegram. Why, the boy's gonna buy back Red for you, no questions asked, just for going out there with him and trackin' Lazlo. And he's even gonna get you a stake to buy that ranch if'n we turn up that gold do-jigger a'his! Seems to me you'd wanta help him out. Kinda like tit for tat."

"Pike," Garner said with a long-suffering sigh, "by the time that money comes—if it comes—Lazlo's gonna be real gone. Even if I wanted to help Quincannon kill himself—which I have got no intention of doing—I doubt if I could even find Lazlo."

"You said as how you thought he was headed to Indian Haunt!"

"Maybe," admitted Garner. "Maybe not. Hell, he could be headed anywhere, and the dust storm's wiped out any trace of him! Few more days, and he could be in Sonora. Or California. Or New Mexico."

Pike pursed his lips. "As I recamember, we was trackin' Sanchez for a goodly six months before we come up with this stud a'yourn."

"That was different," Garner said. "He had my horse."

"And he swiped the boy's cup, too."

"Belonged to the kid's boss man, not him. That's a world of difference." Garner pushed himself down and pulled his hat over his eyes. "Blow out the lamp before you settle in. And don't go kickin' me all night, you old goat.

"I'll kick you if'n I wants to. Seems to me you deserve a good kickin'."

Garner didn't answer, and a few seconds later a muttering Pike blew out the lamp. The bed sagged as he joined Garner on the mattress, and then came the requisite squirming and wriggling until he got himself situated just right.

And, for a blessed half minute, there was silence.

Until Pike said, "Gimme my cards."

"No."

"King, you know I can't sleep without I got my cards on me. Four sevens an' a pair'a sixes. I puts 'em in all my achin' places, an' they keep my juices brewin'."

"Bull turds."

He felt the bed jounce as Pike rolled over. "Fine," came the muffled reply. "If'n I die in the night, I'm gonna tell Saint Peter it was you what done it. Them cards was give to me by a St. Louis mojo woman. There's magic in 'em."

"If those cards are so goddamn special, why you always pullin' 'em out in a game?"

"King," he said with a sigh, "I reckon I ain't admitted this to you before, but, well, I'm weak. I get in a game, and the devil just sits right down and says howdy."

It was an admission Pike made every few weeks, and Garner rolled his eyes before he closed them. "He's not gonna say howdy for a spell, Pike, because you're not gettin' in a game, and you're not gettin' your cards back, either. Not till we get shed of this town." He rolled on his side to face the wall, and also to muffle the sound of Pike's swearing.

"You gonna keep your end'a the bargain and help that boy?"

"Go to sleep, dammit."

10

The next morning, Garner set off for Buster Cree's livery to see to Red. Quincannon wanted to go along. After all, he thought he had a right to see this stallion that he—or more rightly, Mr. Malcolm Peabody—was paying two hundred dollars for. That was, if he was paying anything. Quincannon was nervous about that, too.

But after breakfast, Garner went one way and Pike pulled Quincannon in the other. "King can moon over that horse all by his lonesome," Pike said, wagging his head as they walked down the street. "I tell you, I never seen a fella set such store by a dumb animal. Why, you'd think that stud was a human woman!"

Pike stopped in front of Boudreau's Livery, and Quincannon fought the urge to just keep walking. If that pants-wearing Lisa Boudreau was in there, he might just have to say something to her, something about comporting herself like a lady!

"You gonna stand there all day?" Pike asked. He was waiting in the open doorway. Behind him were the shadowed backsides of their mounts. Quincannon caught a brief glimpse of a man mucking out Faro's stall, and relaxed.

"Coming, Mr. Pike," he said with renewed confidence, and stepped inside.

Pike checked the horses and pronounced them in a fine fettle, then he prodded Quincannon for the cash to pay for another day's board. While Quincannon dug for his purse and counted out the dollar-twenty, Pike fetched their saddles from the rope hooks. He had Millie nearly set by the time that Quincannon finished paying.

"Mr. Pike?" he asked. "What are you doing? I've just paid for another day. And at your request!"

"Get your mare tacked up, boy," said Pike as he checked his girth. "King Garner or no, you an' me is gonna ride out of town a ways, and you're gonna get in some practice with that pistol a'yours."

"Oh! Wonderful, Mr. Pike!" he said. "Splendid!"

He had taken two steps when a female voice said, "You fellas going shooting?"

Even without turning around, he knew that voice belonged to none other than Lisa Boudreau, and he flushed hotly. And it wasn't just because there was something about that girl that got him embarrassed and angry and flustered all at once. It was because he suddenly came to the realization that he would not have recognized Miss Minion's voice anywhere near so quickly.

"Yes'm," Pike said with a grin, which Quincannon knew was most likely at his expense.

In an amused voice, the stableman said, "Hey, that him, sis?"

"Shut up, Darby," she said.

Quincannon refused to look at either of them. They'd probably been talking about his odd dress last night. He knew it had been laughable, but she didn't have to use it for breakfast conversation! He set his chin, then picked up his saddle and began to work.

But she wasn't finished. "If you wouldn't mind, I'd like to go with you," he heard her say, and cringed. "Daddy just gave me a used twenty-two for my birthday. Well,

mostly because he's stove up and spending all his time in
his rocking chair, and he's feeling guilty because me and
Darby are having to do all the stable work. But I'd admire
to try it out."

"Be pleased to have you," Pike said with a grin that
was far too big.

Quincannon resisted the urge to smack him.

"Your friend's still awful quiet," she said.

Quincannon busied himself with the bridle, his head
ducked low. She'd laughed at him over breakfast with her
brother, and now she was after some more amusing stories. The greenhorn and the gun, no doubt.

"Aw, he's just in a tizzy cause them britches a'yours
show that you got two legs, and both of 'em go right down
to the ground," Pike said. He jabbed a thumb in Quincannon's direction. "He's from Boston. Wouldn't you know
it?"

She laughed, and Quincannon wanted to crawl right into
the manger and disappear. Instead, he tried to salvage what,
if any, was left of his pride, and snapped, "Mr. Pike! I'm
certain that the young lady has little interest in where I
come from, and where I will be happily returning once
we . . . we . . ."

He had turned around during his tirade, and at that moment caught his first sight of Miss Lisa Boudreau. Her hair
wasn't in a wild tangle today. Instead, her tawny, sun-streaked
waves were caught back in a pale blue ribbon that matched
her eyes. She was still dressed like a boy, but today, for
some reason, it failed to shock him. What *did* shock him
was the uncommon beauty of her face.

"Once you what?" she asked. Her teeth were white and
nearly perfect, and framed behind lips that were impossibly pink, almost red. Lips that formed a bow shape when
she smiled.

He was dumbstruck, and just stood there with his mouth
hanging open.

She continued to grin at him, but it wasn't a mean-

spirited grin at all. He suddenly realized that he actually
amused her—amused her!—and he colored again. She
didn't see it, though, thank the Lord. She was already
halfway to the back wall and the tack, and over her shoulder, she called, "Hold on there, gents, while I get my horse."

He turned helplessly back toward Pike, who had moved
to Rosie's stall and was tightening her girth. He was chuck-
ling.

Garner led Red out into the sunshine, cross-tied him, lifted
his hoof, and had a good look. The stone bruise was worse
than he had thought. It would be days before the stud was
ready to travel. The cuts weren't as serious, though. He'd
washed them and salved them the night before, and they
looked some better in the light of day.

He'd like to get his hands on Cherry Lazlo, though.
When Pike had climbed the rocks to spy on the late Ramon
Sanchez, Red had looked fine. Still stolen, but fine. What
the hell did a man do to a horse in the space of forty-eight
hours to get him cut up so bad?

He resalved the cuts, and had no more than started brushing Red's shoulder when a shadow fell across the horse's
neck.

"King Garner?" said an officious voice.

Garner grimaced. He knew it was the sheriff before he
turned around. What he didn't know was that it would be
Ed Spencer. He'd gotten old and fat in the years since Garner had last seen him, but it was still Ed Spencer. Pity.

But even Ed Spencer couldn't ruin Garner's mood this
morning. "Mornin', Ed," he said, cocking an elbow over
the stud's back. "Been a while. How's tricks?"

Spencer didn't smile. Garner didn't really expect him
to.

"How long you plannin' to stay?"

Ed Spencer had always been as serious as a funeral, and
by the looks of things, he hadn't changed. His hat was
tipped low over dark, beetling brows, his mouth was set

into a hard line, and the badge pinned to his vest had the life polished out of it. He fairly reeked of determination and bay rum.

"I'm fine, Ed," Garner drawled. "How are you?"

But Spencer didn't twitch. Garner was pretty certain his smiling muscles had completely atrophied about twelve or fifteen years back. Or maybe he'd never had them.

Spencer said, "Fine. I asked how long you was goin' to be in town."

"Depends," Garner said. "I take it you want me gone as soon as possible?"

"That's the size of it."

Garner sighed. He was a law-abiding citizen. There was no paper out on him, anyway. "Mind if I ask why?"

"Don't want no trouble."

"Neither do I," he said. "And Jesus, Ed! Don't you ever change your expression? If you can't smile, frown or some-thin'."

Spencer just stood there like part of the fence. He wasn't the sharpest tool in the shed, not by a long shot, but he'd put quite a few prisoners—the dumb ones, anyhow—into jail with a look. That look. Garner wasn't buying it, though.

"Well, Ed, since you asked so nice," he said, "I'm waitin' on a telegram. Once it comes and I get my horse back, and once he's healed up from this stone bruise, I'll be more than happy to get the hell out of Mormon Wells. Although I'll surely miss your smilin' face."

Spencer mulled this over for quite a bit longer than was necessary, then said, "You always was a smart-assed son-ofabitch."

Garner scowled. "And you never did have a sense of humor. You aren't still mad about that deal with Tom Franken, are you?" And when the shadow of a something akin to a frown flitted across Spencer's face, Garner added, "By God, that's it! That's been more than ten years ago!"

"Thirteen," Spencer said flatly.

"And you're still holdin' a grudge? You beat everything, you know that?"

"He was mine. That should have been my arrest."

Despite Garner's near-giddy happiness—giddy for Garner, anyway—that he'd finally caught up with his horse, Ed Spencer was really beginning to chafe at him. He stood up straight and glared down at the smaller man, and Spencer had to take a step back to avoid staring at Garner's neck.

"You weren't fast enough gettin' there, Ed," Garner said evenly. "You were a half hour too late. Franken drew and I shot him. It's done."

"He was mine," Spencer insisted mulishly.

Spencer was just dumb enough that if Garner had pressed him, it might very well have gone to gunplay. And Spencer would have lost, just as surely as the sun rose in the morning. But the last thing Garner needed was to spend the next few years in prison over some stoic-assed little popinjay of a sheriff. All he wanted to do was to get his horse, get him healed, and head north.

And so Garner took a deep breath and uttered what was, for him, a painfully difficult word. "Sorry."

This seemed to leave Spencer at a loss. Of course, Garner thought, nearly everything did. A town was no better or worse than its law, and if this sawed-off, stupid shit of a sheriff was Mormon Wells's representative, Garner was better putting the place as far behind him as possible.

"I'm not looking for any trouble, Ed," he added, although if he'd had his way, if the day had been any other one but this—when he had Red at his side and things were looking up for the first time in months—he would have picked Ed Spencer up and dumped him in the water trough, headfirst.

"I reckon I'll give you today to get your telegram," Spencer said from behind dull eyes. "You leave first thing tomorrow mornin'."

Garner felt his hands balling into fists. "Well, you sorry little turd!"

Spencer didn't flinch. "Sticks and stones," he said like some idiot schoolboy, and walked away, leaving Garner swearing a blue streak beneath his breath.

He had no more than halfway calmed down when that slimy bastard, Buster Cree, came walking out of the barn with another man. Cree waved a hand at Garner, and called, "You got the money yet?"

Over Red's back, Garner snapped, "This afternoon."

The other man busied himself looking at the horse as he walked up, and said, "He's real nice, Cree. Just like you said."

"And he's taken," Garner growled.

"First money gets him," Cree said smugly. He rocked back and forth from heel to toe, obviously expecting a bidding war.

But the other man caught a glimpse of Garner's face about then. Tilting his head, he said, "You look sorta familiar, mister. Whereabouts you hark from?"

"All over," Garner said curtly. "And this horse is spoke for."

"If you're worried about ridin' a stud," Cree said, oblivious to anything but a pending sale, "we got a feller what'll cut him for you. Does a good job. Ain't had but two die on him this year."

The man, still studying Garner's face, said, "You know, I could swear I seen you someplace before. Maybe it was . . ." And then his face drained of color. He took a step back. "G-Garner?" he whispered. "King Garner?"

"The same. And this horse isn't for sale. And nobody's going to cut him," he added to Cree.

"Just a doggone minute!" Cree shouted. "This here's my horse, bought and paid for, and nobody's gonna tell me who I can . . ." Suddenly he paled as well. "D-did you say King Garner?"

"I'm right sorry, Mr. Garner," the prospective buyer said. He was backing toward the barn. "That's sure a real fine mount you got there. The best of luck with him." When he reached the corner of the building, he turned tail and hustled up the street.

Cree had disappeared in the interim. From inside the barn, he shouted, "The price stands. Business is business!"

"Jesus, boy, watch what you're shootin' at!" Pike barked, and ran to the horses. Lisa Boudreau had dropped and hit the dirt immediately, and Quincannon helped her up. Such a tiny hand! Such a delicate flower!

She scowled at him. Such a pretty scowl! "Cripes!" she said, dusting her trousers. He had grown accustomed to them by this time. They were actually rather charming. "You crazy, or what?"

"I . . . I . . ." he stammered.

"Quit swingin' that thing around!"

He swallowed and let the pistol dangle from his hand. "Yes, of course. Sorry."

"She ain't hurt," called Pike. "You parted Millie's mane in a whole new place, though." He patted Millie's bright chestnut neck a last time, then walked back to them, shaking his head. "The dang horses are in back of us, boy," he said when he reached them. "You're supposed to be shootin' in the opposite direction!"

"I'm terribly sorry, Mr. Pike," he said feebly. "It just . . . went off."

Pike muttered something under his breath that Quincannon didn't quite hear, but Lisa Boudreau did, and she giggled.

"All right," Pike said at last. "You reckon you got that thing under control now?" When Quincannon nodded, Pike pointed toward a prickly pear about twenty yards distant. "See that arm what swings out to the left? The one with all them little pads stickin' up like fingers on top?"

"Yes, sir."

"You see it, too, gal?"

"Sure."

"Ladies first, boy. Shoot at them fingers, Miss Lisa."

She set the rifle into her shoulder, sighted down, and shot the entire arm off.

"Damn!" she said, frowning. "Low and to the left!"

Quincannon, still blinking from the blast of her shot—not to mention her profanity—was next.

"Try the next arm over, boy," said Pike.

Quincannon raised the pistol.

"Set your feet out, like I told you," said Pike. "And squeeze the trigger gentle like. Don't go joltin' it."

Quincannon pushed Lisa Boudreau from his mind, set his feet, took a deep breath, did everything Mr. Pike had gone over—and over and over—on the ride from town, and pulled the trigger.

The little pad at the top went flying.

Quincannon broke out in a grin.

"Hey!" said Lisa Boudreau. "You're good!"

Pike wasn't so easily convinced, however. "Was that what you was aimin' for, boy?"

"Yes," Quincannon said. He was still staring at the cactus. Surely, this had to be a fluke! Perhaps they should just go back to town now, while Lisa Boudreau had something to admire him for. She had the sweetest spray of freckles across her nose!

"Do 'er again," said Pike, jerking him from his reverie. "Next pad over."

"B-but—"

"Next pad over."

Quincannon sighed and drew himself up into the stance once more. He told himself that he'd had his fleeting moment of glory. Now it was back to Quincannon the helpless, Quincannon the neophyte, Quincannon the fish out of water. His all-too-brief moment in the sun was finished. He only wished that Garner had been there to see it. At least Lisa Boudreau had.

"Go on, boy," urged Pike.

Once again, he pushed Lisa Boudreau from his thoughts and concentrated on the task at hand.

He pulled the trigger.

The cactus pad went sailing.

Pike took off his hat. "Well, I'll be diddly-damned!" he breathed.

"You got a first name, Quincannon?" asked Lisa Boudreau.

11

"I'm tellin' you, King, it were near to magical!"

It was late in the afternoon, and Garner was leading Red up to Boudreau's, Pike having brought the cash and business having been transacted. Garner said, "You're fulla sheep dip, Pike."

"Believe me or not, it's the consarned truth," Pike sniffed. "I don't s'pose you believe he got the money, neither. I s'pose you're thinkin' I spun them greenbacks outta watered beer an' thin air."

"Don't much care," Garner replied, and led the stallion into the shadowy, cool interior of Boudreau's. The little gal from the night before was sitting up high on a stack of straw bales, and he nodded to her, then cocked an eyebrow in surprise. Not only was she cleaned up a good bit, but she was lazily swinging her legs and staring off into the distance at exactly nothing. He'd be damned if she wasn't humming, too!

She looked over after a moment, and smiled dreamily. "Howdy, Mr. Garner. You seen Elliot?"

"Who the hell's Elliot?"

She frowned at him. It was a pretty frown. "Your saddle buddy. Quincannon!"

What the hell had Quincannon done out there, anyway? Parted the waters? Pike seemed to think he was the Second Coming all of a goddamn sudden, and this little gal appeared to be past soft on him.

He led Red past, grumbling, "Haven't seen him since breakfast."

"He went on back to the hotel once we was finished at the bank," Pike offered happily. "Hell, I didn't know a body could just send off a telegram and come up rich! How do they jam the cash through them wires, that's what I'm wonderin'."

Quincannon was indeed in the hotel room, sitting on the edge of his cot. One hand was pressed to his forehead, the fingers splaying back through tousled hair, and the other was holding the telegram he'd received from Malcolm Peabody.

He had hoped for a glimmer of understanding, a modicum of comfort, a hint of trust. He'd hoped for just a single word of encouragement, but it seemed this was too much to ask. And he couldn't blame Malcolm Peabody for not offering him a hearty mug of the milk of human kindness, could he? Malcolm Peabody, who rarely left the confines of Boston, and whose sole excursion west had been to the wilds of Reading, Pennsylvania, could have no idea what it was really like in this barbaric land! Occasionally reading a bit of charming or picturesque—or even grotesque—fiction in *Harper's* magazine was no preparation for it.

At least, it certainly hadn't been for him.

Malcolm Peabody could sit behind his burlwood desk in his carpeted office. Nothing to bother him, other than a clerk's voice raised too loudly, perhaps, or his tea being two minutes late. He didn't know what it was like to have a cocked pistol waved in your face, to see men who had been tortured and killed in hideous ways, to see the birds eating their bodies. Malcolm Peabody didn't know what it was like to sit out a storm sent up from hell, or to nearly perish from lack of water, or practically get blood poisoning from a backside so stiff and raw that you wanted to die.

Additionally, he didn't know what it was like to put up with Mr. Garner and Mr. Pike.

All Malcolm Peabody knew was that his Chalice was gone, and it was Quincannon's fault. He'd sent the money. Yes, he'd done that. But he'd made it clear that if the Chalice wasn't retrieved in timely fashion, Quincannon—and all his descendants—would be repaying its cost for the rest of their natural lives. Probably by working in a coal pit.

He closed his fist about the telegram and dropped the crumpled paper to the floor.

He'd been so happy this afternoon! At last, he had found something he was actually good at! Mr. Pike had called him a "natural shootist." And Lisa?

Despite the telegram, his face bloomed with a smile. Miss Boudreau. Miss Lisa Boudreau. Lisa. Had there ever been a more beautiful name? A more beautiful and charming and wonderful girl? And she had called him Elliot, just like that, after less than twenty-four hours of acquaintance!

Why, he had been seeing Miss Minion for three years, and she still—

"Oh, God," he muttered, his smile vanished. Miss Minion.

With the heels of his hands pressed hard to his forehead, he attempted to recount Miss Minion's qualities. He saw her in her simple dresses, which he had once thought elegant, and now struck him as overly severe. He pictured her serving him tea—the biscuit plate balanced on one knee, her finger crooked just so—in the dark parlor of her late father's home.

Everything had its place. If he so much as shifted a piece of bric-a-brac, she'd say, "Oh dear, Mr. Quincannon!" and carefully move it back to its original position.

Once upon a time, he'd seen that as a sign of an organized mind. He was beginning to see it as the sign of a mind with nothing to do, and no wish to find occupation.

He tried to picture her face, her hair. Plain. Lank.

He very nearly went to his saddlebags to dig out her picture and gaze upon her face, then stopped himself. He could not bear to look upon that scowl, not right now. It would only accuse him of being unfaithful, at least in his thoughts. It would only whisper of that smarmy Mr. Peters on the second floor, Mr. Peters who was already a real lawyer, Mr. Peters who always managed to show up when they were strolling the Common on a Saturday afternoon, or drop by their table when they were enjoying their once-a-week crabcake dinner at Malachy's.

Mr. Peters, who always acted surprised to find them. Mr. Peters, who always kissed Miss Minion's glove and did that . . . that *thing* with his eyebrows. And Miss Minion, who always blushed.

And giggled.

He'd like to see Mr. Peters in the wilds of Arizona and cornered by bandits, that's what he'd like to see! He'd like to see him shoot the pads right off a cactus, and not the big pads, either!

Quincannon took a deep breath, then scrubbed at his face with newly callused fingers. This was getting him nowhere. He had to look to the business at hand.

He would not think about Miss Minion's little gold glasses or bulbous nose, or Lisa Boudreau's tight trousers and the way those blue eyes lit up her face. Neither would he think of Malcolm Peabody, who was certainly well past grumpy by this time. He would set his mind to his goal. He would make the Chalice become his focus once more, his singularity of thought. He would find it, he would repair the shambles he'd made of his life, and he would move on.

He rose from the cot and went to the window. The sun was low on the horizon. Soon it would be gone altogether.

"Tomorrow," he said with new purpose.

The three of them would set out once more. There would be no trail to follow, of course, but Garner had said that he knew where this Lazlo was heading. At least, he'd said he had a pretty fair idea: a place called Indian Haunt. Garner was continually gruff and surly, and Quincannon didn't get the sense that Garner liked him one bit, but the man was certainly good at roughing it. He and Pike seemed to know this territory as well as he knew his office in Boston.

He needed them.

And wouldn't Garner perhaps be a tad kinder, now that Quincannon had finally shown his worth at something?

"I tell you, boy, he ain't goin'," Pike said sadly.

Quincannon hadn't seen Garner all morning. Pike had walked up to the stable with him, and Quincannon had truly expected to find Garner there. But no. Faro was gone, too.

"This is disastrous!" Quincannon shouted, once the gravity of the situation sank all the way in. Pike had probably told him a dozen times that Garner wasn't planning to accompany them, but he hadn't believed it, really believed it, until just this moment.

"Not only that," he raged on, "it's criminal! He accepted two hundred dollars from me! Two hundred dollars to buy *that*!" Derisively, he waved a hand at the red horse's backside. "I'll press charges! I'll sue on top of it. I'm just the man to do it, too," he said through clenched teeth, and what he knew was a beet-red face. "By the time I'm done with him, he'll be living in the territorial prison at Yuma. I'll take everything he has and Mr. King Garner will have to change his name to Serf! I won't leave him a button!"

Pike, who was quite obviously alarmed by this sudden outburst, and maybe a little embarrassed—as well he should be—said, "Now, son—"

"Don't 'now, son' me, Mr. Pike."

Lisa Boudreau wasn't there, either, and in his anger-muddled state, Quincannon wasn't sure if this was a good thing or a bad thing. He only knew that for some reason, her absence provoked him even further. Near the end of his tether, he snapped, "I suppose this means you're not coming with me, either?"

Pike shrugged his shoulders, although he had the good grace to look uncomfortable.

In silence, Quincannon marched to the rear of the barn and retrieved his saddle, hurriedly tacked up Rosie and tied on his packs, then led her from her stall. He lifted the stirrup a last time and gave a final yank to the latigo, thinking furiously all the while. Taking Garner to court would drag on for ages, and as enjoyable as it would be to have the man at the defendant's table, he needed more immediate action. So he did the one thing which he knew would bring Garner charging after him.

He walked into Red's stall, clipped a lead rope to his halter, and led the stallion out.

At last, Pike showed something besides foot-shuffling ill ease. He came forward, and shouting, "What you doin', boy?" he snatched the rope from Quincannon's hand.

Quincannon grabbed it back again. He said, "Mr. Garner has breached his contract. Which, as you may remember, Mr. Pike, we sealed with a handshake at the café. I'm certain the waiter and several other patrons will testify to that. Until Mr. Garner sees fit to fulfill his end of the bargain, this horse is my property, to do with as I see fit."

He had no idea if the waiter knew what they'd been talking about, let alone the other patrons, but it had the desired effect. Pike dropped his hand and stepped back, and Quincannon swung up onto Rosie's back, silently praying that he'd got the roan's girth snug enough. He had.

"Where exactly is this Indian Haunt place?"

He fully expected Pike to fold his arms and say, "Ain't tellin'," but instead, the old man's face took on a slightly bemused look. He scratched at his ear, and said, "King's gonna have your hide, boy. You know that?"

Quincannon didn't much care. He was as good as dead most anyway he looked at it, and another fist to his jaw from Garner seemed neither here nor there.

His face must have registered his desperation, because Pike took pity on him and said, "You wanta go due south till you come to a pair'a twin buttes. They's big ol' things, and you can't miss 'em. Reckon it'll take you 'bout a day to get that far, leadin' an extra horse. You goes betwixt 'em, 'cause that's the entrance to Indian Creek Canyon. Once you get in there, you follow along the creek bed for maybe a mile, mile and a half. You'll know Indian Haunt when you sees it." His eyes narrowed. "You be careful, boy. You don't need your hair hangin' from Lazlo's belt. And hold on just a minute."

To Quincannon's surprise, Pike measured out extra oats and filled another water bag, both of which he handed up. As Quincannon strapped them to his already heavily laden saddle, Pike said, "That there's for Red. And you mind him, now, and go easy. That stone bruise a' his ain't healed proper yet."

As Quincannon rode out into the sunshine, leading the big red stud, his last glimpse of the old man was Pike setting his hands on his hips and grinning wide.

"Takin' Red!" Quincannon heard him cackle. "Ol' King's gonna have hisself a whole litter'a kittens!"

"Damn it to hell! You could've told me, Pike!" Garner took off his hat and slammed it to the ground. He looked again at the stall, as if Red would somehow materialize. "What the hell's wrong with you, anyhow, you crazy old coot? How could you let me sit down and eat a steak dinner and sit there smokin' cigarettes and drinkin' beer in the bar till way past dark, when all the time you knew Red was gone?"

Pike leaned innocently against a stall rail. He shrugged. "First off, it were near dark when you come in, King. I can't help it if you spent the whole dang day lollygaggin' who knows where. Didn't you figure it was kinda peculiar

I'd put Faro up for you? Didn't you think it was sorta funny that I'd be snaggin' him from you out front'a the hotel?"

Bad luck, that was Pike. The worst. He should have known better than to leave him with the kid. Too cozy, that's what they were. Pike probably gift-wrapped the damn horse for him with a big gold ribbon!

"You're gettin' back at me for the goddamn cards, aren't you?" Garner said through clenched teeth.

Pike shrugged again. "Mayhap the cards. Mayhap somethin' else. But as long as you're bringin' 'em up—"

"No!" Garner snarled. "And shut up!"

Pike did.

Garner picked up his hat, slapped it against his thigh, then kicked helplessly at the loose straw on the barn's floor. It was either that or Pike. "Sonofabitch. Goddamn sonofabitching whoring shitheel bastard! I was out there riding around in circles and staring at goddamn cactus all blamed day to keep out of Ed Spencer's path, and the whole time my horse was heading south with that blister-butted idiot!"

Pike pursed his lips and slowly shook his head. "Aw, I don't reckon the boy goes in much for whoring, King."

"Close your damn hole!"

"Boy, mister, you sure got some kind of mouth on you!"

He whirled to find Lisa Boudreau standing in the doorway, placidly chewing on a long piece of straw. She turned up the lantern, then sat down on a bale beside the door. "I saw him leaving town this mornin'. That stud horse of yours is sure a beaut! How's he rein?"

"Oh, real nice," Pike said, as if he hadn't a care in the world. "King, here, schooled him slow. I told him he were crazy for takin' so much time with that dang horse, but—"

"Quiet!" Garner was a hair away from pounding Pike into the ground, and paddling the bejesus out of that girl for good measure. "Why is everybody so goddamn *calm*!" he shouted. "The boy's a horse thief! I oughta report him!

Hell, I oughta report the whole bunch of you! You let him waltz out of here with my horse!"

The girl leaned back against the barn wall. "No, we didn't, Mr. Garner. It was his horse, bought and paid for."

Pike chimed in, "Says you didn't hold up your end'a the bargain, so Red's his. Says he's gonna take you to court, otherwise. If I was you," he confided, "I'd steer clear'a that boy when he gets to talkin' legalities."

"Why don't you help him get his Chalice back?" added Lisa Boudreau, and she had the gall to bat her eyelashes at him.

They'd been plotting behind his back. If ever there was a coyote in the henhouse, it was that damn kid! Him and Pike, both the worst kind of luck! Dragged you down, slowed you up, stole your horse! "Quincannon put you up to this, didn't he? I bet you hatched this thing while you were out on the desert yesterday."

"Oh, no," the girl said, smiling. "Me and Mr. Pike cooked it up this morning, after Elliot rode out. See, I think Elliot took that horse to make you come after him. I think he needs you. I think he's bullheaded enough that he'll probably go and get himself killed, too, after what Mr. Pike told me about this Cherry Lazlo. Elliot paid you to help him, didn't he?"

Garner glared at her.

She clucked her tongue. "And you were going to cut him loose, weren't you? You were gonna take his money and then run out on him."

"Oh," said Pike helpfully, "King already done that."

"So why don't you go after him," the girl continued, "and help him rescue that Chalice thing so you can get the reward from his boss and buy your ranch?"

Garner scowled. "Because I'll get killed, that's why. I thought you were a nice little gal."

"You won't, and I am," she replied. "I'm so nice that I had a word with our own peckerwood sheriff, Ed Spencer. He'll be pushing you two out of town come first light. It seems you have quite a reputation. I don't believe he likes you much, Mr. Garner."

"He likes *me* just fine," offered Pike.

"Traitor," growled Garner.

"In the words of our sawed-off sheriff," the girl said, " 'sticks and stones.' I'd get to bed early if I was you, gents." She stood up, brushed the straw from her britches, then lifted the lantern off its hook. She briefly held it out the door. Dust was already dancing lightly against the boards, and Garner saw the sky light up to the east.

She continued, "We got a big blow headed in tonight, but I prophesy that morning's gonna dawn bright and clear, and you fellas'll have some hard riding to do. You need your rest when you get older."

Garner muttered, "Somebody oughta swat your backside."

She smiled at him cheerily. "Try it and die. Night, Lemuel," she said to Pike.

"Night, Miss Lisa," Pike replied.

She blew out the lantern and left them standing in the dark.

"Lemuel?"

Pike gave the stained brim of his hat a jaunty flick. "Don't wear it out."

12

"Aw, shit," **Garner** muttered. He slithered back down the rocks on his belly, to where Pike was waiting with the horses. Of all the blamed-fool idiots ever born, this kid had to be right up there at the top.

Another shot rang out—accompanied by the sound of breaking glass and a great deal of drunken laughter—at the same instant as he slid to a stop at Pike's feet.

"Well?" Pike asked anxiously.

"Bandidos," Garner replied, dusting his shirt and britches. "Six of 'em that I could see. They've got Red tied to their picket line."

Pike stared at him, and he added, "All right, the kid's down there, too."

Quincannon had, in fact, ridden through the gap between the twin buttes the day before, and had proceeded onward, into the canyon, to find Indian Haunt. It was at the rocky bottom of Indian Haunt that the boy was now tied and being used for target practice by the bandidos.

"And?" urged Pike.

"He's still alive. Lazlo isn't, though."

He had seen what remained of Cherry Lazlo, dangling

from a long rope descending from the uppermost window of a cliff dwelling in Indian Haunt. Whether he had been hanged and then scalped or scalped and then hanged was of no consequence. He was dead, his face and torso covered with blood, and dangling in front of ancient mud-walled huts that were stacked, one over the other, in the broad hollow of the cliff face.

The cliff dwelling had been built by long-dead Indians. Anasazi, he'd been told. He didn't much care about dead Indians. He had enough trouble with the live ones. But the rooms that once provided shelter for a vanished tribe had become a sort of occasional trading center for outlaws.

Few people knew about it, for the canyon was practically void of vegetation, and the creek carried water only about two weeks out of the year. No good for cattle, no good for sustaining any sort of life. Not even the coyotes prowled here. It must have been different once upon a time, though. Elsewise, a whole tribe of Indians wouldn't have gone to the trouble of slapping together those stacked rooms, sixty feet high.

Garner had been here only twice before. The first time had been about ten years back while he was trailing Vance Trumbull. Got the thieving bastard, too. And he'd been here with Pike six months ago, on the trail of Ramon Sanchez and Red. Now following Red had brought him back again.

Another shot. No breaking glass this time.

"Think they's runnin' outta Who Hit John?"

"Don't know," Garner answered.

"Well?"

"Well, what?"

Pike rolled his eyes. "What we gonna do, dang it! That boy's gonna take a slug to his skull any second, if he ain't already."

Garner sighed. Visions of cool mountain breezes and long, green grass and gamboling colts, never far from his mind, were shoved aside by a picture of that little gal from town standing over his and Pike's coffins. "And I told them they wouldn't get killed," she sniffled into her hankie.

Garner thought for a moment. "Remember what we did when we came lookin' for Sanchez?" he asked.

"When we come here? To Indian Haunt?"

"Yes, dammit!"

"You don't have to go an' get all snarly on me. I re-camembers."

Another shot and the sound of shattering glass, followed by a loud roar of laughter. Garner slid his rifle from its boot. "Good," he said. "Do it again."

Pike already had his Winchester in hand. "I reckon this time we is gonna be met with resistance?" he muttered.

"You got that right."

Quincannon sputtered into consciousness once again. Some kind of clear liquor stung his eyes and assaulted the cuts in his face. After a moment the fluid dripped pink again from the glass and knife wounds in his scalp.

All around him, filthy outlaws babbled in Spanish, and another one, weaving from drink, his trousers stained by his own fresh vomit, stepped behind the firing line they'd marked with a rock.

"Jorge!" roared the marksman of the moment, and waved his pistol. Another man—Jorge, Quincannon supposed— sashayed over and set another empty bottle on Quincannon's head.

Quincannon, lashed to the rock, incapable of movement, closed his eyes once more and held very still.

Again, the blast came, accompanied by a shower of exploding glass and rock chips. Fresh blood trickled down his forehead and into his left eye, and all around him, men laughed. One of them, a tall man with no front teeth and a lady's plumed hat perched on his head, staggered up to Quincannon and punched him in the stomach. It was the fifth or sixth time the miscreant had underscored his mirth with a poke at Quincannon, and Quincannon would have given anything for five minutes in a room alone with him. He'd show him a good time, all right! He'd feed him that damned blue feather!

After he'd had a drink of water and a nap, of course. At the moment he was certain he couldn't lick a Boston-bull puppy.

They'd come upon him last night. Of course, he couldn't really say they'd taken him captive, because Lazlo had already done that. Lazlo had jumped him before he'd known what was happening, before he'd barely approached the ruins, before he had a chance even to think about drawing his pistol. He'd given a fair account of himself in the ensuing scuffle, but it wasn't good enough, not anywhere near. Lazlo had him hog-tied and the knife to his hairline when the Mexican bandits rode in.

Although he couldn't understand a word they were saying, the bandits must have held a powerful grudge against Lazlo. They had begun torturing him last night while Quincannon watched helplessly. By noon today, they'd tired of tormenting him. They ripped the scalp from Lazlo's living head—the only time the man had made a sound, other than to spit curses at them in Spanish. It was a blood-chilling scream such as Quincannon never hoped to hear again. And then two of them had carried him up into the ruins and hung him out a window.

Then they'd turned to Quincannon.

Ignoring his repeated pleas for water, they'd roped him to this rock and then left him. It was because of the money, of course. Apparently, one of them had found Lazlo's possessions, and they spent the next few hours drinking and crowing over all the gold coins they'd discovered, while Quincannon baked in the full blast of the sun. It was about four when they remembered him, he guessed, although he was so sun-addled by then that it could just as easily have been the next day.

No, not the next day, he thought as a serape-covered arm balanced yet another bottle on his head. He would have been dead if it had been the next day. He was thirsty, so thirsty. He closed his eyes. The lids shut grittily with dust and dried blood.

"Whatever you do, you sonofabitch, don't move," whispered a voice.

Wonderful, he thought dully. English. Now he was hallucinating. He hoped they'd just shoot him through the head when they grew bored with the game. They wouldn't torture him like they had Lazlo, would they?

"Water," he rasped. They ignored him once again.

And again, the blast and the shower of rock and glass.

He passed out.

Garner, dressed in the red serape and tired sombrero he'd taken off the bandido whose throat he'd slit, staggered drunkenly back around the rock, making sure to keep his head low and his face turned away from the others.

There were just three men left. Besides the former owner of the serape and hat, one had passed out—and Garner made sure he stayed that way, by dragging him around a rock and tying and gagging him. Another, who had the bad fortune to surprise Garner while he was seeing to the second fellow's ropes, lay dead beside his compatriot.

Of the remaining three, two were faced off with Quincannon—one standing and presently yelling for something else to shoot at, and the other one sat on his heels behind the firing line, slouched against a rock. The third, a big hombre wearing a woman's hat with a big blue plume, was over with the remuda, between two horses.

The third man bothered Garner, and for reasons other than the hat. He didn't want lead flying anywhere near those nags. More specifically, near Red.

He looked up, high into the rocks of the wall that faced Indian Haunt. The canyon was reasonably narrow here, perhaps fifty yards across, and he spotted Pike with little difficulty. He gave the signal to wait. Despite the grief Pike gave him about his eyes, he could see just fine, thank you,

so long as it was day and it was fair; but even he would
have found it impossible to sight down on that third man.
Not without taking out a lot of horseflesh first.

The slurred cry of *"¡Oye, Esteban! ¡Uno más!"* came
from the other side of the rock. The shooters wanted another bottle.

Judging from the pile of amber and green and clear
shards that lay at Quincannon's feet, there must have been
a whole stockpile of cobwebbed empties in the ruins. But
they'd shot and good-timed their way through those, plus
the bottles they'd brought with them. Aside from the quart
of tequila the rat-bag beside the horses was nursing, there
was only one pint bottle left. Now or never.

He picked it up, then staggered back around the big rock
and into Blue Feather's line of vision. He stopped and
swayed. He wavered and pivoted sickly, the serape he wore
covering the motion as he eased his Colt from its holster.
He staggered again and bent at the waist, his back to the
man with the horses.

The rat-bag in the plumed hat laughed. In Spanish, he
shouted gleefully to the others, "Hey, Joaquin, Pedro! That
shit Esteban is puking again!"

Garner held the bottle out to the side and wiggled it,
signaling to Blue Feather to come get it. He hoped to hell
that Pike was paying attention up there.

He set the bottle out to the side and, still bent at the
waist, leaned farther over. He eased up his hanging serape
and looked between the inverted V of his legs. Blue Feather
lurched toward him, sloshing his bottle, shouting gleeful
obscenities as he came.

Just a little closer, Garner thought as sweat trickled into
his eyes. *C'mon, you greasy sonofabitch.*

The man swayed slowly up to him, his feather bobbing,
and when he was about ten feet away, Garner threw himself to his side. Blue Feather barked out a laugh then
stopped abruptly when Garner rolled to his back and fired.
Too drunk to pull his pistol, Blue Feather fell to his knees,

staring first at Garner, then the stain that was rapidly spreading over his chest. He opened his mouth in surprise, cried, *"¡Condenado!"* and then he pitched forward, dead.

Garner paid only enough attention to be sure that Blue Feather wasn't going to bother anybody again. Pike had begun to fire from the rim a split second after he had, and now Garner scrambled the opposite way around the rock. And nearly ran into one of the bandits.

Garner fired without thinking. The bandido died before he had a chance to bring his gun up.

That left one man, unless Pike had got him.

Garner edged back around the rock, to its rear, and signaled up to Pike. After a moment Pike waved his arm in the sign for all clear, then he backed off and disappeared from the canyon's edge.

Garner relaxed at last. He was boiling hot and exhausted, and he was getting too old for this sort of shit. Wearily, he holstered his Colt, threw off the sombrero, and ripped the serape off over his head. He never had figured out why anybody in their right mind would wear one of those damned things in summer. His shirt was soaked through with sweat.

Sighing, he pulled the knife from his belt and walked around the rock, toward Quincannon.

The Mexican was indeed dead, sprawled on his belly, his arms flung wide, his fingers inches from the butt of his pistol. The boy was unconscious, his head lolling low on his chest. He reeked of liquor.

"Bad-luck little bastard," Garner growled under his breath. Glass crunching under his feet, he cut away the ropes that bound Quincannon's hands, then put his knife away. Water first. Let the ropes hold the sonofabitch up until he could walk.

Garner went over to the horses, and after giving Red a cursory looking over and a pat on the neck, he found a pile of supplies. He pulled a canteen from it, sniffed the contents to make sure it was water, and not mescal or something else. You never could tell with these yahoos.

It didn't stink of booze, and he brought it to Quincannon.

He lifted Quincannon's sagging head and frowned, muttering, "Jesus." The kid's face was pocked with glass cuts weeping blood and fluid. Worse, he must have just missed being scalped, because there was a gash high on his forehead, just beneath his hairline, that ran from his left temple to high above his right eye. Sweat and blood stained his shirt, and the odor told Garner that he'd soiled himself.

For a fellow that only a week or ten days before had been in a nice cool Boston law office, the boy had been through hell.

More gently than he had intended, he held Quincannon's jaw and tipped the canteen to it. "C'mon, boy," he said softly. "C'mon, Elliot. Drink up." And when the kid fluttered his eyes and drank, he said, "That's the way, kid. Easy, not too much. I'll get you freed up in a minute."

"Mr. Garner?" the boy rasped, and brought a hand up to grip the canteen.

"That's right, son. Here, take one more swallow, and then we'll—"

So quickly that Garner barely registered it, the boy's eyes focused past him. He felt something brush his hip, and in the same instant a gun went off, so close that he felt the heat of it in his side.

He jumped back, reached for his Colt, and realized in horror that it wasn't there. In that same second, he saw it in Quincannon's hand, saw the Mexican he'd thought was dead flopping onto his back, his pistol in his hand.

Still staring at the body, his face grim, Quincannon whispered, "Stop shooting at me," before he passed out again. The gun fell from his hand into a dry sea of sparkling glass.

13

Garner rode back down the canyon, passed beneath Lazlo's dangling corpse and the ancient cliff dwelling, and dropped the leather bag of golden coins at Pike's side. It landed with a jingling clank, and the old man looked up from his work.

Pike cocked his head like a dog. "That there sounds like cash money," he said. "Lot of it, too."

Garner got down off Faro and stepped closer, studying the boy's face. Pike had been picking glass slivers from it when he left to reconnoiter the canyon, and the old man was still at it.

"A good bit," he said. "Didn't count it. Looks to me like Lazlo sold off the boy's gold jug. Didn't get that fortune he's always ranting about, though. Found three set of tracks goin' the other way, real leisurely. Reckon those were the buyers'." He tipped his head toward Quincannon. "How is he, anyway?"

"Better, I reckon," said Pike. "I pick out the glass, he wakes up and asks for water, I give him some, an' then he passes out again and I pick out more glass. Think I .'bout got 'er all, though. Dad-blasted stuff, anyhow! I keep on stickin' my own dang self!" He held up his hand. The fingers were dotted with blood, and after a moment he stuck them in his mouth. "They smarts somethin' awful!" he said around them. "Is we gonna follow 'em?"

Garner ignored the question and pointed to the boy's bandaged forehead. "What about that knife wound?"

Pike removed his fingers from his mouth with a *pop* and, after a short search for a relatively clean place, dried them on his shirt. "That was a bad 'un." He shook his head. "Cut clean down to his skull. Happened yesterday by the looks of it, and the blame thing was startin' to heal open. Cut 'er a fresh edge with my shavin' razor and stitched it up with a hair from Red's tail."

Garner frowned. "Why Red?"

"'Cause I knowed it'd make you so dang happy, that's why."

Garner grunted. "How about him?" He nodded toward the trussed bandido who lay against the rocks at the edge of their campsite.

"Ain't made a peep. Likely still higher'n a kite." Pike grinned. "He's gonna have him a real surprise when he wakes up, ain't he?"

Garner stood up. "If you're done playin' nursemaid, see if you can find enough sticks to make a fire and get supper started. There's a dead mesquite down the canyon about sixty, seventy yards."

Pike scowled. "Why don't you jus' tell me to run to Tucson and whittle up some ironwood for you? Mesquite's near about as hard to chop when you ain't got no ax!"

"Didn't ask for a bonfire," said King as he led Faro toward the picket line. "Just snap off some twigs. I'm gonna see to the horses."

"You're gonna bill an' coo with that ol' red horse, that's what you means," he heard Pike mutter behind him.

He had no more than tied Faro to the line when, suddenly, night fell upon the canyon. Once the sun dipped below the western rim, it was just like someone had blown out a lamp. But the moon was half-full, and so far, the sky was cloudless. Maybe the storms had blown themselves out for a few days.

He fed and watered the horses, feeling his way up and down the line more than seeing it. He was tired to the bone or somewhere past it, so it took him quite a while, especially considering the extra time he spent with Red. Despite having been led over twenty-five miles through rocky terrain, he didn't look half-bad. Garner supposed that resting all day today had helped.

By the time he stumbled back through the darkness to Quincannon and Pike, the former was sitting up, looking woozy, and the latter had a fire started. Ham slices in an iron skillet were beginning to sizzle.

Pike was concentrating on the small pot of beans. It was just coming up to a bubble, and he carefully measured spices into it, pinching them from tiny, unlabeled pouches he pulled from his goody bag.

"Smells good," Garner said. He sat down across the fire.

"She'll smell better once them fixin's get a chance to settle in and them beans is cooked soft," Pike replied. He closed the bag, then tipped his head toward Quincannon. "I give him some jerky to tide 'im over. How you doin', there, Elliot?"

"Fine, thank you, Mr. Pike," Quincannon said before he warily turned his attention toward Garner. "Before you launch into another of your tirades, Mr. Garner, I'd like to say thank you. For saving me, that is. And I'm sorry I took your horse."

He paused to take another gulp of water from the canteen, then added defensively, "Although I was perfectly within my rights, because at that time you had failed to fulfill your part of the bargain. However, since you are back on the job, and very probably saved my life from those miscreants, I'll now consider him one quarter yours."

Muttering, "Christ on a crutch!" Pike stood up and moved back from the fire and out of the way.

But Garner remained silent. He glared into the fire, his jaw muscles working overtime.

"Now, King, you gotta remember that he ain't proper back in his head, yet," soothed Pike from a safe distance.

"I assure you, Mr. Pike," said Quincannon, "I'm thinking properly."

Garner looked up at last, and into the face of the battered boy with the set jaw. Quietly, he said, "All right."

"What?" yelped Pike from the shadows.

"You heard me, you old geezer," Garner snapped.

"V-very good, then," croaked Quincannon. He sounded for all the world like a puzzled frog. He appeared to try to raise his eyebrows, then winced and touched the bandage Pike had tied around his forehead. "I must admit, Mr. Garner, that quite frankly I didn't expect you to acquiesce so readily." He leaned back, exhausted. "I—I'm . . . grateful."

"You already said that. And drink some more'a that water. You sound like you swallowed a mile of river gravel. You look like hell, too."

Muttering, "I'll be double-dog-damned," Pike crept back to the fire and sat down with a thump. He gave the beans a stir. "What's this blamed world comin' to?"

"You makin' biscuits?" Garner asked conversationally.

Pike's head jerked back and he snapped, "Of course I'm makin' biscuits! Don't I always make biscuits?"

"You don't have to get mad, dammit."

"Well, somebody's gotta get mad!" Pike said, and he popped to his feet again. "Don't seem natural, nobody yellin'!"

"Oh, sit down!" Garner growled.

Pike snorted, then grouched, "Well, that's some better, I reckon. Least you sounds like yourself."

Garner ignored him. "I'm only doin' it," he said to Quincannon, "because you're either too goddamn pigheaded or too stupid to quit. Haven't decided yet. And it seems like you're dead set on gettin' yourself in the most trouble you can find."

He twisted toward Pike. "And because you're such a damn jabbermouth that I'd never hear the end of it if he went and got himself killed. Besides, seems to me that a whole lot less people get dead when we're keepin' him clear of trouble than do when we're gettin' him out of it. And sit down, for Christ's sake!"

"All right, all right!" Pike muttered, and sat down again. "Don't need to get your knickers in a twist."

"Either way," Quincannon said softly, "I'm beholden to the two of you. Both myself and Mr. Malcolm Peabody."

"Then shut the hell up about Red," Garner said. "About parcelin' him out in pieces." He stopped, then grumbled, "A quarter here and a half there. You make it sound like I was buyin' him from the butcher for the damn roastin' pit!"

"Sorry. I won't mention it again, sir."

"Good." Garner poked around his pocket for his fixings, and began to roll himself a smoke. "Found tracks of three riders headin' out the back way. Reckon those are the ones that have your gold cup."

"The Iberian Chalice."

"Whatever," Garner said. He lit his smoke with a twig from the fire, then tossed it back. "Pike show you the money?"

The boy nodded. "I can only guess at the amount he received for the horses back in Mormon Wells, of course, although I assume he got a good bit less for the other horses than he did for your stallion. He truly is magnificent, Mr. Garner."

Garner felt a sudden surge of pride, although he didn't know why he should. The little idiot wouldn't know a plow horse from a pacer.

Quincannon sipped at his water again and continued, "In any case, he couldn't have sold the Chalice for more than four hundred dollars, five hundred at the outside. There was less than nine hundred in the bag. I should have to say, gentlemen, that this Lazlo was a financial idiot."

He said it in a voice laden with disgust, as if being bad with money was a far greater sin than the multitude Lazlo had committed in the past. Pike looked at Garner and Garner looked at Pike, and neither of them could think of a thing to say.

They sat there in silence for a time, listening to the drunken bandit snore and smelling biscuits baking and ham frying, and at about the same time that Pike reached for the ham skillet to set it off the fire, Quincannon said softly, "Have you killed a great many men, Mr. Garner?"

Garner thought he knew why the boy was asking, but he said, "My share, I reckon. Killed a few more today to save your fool hide."

Quincannon didn't look at him, but stared at the fire instead. "Do you ever become . . . steeled to it?"

Pike opened his mouth, but Garner silenced him with a look. He said, "When they're men like these ones today, yes. I reckon you know better than I do what they did to Lazlo, up there." He tipped his head backward, toward the suspended corpse. "Looks like they did him bad. Not that the sonofabitch didn't deserve it."

"No man deserves what they did to him," Quincannon said quietly.

"Maybe, maybe not," Garner replied. "I suppose I'm not the judge'a that. But they were having their fun with you. Cut you up pretty bad. Pike was pickin' glass out of you for over an hour, and trust me, boy, you don't want to see your face."

He tossed his cigarette away, then continued, "I don't reckon that when they were done, they woulda just set you on your horse and sent you on your way. No, boy. It was them or us. Me and Pike, we chose us. So did you. Simple as that. Although," he added, turning toward Pike, "if somebody had done his damn job right in the first place, somebody else wouldn't've had to be cleanin' up after him."

Pike threw the bean spoon down into the dirt. "I just knowed you'd be bringin' that up sooner or later! King, I swear to God I thought he were dead. Hell, he fell right down and everythin'! An' why didn't you check him when you come out around that big ol' rock instead'a fetchin' water for Elliot, here? Seems to me that makin' sure that Mex weren't playin' possum'd be the first thing a fella'd do!"

It should have been. But he didn't want to admit that he'd been too damn tired. Or that he'd been too concerned about the boy. That seeing him strapped to the rock half-dead, covered in his own blood, with that wicked knife wound to his forehead, had brought a whole new—and wholly unwelcome—feeling over him.

Guilt.

So he snarled, "That'll be the last time I trust you when you signal the all clear, old man. Those damn beans ready yet?"

"No," said Pike, and proceeded to pick up the spoon and angrily wipe the dirt from it.

"It bothered me," Quincannon said, so softly that Garner had to strain to hear the words. "I know he was a bad man, but it bothered me. Not at the second I pulled the trigger, but later. When I saw him leveling his pistol at you, I just grabbed for your gun and fired."

He paused, and Garner waited. "No, that's not correct," he continued at last. "At first, I thought he was going to shoot at me again, shoot another bottle. It was just after I fired that I realized he was aiming at you, not me. And that seemed . . . well, it seemed worse, somehow. But to take a life, even the life of one of these . . . these animals . . ."

Just then, the bandit let out a tremendous fart, snuggled into his ropes, and began to snore again.

"Elliot," said Pike after a moment, "somehow, I think the Lord's gonna forgive you." He dipped his newly cleaned spoon into the pot and smashed a bean against the side. "Vittles is ready," he announced.

That night, when Garner was asleep and Pike was down the canyon, keeping guard, the wind whipped the upper reaches of the canyon and set Cherry Lazlo's body swinging and twisting. Quincannon lay awake in the stillness at the floor, where the wind didn't reach.

His entire head felt like a large throbbing lump of ground meat, and additionally, he was beginning to wonder if it wasn't his fate to die of thirst. After all, he had nearly accomplished it on two separate occasions in just the last few days. Third time's the charm, isn't that what they said? He was still in the grip of a powerful thirst. Pike had refilled the canteen for him so many times he'd lost count, and he was nearly through it again.

He had replayed the killing in his head over and over. It was sketchy at first, but he thought he had it clear now. The feelings, if not the actual details.

It seemed he was living in a world populated by bad men, with only degrees of badness to tell them apart. Pike, he decided, was only a little bad. He hadn't decided about Garner yet, although he was beginning to suspect he wasn't nearly so bad as he'd originally thought. But Lazlo—and the bandits who had captured him—were very bad indeed.

He had felt sorry for Lazlo in the same way he would feel the pain of a tortured animal. Last night, he hadn't wanted them to stop stripping the skin from Lazlo's chest and arms so much as he wanted them to kill him and get it over with.

That they might let Lazlo live—or that they *should* let him live—had not occurred to him.

And today, when he shot that bandit? It had bothered him, yes, but not nearly so much as he would have suspected. It was just that he had done it so quickly, without giving it a second thought. Of course, if he had given it thought, then he and Garner would both be dead.

Mr. Garner was correct when he said that a man had to make a choice. This was a harsh land, as divorced from Boston as was the distant landscape of Mars. Actions that would be deemed reprehensible east of the Mississippi were matter-of-fact out here.

Quincannon sensed, however, that some things remained the same, if not more so. The bonds between men, for instance. Pike and Garner, for example. Despite all their bickering, despite their differences, they stayed together. Perhaps it was habit, but Quincannon suspected it was something different, something grander than even Pike or Garner suspected.

Quincannon had never had a friend. Oh, he'd had acquaintances, certainly! But never a true friend, one who would lay down his life to save Quincannon's. Never one Quincannon would sacrifice his own life for.

Today, a split second after he had fired, after he had spoken, when it belatedly sank into his muddled brain that the bandit had been aiming at Garner and not him, he had been filled with a rage the likes of which he had never before experienced.

Was this friendship? Could it be that he actually liked Garner? Admired him?

The thought was upsetting, and he closed his eyes. *No, it was just us against them,* he thought. As in a war, it was just saving your comrades from the enemy, that was all. You protected your brothers-in-arms because they protected you.

His eyes jerked open at a scraping sound. It was the Mexican. He'd finally come awake. The man was mumbling behind his gag, and Quincannon got up and warily went to him. He removed the gag, and the man started babbling in Spanish.

"I don't understand you," Quincannon said, and cast a glance toward Garner's sleeping form.

"¡Mierda! ¡Agua, agua!" the bandit snarled, and tried, without success, to spit in his face.

Now that he had a closer look, Quincannon remembered him. This was the man who had taken the strips of flesh they peeled from Lazlo. He'd taken them and thrown them in the fire at Lazlo's feet, laughing.

Quincannon sat back on his heels, careful to shield his gun even though the man was hog-tied. Anger came over him in a wave, and he thought that this man did not deserve to live. For a moment he rested his hand on the butt of his pistol.

"Gets easier, don't it?" Garner said, behind him.

"I—I wasn't going to," Quincannon said lamely, and removed his hand. Although if Garner hadn't spoken just then, he honestly didn't know what he would have done.

"Give him some water."

"Sí. Water. *Agua,"* croaked the bandit.

Quincannon fetched the canteen and held it to the man's mouth. He was recapping the canteen when the man said, with great difficulty, "I am have to make piss."

"Nobody's stoppin' you," said Garner, and rolled over.

Smiling to himself, Quincannon put the man's gag back in place and went to his bedroll. Garner was already snoring.

14

By the time they ate breakfast and packed the horses, the sky above was gunmetal with the coming dawn.

"What about him?" Quincannon asked, giving Rosie's girth a final tug. He tipped his head toward the bound bandit. His thirst had been quenched at last, but his voice was still on the sandpapery side. He hadn't shaved. Pike said he didn't trust him to look in the mirror.

"Go cut him loose," said Garner, and handed over his knife. "I'm leaving him supplies and one pony." He snugged another horse's lead rope. "That, and a shovel. He can bury his buddies if he's of a mind. Tell him that in American. He understands it good enough."

Quincannon did as he was told, and then the three of them—plus a long string of horses—rode down the canyon. The remaining bandit's echoing curses followed them for a good while.

"I got half a mind to just ride back there and plug 'im," Pike muttered around the biscuit, left over from breakfast, that he was devouring.

Garner ignored him, and turned in his saddle. "What happened to Lazlo's scalp?" he asked Quincannon.

"The one with the feathered hat wore it for a while," he replied, and his stomach lurched at the memory. "The one who was using me for target practice when you came— the one I shot—had it last. Maybe it was on his belt. I don't remember."

"Not no more, he don't," Pike said with a grin. Reaching behind him, he patted his saddlebags. "Reckon we can get ourselves a few free drinks off'n that cherry-colored mop, can't we, King?"

Garner made no reply.

They rode through Indian Creek Canyon for better than an hour and a half, and the trail of the traders was clear. It had been windy last night, though, and Quincannon feared that once they came out the southern end of the canyon, they'd find the tracks blown away.

He needn't have worried. The wind had been working at them some, all right, and they were faint, but there was still enough trail to follow. Even Quincannon, who was the first to admit that he was no hand at tracking, could make out the line of broken brush stretching across the land ahead.

They pushed on until about noon, when they came to a small spring surrounded by palo verde and mesquite.

"Just jerky and biscuits, Pike," Garner said as he dismounted. "Quincannon, give me a hand with these horses. I wanta take Red and that dun gelding with us. Start bringin' the others over here so I can pull their shoes, then get their halters off and shoo 'em out of here."

"I beg your pardon?" Quincannon asked in surprise. "Shouldn't we take them to a . . . to a barn somewhere? Can't we sell them?" Although two of the bandits' mounts looked like they'd seen better days, the rest were quite nice. At least, they looked nice to him. Perhaps there was something Mr. Garner's expert eye had seen that he'd missed.

Garner sighed. "You see any barns? We're taking the dun gelding because he'd the strongest of the lot. Pack-horse. We could sell the rest of 'em for thirty, maybe forty dollars a head if we were going to a town, but we're not, and they'll just slow us down. They've got water here, and halfway decent graze. You overly attached to that strawberry roan a'yours?"

Quincannon blinked. "Rosie? Why?"

"Because she's old. If I were you, I'd turn her out and take that black-bay gelding. He's only five, and he looks to be fair put together."

Quincannon was horrified. Rosie? Turned loose with these Mexican horses? Why, she didn't even speak Spanish! The second he thought it, he colored and thanked the Lord he hadn't said it out loud. He said, "Thank you, but I'm satisfied with the mount I have."

Garner shrugged. "Your choice. Now get that hammerheaded sorrel on the end."

One by one, Quincannon brought Garner the horses, and horse by horse, hoof by hoof, Garner clipped the nails with a wedge and nippers, then pried off each shoe.

When Garner, dripping sweat, was halfway through the third horse, Pike wandered over with some hardtack and jerky. "Don't know why you're takin' the time to pull them shoes," he commented.

"'Cause if they're gonna be turned out wild, they oughta be wild all the way," Garner said.

Pike winked at Quincannon. "He's right funny about his horses," he confided. "Anybody's horses, come t'think of it."

Distastefully, Garner looked at the hardtack in his hand. "What'd you do, old man? You eat all the breakfast biscuits?"

"They was only eight or nine of 'em left," sniffed Pike. "Weren't enough to save."

Quincannon felt a grin coming on, but the pain that arrived when he stretched his face wiped the smile right off it.

"Them Mexes had plenty'a cornmeal and some lard," Pike went on, heedless. "Now, lard ain't so good as a mess'a bacon grease, but I could make us up a batch'a corn dodgers if'n you want."

Garner shoved the hardtack in his shirt pocket. "You're a good cook, Pike, but I hate those damn corn dodgers of yours," he said, and bit off a chunk of jerky. "Especially with lard," he said around it, "and not even with bacon grease. They're not fit for livestock, let alone human beings." He pushed the rest of his jerky in with the hardtack, and moved around to the horse's off side.

"If you doesn't like 'em, just say so," Pike said over the horse's back.

"You gettin' deaf, too?" Garner bent to his work again, with an, "Easy, girl. Gimme your damn foot."

Quincannon was still holding the lead rope, and Pike turned his attention toward him. "How 'bout you, boy? You like corn dodgers?"

Quincannon didn't have the slightest idea what corn dodgers might be, but since Garner had expressed such distaste for them, he said, "I don't believe so, Mr. Pike. I thought your biscuits were quite good, though."

"What there was of 'em," muttered Garner from the other side of the horse. There was a dull thud as the third shoe popped off and hit the dust. He moved to the last hoof.

Either Pike didn't hear him, or he pretended not to. "It were country like this where me and Sam Akers found them boys what had tangled with Jackson Woodrow," he said thoughtfully. "That were a few years back, afore I started ridin' with King. Had their heads cut right off, all four of 'em, and a couple was missin' arms an' legs. Sam an' me had us a hell of a time matchin' up the parts so's we could bury 'em." He scratched his head, and his hat bobbled up and down. "Mighta been this same locality, now that I get to thinkin' about it."

"Jackson Woodrow?" Quincannon asked. He was gnawing on his hardtack, and sincerely wishing that Pike hadn't eaten all of those lovely powdery biscuits. As for the hardtack, dogs would probably adore the thick, hard, tasteless crackers, but they were barely fit for human consumption.

"Oh, Woodrow's a bad 'un," Pike said with a shake of his head. "Makes your ol' buddy Cherry Lazlo look like he's bringin' Christmas baskets. One time, I heared that him an' his boys took out a whole village'a Mexicans. Killed the men right off—beheaded what ones they hadn't shot—then did bad by the womenfolk. Killed 'em after, and the kids, too, afore he burnt the place to the ground. Rode around for the next week with a baby's head on his saddle horn. They said he done it just 'cause he was bored that day." Pike sniffed. "'Course, ol' Woodrow never cottoned much to Mexicans."

Quincannon gulped. "A b-baby's head?" he asked weakly.

Garner stood up. "This one's done. You can turn her loose, boy. Jackson Woodrow got killed last winter, Pike. No sense talking about him."

"Where'd you hear that?" Pike asked.

"One'a Gussy Simpson's boys, over to Yuma. You hear me, Quincannon?"

"Yessir." He began to fumble with the halter. A baby's head. Good God! "Th-those men you found. How did you know Woodrow was responsible?"

"'Cause them body parts was chopped off," Pike said conversationally. "Ain't nobody uses a saber like Jackson Woodrow. Real clean like. Now, Bad Bobby Blake, he's fond of a knife and he'll whack off a hand or a foot, but Woodrow—"

"Shut up, Pike." Garner appeared at Quincannon's elbow and shoved him out of the way. "Don't listen to him, boy," he said. "The old coot just likes to hear himself talk." He slid the mare's halter off, then smacked her on the rump. She trotted off about twenty yards and began to graze.

"As I was sayin'—" Pike began.

"You were sayin' a bunch of horseshit," Garner interrupted. "Jackson Woodrow's dead. Got himself shot off a running horse down in Sonora and the damn nag dragged him for two miles before they caught up with it. Peeled all the hide right off him, and I say God bless every cactus that took a piece of his flesh. Bad Bobby's in jail over in New Mexico for cuttin' up a rich man's son. If you'd spend half the energy you use flappin' your lips on makin' biscuits, we'd be in baked goods from here to Judgment. Bring me the chestnut, Quincannon."

"You don't have to go an' get all testy with me," Pike grumbled. "And while we're talkin' about time, you're sure wastin' a lot of it babyin' these here nags. Why, by this time we coulda found them fellers what's got the boy's jug! We coulda jumped 'em and had us a little shoot-'em-up and been ridin' back all happy and fulla ourselves!"

"And I could've been finished pullin' these shoes if I didn't have to stop and listen to you, you old windbag. Quincannon! Quit lollygaggin' and bring me that chestnut!"

They made better time once they'd left the spring and the other horses behind, although Garner was still going easy, probably to save wear and tear on his stallion's stone bruise. Garner led Red, who was burdened by exactly nothing, and Pike led the dun, which was packed high with the dead bandits' supplies. Garner had said that they had enough water to last nearly a week, and enough food to travel for two, if need be.

Quincannon sincerely hoped it wouldn't be that long.

He was having a hard time putting the grisly image of that baby's head out of his mind. He wished that Pike had never mentioned it. He tried telling himself that it was just something Pike had heard, something that had probably been embellished several times along the way. But still, he couldn't shake from his head the picture he'd conjured.

And the name Jackson Woodrow just didn't match up with such barbarity! A man named Jackson Woodrow should have been a politician or civic leader. Bad Bobby Blake, on the other hand, sounded like a character from a dime novel.

Hoping to distract himself from unpleasant thoughts, he urged Rosie forward and rode up even with Pike. Garner was riding about twenty feet ahead, following the trail, showing them the way.

"How you doin' there, Elliot?" Pike asked before Quincannon had a chance to open his mouth.

"Fine, sir," he replied, although it wasn't the truth. "I was wondering. You said you used to ride with a man called Sam?"

As Quincannon had hoped, the question set Pike off on tangent. "Sam Akers," he began. "Quite a piece'a work, ol' Sam. Him and me rode together for nigh on three years. Fought Apache in the New Mexico and Arizona territories, we did, afore they got reservationized. Fought some ornery white men, too. Now, Sam used to have him this fiddle, an' he played it good. Best I ever heared. Why, one time I seen him—"

"Aw, hell, Pike," said Garner. He'd apparently heard them talking and waited until they caught up with him. He was keeping pace with them now. "Sam played that fiddle flatter than a pancake, and you know it."

"Sounded sweet to me," Pike sniffed. "When'd you ever hear Sam playin', anyhow? I didn't even know that you knowed him!"

"He got drunk and pulled it out in a saloon down to the town of Deuce about six years back," Garner said, a little too happily. "Played three bars of 'Turkey in the Straw,' and they nearly tarred and feathered him. That was sayin' a lot for those Deuce boys. They hadn't heard a fiddler for so long you woulda thought they'd put up with a bow drawn over a rusty saw."

Quincannon smiled—or tried to—but Pike frowned. "Well, he sounded sweet to me. Mayhap you caught him on a bad day, King."

"I believe you're tone-deaf on top of color-blind, Pike.

Tell Quincannon, here, what became of your old pal Sam Akers."

Pike shook his head. "Well, poor Sam were taking out after a stray calf at a dead lope—we was working for day wages over on the Double T that spring—and Pepe Lopez plugged him by mistake. Shot him right through the head. You couldn't blame Pepe. He were aimin' at a quail that had flew up and Sam rode right into his line'a fire. Why, he felt so bad he sat right down and bawled. Everybody loved 'ol Sam."

"Unless they'd heard him play that fiddle," said Garner. "Why don't you tell Quincannon what happened to Dave Thurgood?"

"Who's Dave Thurgood?" Quincannon asked. The conversation was, at least, taking his mind off infanticide.

"Oh, Dave was the fella that Pike rode with before Sam. Tell him, Pike."

Pike shot Garner a nasty look, but he said, "Comanches got him, over Texas way."

"And Pablo Ortega?"

Quincannon said, "Who—"

"Before Thurgood," Garner said before Quincannon could get the question out.

"Pablo got himself hanged," said Pike crisply. "You knows that, King."

"The point being, kid," Garner said, "that every man Pike's ever ridden with has met his Maker a whole lot sooner than he expected. Don't bode too well for us, now, does it?"

With that, Garner kicked Faro out ahead again, and didn't slow down until he was a good thirty yards off. Which left Quincannon with Pike and nothing to say.

After a moment Pike took up the conversational slack. Quietly, he said, "I reckon I can't help it if them fellas up and got themselves killed, Elliot. Every one of 'em was like a brother to me. You rides with a feller for a year or three, it gets thataway. But better them than me, that's what

I figures. King says as how I'm bad luck, but I'm gettin'
to be an old man and I'm still livin', ain't I? I'd call that
good luck."

He patted his pockets and grinned. " 'Course, I got my
mojo playin' cards back. Reckon that helps."

Quincannon was looking ahead. "Why has Mr. Garner
stopped?"

Garner had not only come to a halt, but he had dismounted and was kicking at something on the ground,
something down in the brush. By the time they'd closed
the distance between them, he was swinging a leg back
over Faro.

Puzzled, Quincannon asked, "Mr. Garner? What seems
to be the—" He stopped talking.

There was a body on the ground. The man, who had to
be one of the group they were tracking, was not long dead.
Two arrows protruded from his back.

"Aw, turds," Pike muttered under his breath.

"Apache," said Garner grimly.

15

Pike scratched his head. "Kid, is there anybody in this blue-eyed world what *ain't* after that jug a'yourn?"

"Weren't after any jug," said Garner. He was squinting left, then right, trying to make sense of it. The man's mount was nowhere to be seen. Garner figured it had either run off or been led off by the Apache.

He tossed Red's lead rope to the boy. Then, his eyes on the ground, he rode thirty or forty yards to the east, scanning the tracks, finding the shallow arroyo where three Indian ponies had stood for a long time, waiting, and where they'd sprung up and dashed to the chase. Next, he circled past Pike and Quincannon to the west and stared out across the desert.

When he trotted back to them, he said, "Near as I can figure, there were three braves. Scouts, maybe, or a hunting party. I imagine they just stumbled across these boys and decided to have a little fun. I reckon they surprised 'em right here and killed this fella, then they all took off at a dead run that way." He swung his arm and pointed.

Quincannon, whose swollen face currently looked to have been lumped together out of rocky clay by a blind

man, said, "Hunting party? What on earth could they have
been hunting out here? And I thought you said they were
all on the reservation!"

"Pronghorn, most like."

"But we haven't seen—"

"We passed two herds this morning. You're just not
lookin'. And just because the U.S. government tells those
boys to stay put, it doesn't mean they have to listen. Some
mother's son and all his pals jump the reservation about
every ten minutes."

Quincannon colored and said, "Oh." Wonderful. Now
they had to worry about wild Indians, too.

"What you thinkin' we should do, King?" asked Pike.

Actually, Garner was thinking that they should just forget all about it and head back north. But he knew that
Quincannon, pigheaded fool that he was, would have none
of it. He'd just say, "Thank you very much, sir," and go
on alone. Garner frowned. On top of everything else, he'd
probably have to fight the kid for Red, and he'd probably
kill him.

And Garner wasn't about to sit through another session
of watching that stalwart, stiff upper lip, or listening to
Pike whine and carry on about how they couldn't leave the
poor little bastard all on his lonesome.

Last night, when he'd found Lazlo's money pouch, it
had occurred to him that this was more than enough money
to buy himself a spread, a nice one. He'd even gone so
far as to stuff the bag of coins into his pack, to plot how
he'd wait until the middle of the night, then sneak out with
Red and the gold and take his sorry behind north, and in
a hurry.

Let Pike take care of the boy, he'd thought. An old fool
leading a young one, or vice versa.

But then he'd got to thinking about Pike, about the times
the old codger had saved his bacon. And he thought about
the boy, how he'd gone through a world of hurt and no
water and a face cut to ribbons just to right a wrong. Gar-

ner supposed some of that old lawman shit had kicked in, too. It was a curse.

In the end, he'd tossed the gold at Pike's feet. He was in it now, real permanent, and for good or for bad. Probably for bad.

So he said, "We're followin'. You happy?"

Pike grinned. "'See there, Elliot? King's gonna get them Apache."

Garner grunted. More likely, the Apache were going to get him. One of these days they'd have to, if only to even out the score a little.

"Thank you, Mr. Garner," the boy said. Garner couldn't decide whether the kid looked relieved or scared. It was hard to tell anything with that swollen face of his.

"I don't suppose you saw my Chalice while you were scouting around?" Quincannon asked. "It would save us all a good deal of trouble if—"

"No. And yes, I looked."

The trail didn't appear to be more than a few hours old. There was a light breeze that afternoon, but the tracks weren't much affected yet. They caught up with the riderless horse, a dirty rose gray, about forty minutes later. Apparently, he'd just kept on running with the mob until he got tired.

He was spooky, and wouldn't be caught. Garner had to throw a rope over him, then he stripped off his tack and turned him loose. They were hurrying now, and there was no time to pull his shoes.

Garner was beginning to wish that he'd pulled Red's and left him back there with the other horses. The Apache loved a good horse, but they weren't above killing one if it would slow a white man down.

Too late to do anything different. That was the story of his life, wasn't it?

They followed along at a jog for about a half hour— probably eight or ten minutes of fast traveling for those Apaches and the boys they were chasing—and then the trail changed. One set of shod hooves veered off to the south, followed by two Apache ponies, and one shod horse cut to the west. Only one set of pony tracks followed him.

"Which way, you reckon?" asked Pike.

"Flip a coin."

Quincannon was the only one with any cash money in his pockets, and he tossed a coin in the air. He caught it on the back of his forearm and, still clasping it, said, "Tails, we go south?"

Garner nodded.

Quincannon peeked under his hand. "Heads," he said. "We go west."

They came across the body an hour later. Like the fellow they'd found before, he was white. Unlike his friend, the buzzards were already down and at him, probably drawn by his horse. The sorrel gelding—bright sorrel, like Red—was caught in his reins, which were tangled and snarled around his leg. His head was snugged close to his right knee. One of his hind legs was snapped below the hock, and the hoof dragged uselessly. He'd been spurred bloody. White ringing his eyes, he staggered helplessly about twenty feet from the body.

Garner stepped down, then looped Red's lead rope around his saddle horn. He tossed Faro's reins to the Quincannon. "Hang on to 'em for a minute," he said quietly.

"Ho, son," he murmured. Thigh-high brush scraped and tore at his legs as he slowly walked toward the horse. Snorting, the gelding wrenched his head back and forth and tried to back away, but only succeeded in halfway falling down.

"Ho, son. Easy, son." Garner stepped over what remained of the contents of the dead man's saddlebags. It beat him how that Apache could have gone through the packs—had his hands right on that suffering horse—and not put him out of his misery. For the life of him, he'd never understand how an Apache thought, not really.

"Atta boy," he said as he reached the horse, and took hold of him by the cheek strap. "Easy, fella."

Quickly, he unsnarled the reins that bound the gelding's head to his knee. The muscles in the horse's neck relaxed as his head lifted into a more natural position. Despite the grievous injuries to his flanks—and the worse one to his leg—he nuzzled Garner gratefully and nibbled at his pockets, making little whickering sounds.

King reached for his knife. He couldn't risk a gunshot, not without knowing where those Apache had gone to.

"Good fella," he soothed, and ran his palm slowly across the horse's forehead. He straightened the forelock. "Easy, now. You got yourself a busted leg, you know? I'm sorry, boy."

And then, gently, he lifted the horse's chin and plunged his blade, very deep and very quickly, into the jugular vein.

Blood gushed hot and red over his hand, his arm, but Garner barely noticed. He kept talking to the horse, kept touching it as it went down, first to its knees with an immense groan, then down all the way. "Easy, son. Easy, son. I'm sorry."

He kept talking long after it was dead.

Pike shooed away the vultures. They rose up in an angry, squawking cloud, and he went in for a look at the body. Quincannon's eyes, however, were on Garner. He had almost yelped when Garner had cut the horse, almost called out to him to stop it, for the love of God! But then he realized that the sound of a shot would likely bring the savages down upon them. Garner was doing the only humane thing possible, under the circumstances. The horse's leg had been badly broken. There was no hope for it.

"That buck got in close for this'n," Pike announced, and Quincannon turned toward him. Pike was just standing up, brushing his hands on his shirt. "Knifed him good."

"He's dead?" Quincannon asked. He fervently hoped so, especially considering the buzzards. "Does . . . does he have my Chalice?"

"Yup, he'd dead, and nope, he ain't got it on him,"

replied Pike. "Knife took 'im right through the pump. King still foolin' with that horse?"

Garner stood up then, and came toward them. His shirt, which had been pale blue, was now spattered deep red and glistened wetly with the horse's blood. No one said a word as he walked to their packhorse, pulled down a full bag of water, and poured it over himself.

At last he mounted again. "No cup, kid," was all he said before he clucked to Faro and rode out in the lead.

It puzzled Quincannon that Garner would be more upset about putting a dumb animal out of its misery than about killing those men the day before. After all, the horse had no future, did it? It could feel pain, certainly, but it couldn't think. It was just an animal.

Any one of those bandits, on the other hand, might have eventually reformed. He might have gone on to lead an exemplary life. For all Quincannon knew, one of those miscreants, if he had lived, might have one day sired a child who would become a doctor or a lawyer or a politician. A famous man, a good man.

But then, Quincannon had killed one of them, too.

The subject bore further thought. Not at the moment, though, for Pike was speaking to him.

"Beg your pardon, Mr. Pike?" he said.

"I said, you're sure gonna have a tale to tell that gal a'yourn! Provided we doesn't get ourselves killed, that is."

Quincannon nodded. "Yes. Yes, I will," he said, smiling as much as was possible without splitting open his face in sixteen different directions. He was thinking about Lisa Boudreau and her blue eyes and that spray of freckles across her pert nose.

Mr. Pike's face took on a decidedly ornery expression. "We is talking about the same gal, isn't we?"

"Well, certainly! I . . ." He felt heat flooding his face, pushing uncomfortably at his scabs. "Oh." Miss Minion.

Pike chuckled. "I'd have to say that red ain't your natural color, Elliot. Hey! Whoa up there, Millie!"

Pike reined up the mare in time to avoid a slow collision with Garner's horse. Garner was staring at the sky to the south, where a thin, barely perceptible wisp of smoke rose from a distant hill.

"Reckon King's found them braves, Elliot," Pike said. He took advantage of the halt to drink from his canteen.

Garner reached back and slipped his spyglass from his saddlebag. "Third one was cuttin' back to meet up with the first two."

Quincannon's breath caught in his throat. He hadn't expected to actually catch up with the Apaches. After all, in his experience with Garner and Pike—until recently, that was—they seemed to trip over the aftermath of bad men's deeds, not catch them in the act.

Spyglass to his eye, Garner silently studied the distance. At last, he collapsed the glass and put it away. "All right," he said, and his face was grim. "Keep it slow."

Quincannon began, "Shouldn't we, that is, if they've built a fire . . . I mean . . ."

Garner turned toward him. "Spit it out, boy."

"If they've built a fire, then they've probably already caught that last bandit, haven't they?" When Garner didn't speak, he pressed on. "Well, they might be hurting him! Shouldn't we—"

Scowling, Garner raised his hand. "Hurting him? Kid, you haven't even scratched the surface of it. But even if we went chargin' over there full bore, we wouldn't get there in time to do that fella any good. Plus which, we'd be giving those Indians an invite to do the same to us. You have any idea how much dust five galloping horses can raise?"

Quincannon didn't say anything.

Pike, however, said, "You reckon them savages is cookin' that feller alive, King?"

Garner didn't answer, only started his horse moving again. Pike and Quincannon followed.

"I seen Apache do some right dastardly things to a man,"

Pike continued, seeing as he had a captive audience in Quincannon. "They'll strip the hide off a living man, kinda like what them Mex boys did to Lazlo, 'cept Apache can stretch it out two, three days. Tie him upside down and peel him for fun. They'll slice off his pecker and shove it in his mouth whilst he bleeds to death. 'Course, if they's in a hurry, they'll just find 'em an anthill and stake a feller out on it. Maybe slash his eyelids, too. Why, one time—"

"Stop it!" cried Quincannon in desperation.

He was nearing the end of his tether, and beginning, for the first time, to wonder if this quest he'd taken on was worth the cost. Two weeks ago, he would have been staggered with horror at the idea of a man being stabbed through the heart by an Apache knife. Any knife, for that matter. It struck him that he was beginning to think of that as a relatively nice way to go.

He said, "Please, Mr. Pike! Do you have to confide every ghastly affront to mankind that you've ever heard of? I'm still half-sick over that story about Jackson Woodrow and the baby's head!"

"Oh, that Woodrow, he were a real snake," Pike went on gleefully, and with no regard whatsoever for Quincannon's roiling stomach. "'Course, white boys is worse when it comes to what happens after a feller's dead. Apache and Comanche—Yuma, too, when they was runnin' around wreckin' havoc—are worse when a feller's alive, what with all them things they think up for makin' a man scream. Why, Comanche'll stake a man down, then cut a little hole in his belly and pull out all his ropy innards while he watches. They'll string 'em out twenty, thirty feet, then leave him there so's he can watch the coyotes eat him alive."

White-knuckled and speechless, Quincannon gripped his saddle horn.

"But whites?" Pike went on merrily. "Why, some'a them soldiers in the U.S. Cavalry used to make tobacco pouches outta women's privates—men's, too—and—"

"Pike!" shouted Garner from up front. "Close your damn hole!"

Pike sniffed. "Seems to me everybody's gettin' awful touchy all of a damn sudden."

The line of hills grew closer, but Quincannon despaired of ever reaching them. Things were so vast in this wild country. And he was thinking, as they rode, that right up until Mr. Pike had mentioned his girl—and he had thought, belatedly, about Miss Minion—he had not given a thought to anything east of the Mississippi all day.

This both puzzled and amazed him. Until very recently, his entire existence had been books and studies and quiet offices, attending his classes at night, and keeping Miss Minion's company on Saturday evenings and Sunday afternoons. He had never thought it would be—or should be—any other way.

Granted, he would rather have had different business out here. Chasing after the most vile and reprehensible criminals imaginable—no, past imagining—was a labor with which he hoped never again to be saddled. Mr. Pike spoke casually of murderous bandits and Indians in the same manner that most men of Quincannon's acquaintance would speak of some long-ago court case.

But perhaps, he thought, it was the same thing to Pike. When one lived in a land where the law was practiced and upheld only in rare and isolated areas—and where, for the greater bulk of the countryside, there was no law to speak of—men became inured to the idea of risking their lives on a daily basis. They became, for all intents and purposes, laws unto themselves.

Oddly enough, Quincannon was finding that he could live with this idea.

And the land itself, which at first had seemed a monotonous, endless vista of thorns and nettles and rocks—everything either hard or sharp—was now coming into a different sort of focus for him. He was seeing the subtle modulations of land, the variations of color. Not forty-five minutes after Mr. Garner had commented that he wasn't looking hard enough, he had made out a pronghorn herd in the distance. It was small—four does and a buck—but he had seen them. The buck, unafraid, had lifted his elegant, alien-looking head and watched as they rode by.

For the first time, he wondered if Boston might seem unduly tame when he reentered it.

Up front, Garner abruptly veered from the trail—and the distant smoke—at a right angle. Quincannon was alarmed at first, thinking that he might have sighted the savages. But when he didn't alter his speed, Quincannon relaxed a bit.

He didn't lead them far. After about a hundred yards or so, he stopped Faro and dismounted, and once again handed his reins up to Quincannon. This time, Quincannon knew the reason. He'd been so lost in thinking about pronghorn and the subtle shades of brown and green that he hadn't noticed the circling birds until just then. Always, the birds.

He steeled himself, waiting to hear that Garner had found the last of the bandits. He hoped to hear that they'd found the Chalice as well, even though the chances were so slim as to be inconsequential. Mostly, he was dreading the thought that his Chalice—Malcolm Peabody's ancient, priceless, goddamned Chalice—was now in the hands of red savages, as opposed to white ones. How did one begin to bargain with Apaches, anyway?

He comforted himself that this white man, at least, wasn't suffering the hot embers of the fire. Its distant smoke still spilled thinly into a blue-white sky.

Garner threw a rock, and the buzzards rose from the knee-high brush with a rustle of wings and their now familiar squawks and complaints at a meal interrupted. He walked in a few feet, then squatted down.

Pike asked the question that been on Quincannon's lips. "Is it one'a them fellers, King?"

Quincannon could see a scrap of sun-beaten, yellow cloth, nothing more.

Dusting his hands, Garner stood up and walked back. "Apache," he said. "Took a slug to the shoulder, but I reckon the tumble from his horse killed him. Busted neck. Pony musta run off."

"Well, by gum!" crowed Pike. "Looks like that last feller whittled down the odds for us!"

Not enough, thought Quincannon, eyeing the smoke tatters wafting heavenward on the horizon. *Not enough.*

16

It was nearly dark when they reached the first low, rolling hill, and the thin trail of smoke had long since ceased to mark the sky. Quincannon had voiced his relief, but Garner wasn't so certain. Those Apache braves might have finished their business and just ridden away, but why hadn't they come back and picked up their fallen buddy? Unless circumstances gave them no choice in the matter, they didn't leave their dead for the coyotes and vultures, at least not right away. That dead Apache would have to be hauled back to the village and be touted for his bravery before they ceremonially disposed of the body.

Which got Garner to thinking about the Apache campsite. This plagued him, too. It was likely they were camped less than a day's ride off, two at the most. He hoped these braves had just ridden out that morning, and that nobody was going to come looking for them for a while. But right now he had these hills, and the threat within them, to worry about.

It was far from the smartest thing to do, riding up like this, bold as you please, but there was no cover. They didn't have any choice.

So for the last hour or so, he'd been doing what little he could: scanning the land ahead, both with the naked eye and with the help of his spyglass, looking for anything out of the ordinary, any sign that their approach was being watched.

He hadn't seen anything so far, but that didn't mean much when it came to Apache, who were the toughest, sneakiest, guerrilla fighters he'd ever had the displeasure to tangle with. They could turn themselves right into rock and brush—or thin air—if need be. It occurred to him that if the Union had been smart enough to sign up a few Apache warriors, the War Between the States would have been over in about five seconds flat.

Of course, it would have been a good bit bloodier, and that was saying something.

He swung his horse toward the east, following the base of the hill, keeping to the flat, and the others followed. They hadn't said a word for the last fifteen minutes. Quincannon looked good and scared, which to Garner's mind was the correct response to Apache. Pike looked half-asleep. Well, he'd come alert if there was any trouble. One thing about Pike, you could always count on him in a scrap, so long as it wasn't with a white man over cards. The damned fool always sat there, grinning like an idiot and waiting for Garner's name—or gun—to protect him.

Jackass.

They followed the curve of the hill, then climbed slowly to the place where it dipped to meet a second hump of land. The only sounds as they traveled were the squeak of leather and the muted dig of hooves into clay and rock. The terrain before them was all soft rolling hills and gentle valleys. It looked to be a somewhat kinder land than the flats they had just left behind, but the shadows were growing deeper. He had no wish to be caught in here once the sun went all the way down. At least, not unless he knew what they were up against.

Before they came to the next breast of land, Garner held

up his hand and signaled the others to wait. He dismounted, pulled his spyglass from his pack, then handed Faro's reins and Red's lead to Quincannon. Sweat and blood had seeped through the bandage on the kid's forehead and dried in stringy, rust-colored trails down his face, but the swellings on his cheeks and nose, where he'd been punctured by flying glass, looked to be going down some. He was as white as milk, but the set of his jaw was determined.

Garner gave him a brief nod of encouragement, then got to business. He climbed the hill, dropping to his knees and then his belly as he neared the top, and crawled the last few feet like a gecko on a wall. The wind shifted just as he gained the vantage point he was seeking. It was very faint, but he could smell it. Cooked flesh.

Reluctantly, he pulled the spyglass from his pocket and began scouting the land before him. And two minutes later, through a crotch of land, he saw it: far away, in deep purple shadow, stood a lone ironwood. The lightning-struck tree was long dead and skeletal. It had been split nearly down the middle, and was leafless and bare save for the two unmistakable forms dangling upside down from its limbs.

"Aw, Christ," he muttered, and looked again. It was still the same. He collapsed the spyglass and skittered down the hill.

"See 'em?" whispered Pike, who had taken advantage of the stop to water the horses. Quincannon looked up expectantly. He was watering, too, and held his hat, filled with water, to Red's muzzle.

"Yeah," Garner said. "I saw 'em." He ran a hand down Red's leg and lifted the hoof. He prodded the frog. The horse didn't flinch.

"And?" hissed Pike.

He let down Red's leg and patted his gleaming shoulder. Red was a good horse. Didn't act like a knot-head stud unless there was a good reason. He hadn't so much as nickered in all these days. Well, Red knew about mares, and

he knew there wasn't much point in getting all excited if
they weren't in season. And that hoof was good as new.
One good thing today, anyway.

"Dammit, King!" said Pike in a loud whisper. "What's
them heathen up to?"

"Not much of anything, anymore," he replied grimly,
and swung up on Faro to a squeaky complaint of leather.
Pike stuck a foot in his stirrup and mounted as well.

"Mr. Garner?" said Quincannon as he stepped up on
Rosie. The boy was getting off and on just fine. "What do
you mean? What did you see?"

Garner gathered his reins. "I don't know who we're
chasin', kid, but he's real bad business."

Silently, they rode over the next long, low hill. The land
was beginning to take on a character that was slightly more
lush. Quincannon might not have noticed the change several days before, but he did now. There was a stunted,
brushy tree every now and again, and the vegetation was
slightly greener and thicker.

The sun didn't wait for them. The shadows grew longer,
and by the time they rode down into the valley—after Garner stopped them two additional times and climbed higher
to reconnoiter the land ahead—it was dark.

It wasn't dark enough to hide what had taken place in
that long scoop of land, though. The moon picked out details on the old lightning-struck ironwood, and on the two
men hanging from it.

They were Apache, judging by what was left of their
clothing. They were strung up by their feet, arms tied behind their backs, so that they dangled about eighteen inches
off the ground. Below their skulls, or what was left of
them, the black and ashy remains of two small fires marked
the dust. The sickening scents of burned hair and scorched
human flesh and sizzled brain hung heavy in the air.

Quincannon managed to dismount before he vomited.

His head still near his knees, he heard Pike's muttered, "What kind of a sonofabitchin' bastard does this?"

Then Garner's terse, "Let's get 'em down. Quincannon, once you get yourself squared away, see to the horses."

The nausea came again, flooding Quincannon's throat, burning his mouth and his nose. At last he stood up, facing away from the tree while he tipped his canteen with shaking hands, then rinsed his mouth and spat. How had a white man done this? How had a lone white man captured two Apache braves?

From everything Pike and Garner had told him, he had come to understand that one Apache was worth any three whites. They were clever and vicious and determined in any scrap. How had they come to be caught, and why on earth had this white man tortured them so cruelly?

Whoever he was, he had done his worst and moved on. The fires were long dead, and there were no horses. No one needed to tell Quincannon that his Chalice was gone, too, in the clutches of this nameless monster.

Sick at heart and still queasy of stomach, he at last strung a picket line and began unsaddling the horses.

He was about halfway through feeding when Garner walked up and grabbed a bag of oats. He measured some into a nose bag. "You feed Millie yet?"

Quincannon shook his head.

"That was a pretty tough thing," Garner said. He buckled Millie's feedbag and paused with his back to Quincannon. "A feller has business in the wild places, he's got to get used to 'em."

Quincannon didn't reply, just stood there waiting.

Garner said, "I reckon some things are harder to get used to than others." He bent to pick up the oats again, and fixed another feedbag. "Who's left?"

"Just the dun," replied Quincannon. A night bird cried overhead, and a chill took him. "Mr. Garner?"

Garner strapped the bag on the dun's nose. "What?"

"Why horses? I mean, it seems to me that you get on

a lot better with horses than you do with people. No, I'm sorry. That's not right. What I mean to say is—"

"I know what you mean," Garner interrupted. "I respect 'em, boy. And I take pity on 'em, too." At last, he turned to face Quincannon. He hung an arm over the dun's withers. "See, a horse can't choose. If he could, he'd be free all his life and knee-deep in sweet grass and never know a saddle or bridle. He'd run when he wanted and roll when it pleased him, and die on his own terms. But men, they make all his choices for him. And the horse, he makes the best of it. Horses make do."

He paused to stroke the dun's neck. "They can make do with some clown who spurs 'em bloody, and they'll make do with idiots ridin' 'em into war. And most of the time, they'll do their best. You understand what I'm sayin'? They got no choice. They die in the traces with busted knees and they get butchered for food. Folks chop their tails off and crop their ears for fashion. People ride 'em till they drop and whip 'em 'cause they didn't go farther, but they still do their best."

Garner paused a moment and took a breath. Moonlight picked out his hand as it slowly fingered the dun's mane. "When it came to creating, God made no finer or more willing creature than the race of horses, mankind included. I reckon that deserves some respect. I don't cotton to that part in the Bible, where it says about people owning all the beasts and doing with them as they see fit. I don't think that even the Almighty would assign ownership like that, without givin' a test to see if mankind was fit."

He paused, and gave a rare, brief grin. "'Course, I'm the one who's wantin' to have a horse ranch and raise up horses to train and sell. What the hell do I know?"

Quincannon just said, "Oh." He fully expected Garner to turn and walk away, but he didn't. Instead, he thumbed back his hat.

"What kind of law you practice, Quincannon?"

"N-none, right now." For some reason, the question un-

settled him. "I'm only a clerk until I complete my school-
ing and pass the bar. But Peabody and Strauss—the company for which I work—handles primarily civil litigation."

"Speak English."

"That is, I mean, the firm doesn't handle criminal cases.
Well, last year, when Mr. Ernest Pendergast's son was ar-
rested for malicious mischief and stealing a lady's purse,
we defended him. But it's mostly wills and mergers, people suing other people."

"You get him off?"

"Who?"

"This Pender-whatever's kid."

"Mr. Strauss did," he replied, and for some reason he
felt embarrassed. Ernest Pendergast, Jr. was a spoiled college boy, who'd gotten drunk and raised Ned on the Common, stealing purses and tossing them in a rubbish bin
down the way. All the ladies but one had declined to press
charges after their bags were returned, fatter than when
they'd lost them, and Mr. Strauss had been good friends
with the judge. He added lamely, "Mr. Pendergast is one
of our most important clients."

Garner patted the horse on the neck. "Pike's got a fire
goin' and beans about to bubble. C'mon when you get
finished up." He walked away, toward Pike's crouched
silhouette and the fire he had started in a little clearing
far from the tree.

Quincannon stood there a moment, feeling odd and rather
ashamed, as if he had somehow let Mr. Garner down.

By the time Pike declared their supper fit to eat, and just
when Quincannon was thinking that he never wished to eat
again, he found that he was ravenous. The stench of death
had been scoured from the valley by a soft wind, and it
helped that Pike and Garner had moved the bodies far away
and covered them, or so Pike said, with a blanket.

"Covered 'em with one of them Mex blankets what we
picked up back there at the canyon," he said around a bis-

cuit. "Figure them Apaches is already so dang mad at the whole Mexican nation that a little more mad on top of it can't hurt much."

"You think they'll find them, then?" Quincannon asked.

"Yup," Garner said, then snarled, "You eat the last of the ham? You did, you old buzzard!"

"You shoulda spoke up earlier, like my mama used to say," Pike replied huffily. "From now on, we're gonna need to shoot our meat. Less'n you wanta eat jerky. Got lotsa that."

"Well, gimme some more beans, then," Garner said tersely, and stuck out his plate.

" 'Gimme some beans, gimme some ham,' " Pike mimicked as he spooned a pile of beans onto Garner's plate. "Don't know who it was made me your servant."

Quincannon figured this was as good a time as any. He set his plate aside, cleared his throat, and said, "Gentlemen? I think we should give it up."

Pike arched a brow so high his hat wiggled. "What'd you say?"

"We must be nearly in Mexico by now," he went on, rushing the words, as if a wall of them could keep him from being interrupted. "We cannot legally pursue this brigand beyond our national boundary. I believe we should set back for Mormon Wells in the morning. I shall wire Mr. Malcolm Peabody that I have failed. He can fire me if he wishes. He can press legal charges. I don't care. I will not slap the law of the United States—or that of Mexico—in the face."

Both men stared at him.

"I—I won't," he stuttered. "Really!"

Garner set down his plate. "First off, kid," he began in a tone that was far more conversational than Quincannon's, which he feared had ended on a note of hysteria, "nobody's painted a damn line in the dirt or anything. And we're not law officers. We could chase this sonofabitch down to Peru if we were of a mind. Stop makin' stuff up."

Quincannon opened his mouth, but Garner snapped,

"Shut up," before he could say anything. He closed his mouth with a *click*.

"Second of all, what happened to all that 'honor' shit you were jabberin' about twenty-four goddamned hours a day, back at the beginning? Third, you're scared. Admit it."

Quincannon sat erect. He'd been caught out, but he was going to take it like a man. "Of course I'm scared! Do I look like an idiot?" Pike started to say something, but Quincannon hushed him with a look. "Before, I thought I could buy my honor with my life if need be, but I've seen enough of killing. Look at what this man, this lone man, has done!"

"Strung them Apache boys up and whittled whilst they screamed," Pike said quietly, and helped himself to the beans again. "We found the shavin's over there," he added, and pointed out into the darkness. He stared at his plate. "Believe I got these beans a tad salty."

"You see what I mean?" Quincannon cried. "Excuse me for saying it, Mr. Pike, but I have no wish to become like you. I've seen a man scalped while he was still alive, seen him tortured and hanged! We've come across awful things, unspeakable things, and a man has died at my own hand! This last, this was the finish."

He turned toward Garner. "You said that there were certain things a man had to get used to if he was to have business in the wild places. Well, I don't intend to get used to them. I don't even know that I'm fit to practice law anymore. But I do know that we're going no further, because the trouble is, I find myself . . ." He paused, wiping sweat from beneath his bandage, then tearing it away impatiently.

"You're gettin' a little too used to 'em to suit you," Garner said quietly. "That it?"

Quincannon let out a big breath, as if something enormous had just fallen from his shoulders. "Yes."

"Well, what's wrong with that?" Pike asked, his spoon paused in midair and dripping. "I never heared'a such a thing! Also, I never in my life met such a magnet for trouble and wild times as you, Elliot. Why, we turned up more deceased bodies in the last week or so than me and King has seen in practical the whole of our acquaintanceship." He thought for a moment. "The last year, anyways. I tell you, it's plumb excitin'! You break this deal now, and it'll be a . . . a whatchacall. There won't be no dang endin' to it, that's what! I likes things what get finished up neat an' tidy."

"Better no ending than we all die like those Apache, Mr. Pike," Quincannon said. Relief that it was over had made him feel as if he were floating. That, and this knowledge that his experience hadn't been normal, after all. He was almost giddy with it!

He thought about Mormon Wells and about Lisa Boudreau, and about the wire he would send to Malcolm Peabody. He could face anything, even that telegram, even the aftermath. A man's honor wasn't such an important thing, was it? Not when you compared it with the blood it cost, and the pain. Everything would be all right. Everything would be simple after this.

"I never heared the like!" Pike continued to fume. "Seems to me that when a feller's number's up, it's up. Elliot, I swear I'd druther take a bullet or blade than croak all boring-like in a feather bed!"

Garner had remained silent, but he seemed to be studying Quincannon. At last, he gave a curt nod. "It's your party, kid. You call the shots. Hell, I didn't want to come in the first place!"

"Good." Quincannon had never meant a single word so much in his life.

"All right, then, it's settled." Garner stood up and stretched. "I'll take the first watch. Pike, I'll be rollin' you out about midnight. Quincannon, Pike'll wake you up 'long about three."

17

Quincannon slept fitfully, despite his decision. He dreamed that he returned to Boston, expecting—for some reason known only to the gods of slumber—a hero's welcome. Unfortunately, he didn't get it. He stepped onto the train station's platform, and was stoned by the populace at large. Standing atop the depot roof with a phalanx of drab-skirted sisters, Miss Minion tossed a rock that hit him in the face.

He dreamed about Lisa Boudreau then, a much nicer dream, until he told her he'd given up his quest for the cup. And as he told her, he seemed to grow smaller and smaller until he was half his former size, at which point she picked him up like a doll, and pitched him in the water trough.

He thought that he must have hit his head as he fell, for quite suddenly his dreamscape went from Lisa Boudreau and the dusty streets of Mormon Wells to stars, nothing but blackness and stars, and then there was nothing.

Sometime later, he woke with a jolt.

The first thing he realized was that it was nearly light, and than he'd been sleeping on his side. He never slept on his side!

And just as it was seeping into his brain that he was supposed to be standing guard, just as he was about to groggily hiss, "You didn't wake me!" to Pike, who was staring at him, really staring, a scream built in his throat, a scream that was so mindless and overwhelming that no human was capable of making it.

It emerged as a long, high-pitched wheeze of air that emptied his lungs just as, out of nowhere, a boot appeared and kicked Pike's head. The head, severed just below the jaw, rolled several feet and came to rest in the ashes of their fire. The eyes were still open, still staring. Still accusing.

Quincannon tried to lurch to his feet, but his hands and feet were tied and he didn't make it more than an inch.

A voice, well-spoken and mannerly, said, "Be still, boy."

With a jerk, he turned his head and, in horror, looked up the leg that had kicked poor Mr. Pike.

The man wore no hat. He was tall and slender, and attired in a dusty black frock coat, a brocade vest of bright jade, and blood-spattered pants. His steel-gray hair was long and plaited down his back, and his face was clean-shaven, his nose aquiline, nearly elegant. A pistol rode one hip, and a long saber trailed from the other.

And there was no trace of sanity in his eyes. They were cold and gray and mad. Utterly mad.

This was the man who had burned the Indians alive, listened to them scream while he whittled, the man who had beheaded Mr. Pike. Of this, Quincannon was instantly certain.

He hadn't realized he was holding his breath, but when he suddenly inhaled, the air he took in was sour, filled with a hopelessness past dread, past terror.

Casually, the man pulled a silver case from his pocket, extracted a slim cigar, and bit off the end. He lit it and shook out the match. "And what might your name be?" he asked, as if this were Boston, as if this were broad daylight on the Common.

Quincannon didn't answer, and after a moment the man, still smiling, pulled back his boot and gave him a savage kick. There was a loud *pop* in his shoulder, and pain knifed through him.

"I asked your name, young man."

Eyes closed against his agony, he hissed, "Quincannon," through clenched teeth.

The man snorted. "Quincannon, did you say? Not Elliot Quincannon of the Boston Quincannons!"

Quincannon swallowed dryly against the vomit that threatened to rise up his throat.

The man laughed. "My gracious!" he finally said. "It is, indeed, a small world. Well, well."

And then he turned and walked away, as if on some urgent business.

His breath coming in shallow pants, Quincannon listened to the soft crunch and swish of brush as the man walked away. Was this how it was going to end? Strung upside down from an ironwood with a fire slowly cooking his brains while he struggled helplessly against his bonds? Would he smell his own hair singeing? Would he still be alive when his skull burst?

Mr. Pike was already dead and past caring. Pike, who had been kind to him, especially in the beginning. Pike, who had eaten all the biscuits and had gleefully told him stories that turned his stomach; Pike, who had taught him to shoot a pistol, rubbed salve over his pitiful backside, sheltered him from the storm, and who had teased him about Lisa Boudreau.

He hoped to God that it had been quick, that Mr. Pike had never seen it coming.

Only then, at the sound of a low moan behind him, did he remember Garner. Slowly, his head pounding in time with his shoulder, he tried to turn over. It was difficult, for his feet were tucked up behind him and bound by a short rope to his hands, and his left arm was utterly useless.

But anything was better than staring at the severed head

of Mr. Pike. Or at his body, which Quincannon had just realized lay across the valley floor. He could see just a snatch of blue cloth.

After some work, he managed to roll over. He was convinced his shoulder was broken. Something inside grated with every breath he took.

Garner lay a few feet off, his hands and feet bound. His hat was gone, and dried blood matted dark hair to his forehead. His eyelids fluttered slightly.

"Mr. Garner!" Quincannon hissed.

There was no reply.

"Mr. Garner!"

Nothing.

Don't vomit again, Quincannon told himself. *Don't piss yourself. Don't worry about Mr. Pike or Mr. Garner right now. Don't panic. Breathe. Think, dammit!*

It was easier said than accomplished, but gradually, Quincannon slowed his breathing. If nothing else, it eased the pain in his shoulder. Slowed down the thudding, anyway. He attempted to order his thoughts.

First, he decided, he had to determine the proximity of any weapons. Another shoulder-wrenching roll, and he was back in his original position. Taking care not to look in the direction of Mr. Pike's head, he craned his neck and scouted the pile of blankets that had been their bedding.

The man had been careless, or more probably supremely sure of himself. All of their weapons had been tossed in the haphazard heap, along with their bedding and the saddles they'd been using as pillows. His handgun, at least, was on the ground at the edge of the pile. Its butt peeked from beneath Pike's old iron skillet. Unfortunately, it was a good ten feet away.

His heart sank lower, if that were possible. Even if he could somehow manage to get over there and coax the gun into his hand, firing it—and hitting anything besides himself—would be a magician's trick. He was no magician.

Somehow, he had to free himself.

And then it came to him. He had a knife, by God! He'd bought the little pearl-handled pocketknife back at the store in Rusty Bucket—Lord, it seemed the distant past!—and he was fairly certain he'd stuck it back in his pocket after all the pants changing and clothes washing in Mormon Wells. He'd never used it, never so much as opened it. They'd used that big blade of Garner's every time a knife had been needed.

Garner groaned again.

Busy trying to reach his back pocket, Quincannon ignored him. But the ropes were too tight, and his broken shoulder put him at a distinct disadvantage. If he could sit up, sit on his knees, perhaps with the accompanying slack in the rope . . .

Grimly, he began to rock, his shoulder and his head complaining with each movement. *Sonofabitch!* he thought as he struggled. *Get up, you sonofabitch!*

Seeing Garner's head wound coupled with the pile of rubble to which their campsite had been reduced, he was convinced that this man, this devil, had coldcocked both of them. How else to explain his pounding head, the fact that he hadn't come awake until far too late?

The man had killed Pike first, he was sure of that. If he did it stealthily, it would have made little noise. Then he'd come into camp and bludgeoned them both, hog-tied them, and gone through their possessions at his leisure.

At last, Quincannon rolled up on his knees and sat panting, his eyes closed, waiting for the pain to subside to a bearable roar.

He looked up a moment later, at the sound of footsteps—and singing. The man walked up the center of the valley, and he was singing "Danny Boy" in a pure, clear tenor. At any other time, the sound of that voice, dripping with sentiment, and that old Irish song might have moved Quincannon to tears. Now it only filled him with horror. He realized he was shaking, and couldn't make himself stop.

The man stopped about thirty feet away and broke out in a grin. "Sitting up, are we, Elliot?" he called gaily. "Excellent, excellent! If you'll bear with me, I have a bit of business to attend to. Then I'll be along and see to you. Never fear!"

The song resumed. " 'But come ye back, in sunshine or in shadow . . .' " he sang as he made his way toward Mr. Pike's body. He pulled his sword.

Still trembling, Quincannon began to fumble at his pocket. As he'd thought, the rope connecting his feet and his hands had gone slack. He poked a thumb into his pocket and touched the upper rim of his watch. Cursing, he felt the outside of the pocket, and felt the small outline of the knife down deep, below the watch, pressed against the bottom seam of his pocket.

He began to work the watch out.

He heard an odd sort of chopping sound, just one, and looked up in time to see the man tossing Mr. Pike's severed arm to the side. He had begun the tune again, and sang dolefully, " '. . . the pipes, the pipes are calling . . .' " as he raised his sword again.

This time, Quincannon couldn't stop himself from retching. Acid vomit spilled from his mouth, spattered his shirt and his thighs.

He kept on working at that watch, ignoring the taste of bile. After what seemed years, but probably wasn't more than a few seconds, it popped from his pocket and fell between his legs. He began inching the knife up.

Weakly, Garner muttered, "Kid?"

Quincannon twisted toward him just as the little knife cleared the top of his pocket and dropped into his cupped and waiting hand.

But Garner wasn't looking at him. He stared out across the valley, at the singing madman who was slowly dismembering their friend. "Pike," he breathed, and closed his eyes. "Aw, Pike."

Quincannon tried to open the blade with his one good

hand, and nearly dropped it. He steadied himself, and tried again. This time, he pried it open.

"Jackson Woodrow, you sonofabitch," Garner shouted suddenly. It was loud enough that Quincannon nearly dropped the knife again, loud enough that the man looked up from his labors.

Quincannon supposed he had known it was Jackson Woodrow when he'd seen the sword on his hip, but hoped he was wrong. The man's response put all doubts to rest.

He stood, raising his sword and waving it at his side. Pike's blood spun out in little rivulets from its tip, spraying the weeds. "Good morning, gentlemen!" he called merrily. "I see everyone's awake! Be with you shortly."

He turned again to his gruesome work, this time giving voice to "Old Black Joe."

Garner said, "Looks like this is it, kid. Goddamn sonofabitchin' bastard!"

"Perhaps not, Mr. Garner," Quincannon said. His shoulder was on fire and he had managed to stab himself in the wrist, but he had opened the blade and turned it to business. The bound position of his hands made sawing clumsy, but he persevered. "Look at my hands."

"All I can see is blood. Jesus, boy, what'd he do to you?"

"A knife!" Quincannon whispered through the pain in his shoulder, his head, and now his hand. They seemed distant, only petty annoyances. "I found my pocketknife!"

Garner gave a little huff. "What are you tryin' to do, cut your damn hand off?"

Quincannon ignored the question. "He knew my name. I mean, my first name."

"Who? Jackson?"

"No, Ulysses S. Grant." He stuck a finger alongside the blade and felt severed fibers. Not enough. There were three ropes around each wrist, and he had barely made a dent in the first. He began to saw again.

"Don't be a smart-ass," Garner said. "The bastard

must've staked his ponies out a couple valleys over. Must've snuck back last night and listened while we were talkin'. Dammit!" With a grunt, Garner rocked himself up into a sitting position. "I should've heard him sneakin' around out there! Arm's gettin' too short to read the newspaper, and now I'm goin' deaf, too!"

"But he knew I was from Boston," Quincannon whispered. He would have given anything for the use of his left arm. It hung from his broken shoulder like so much meat. "How could he know that? And are you sure it's Jackson Woodrow?"

"I'm sure," Garner said grimly. "Guess those stories about him gettin' shot off a running horse down in Mexico were a bunch'a crud. Aw, no . . ."

Quincannon followed Garner's line of vision to their fire. And Pike's head. He turned his face away quickly, but Garner continued to stare. "Sorry, you old goat," he said softly. "Guess those ol' mojo cards'a yours didn't work out, after all." Garner paused, then snapped, "You through that rope yet, boy? Now'd be a real good time." He was all business again.

"No, I . . ." Quincannon moved the wrong way, and pain flooded his shoulder again. "It's a new knife," he said, grimacing. Sweat ran down his forehead, into his eyes, and clamminess had overtaken his body. "I guess they don't come from the maker presharpened."

Garner swore under his breath.

Quincannon didn't look at him. He just kept sawing.

18

Jackson Woodrow had stopped his singing, and as he crossed the valley toward them, calmly scrubbing the blood from his sword blade with a handful of yellow weeds, he whistled "The Battle Hymn of the Republic."

Garner watched his progress with a cold disdain that was miles past fear. Fear for himself, anyway. He would have thrown himself on that blade if it could've gotten him close enough to reach Jackson's throat. He'd choke the crazy sonofabitch until his head popped off, and keep on choking him long after they were both dead.

Beside him, the boy still worked at that rope. Garner couldn't see the knife, because Quincannon had the blade between his hands and his body, and the knife was so small that his hand covered the rest of it. That was good, because if Jackson checked their bonds, he likely wouldn't see it.

Of course, he'd see all that blood, and he just might take a look to see where it was coming from. Quincannon had poked himself but good, and the ropes were soaked and dripping red. How he could have done that much damage with a blade that was only store-sharp was beyond Garner. The kid should have sat himself right down and honed it, first thing.

There was another thing to be ticked off about. Besides Pike. Besides Woodrow.

At least his horse was all right. Woodrow hadn't touched the string, from what he could see. Of course, he always was a lot more bent on chopping up people than animals.

"Watch yourself, kid," he whispered just before Woodrow stepped into the little clearing they'd made for camp.

Jackson Woodrow, having finished the song—and the blade polishing—slid his sword back into its sheath. The sun at his back, he smiled broadly and crossed his arms, hugging his shoulders.

"Well," he pronounced. "It seems to me that you have come down in the world somewhat, Garner."

Garner squinted. "Can't say as it's too nice meetin' up with you again, either."

"Tut-tut," said Woodrow with a shake of his head. "Always the same. Never a kind word." He squatted down on his heels. "It has been a goodly amount of time. What, ten, twelve years?"

"More like eighteen."

Beside him, Quincannon piped up, "You *know* him?"

Woodrow answered for him. "Land sakes, yes! And I believe you're right, Garner. It was in sixty-two that we met. For our younger members," he added, looking at Quincannon, "that was during the War of Northern Aggression. Or the War of Secession. Or the War Against Slavery. Take your pick. Wasn't that a jolly time! You know, most men failed during that war. Died or were wounded or went crazy or, at the least, went down to skin and bones. Me?" He patted his stomach. "I wasn't proud where my meat came from. I put on twenty pounds!"

Quincannon went whiter than he already was and sagged against his ropes, and Garner hissed, "Hang on, boy." What he meant was, "Hang on to that knife!"

"And your traveling companion, King Garner?" Jackson

continued. "He was quite the wild one back then, my boy. You'd never know it to look at him now, but he was one rip-roaring sonofabitch, if you'll pardon the expression. Had quite a reputation even then. Came all the way from the wilds of New Mexico to join the fight, then decided he didn't like it and went home. Without permission as I recall, isn't that right, Garner?"

"What's your damn point, Woodrow?" Garner growled.

Jackson laughed. "Touchy, are we?"

Garner could tell by the subtle, rhythmic, almost imperceptible twitching of Quincannon's elbow that he was still working at that rope. He didn't dare look down to see if he was making any progress, though.

He said, "Why'd you burn those Indians, you sick bastard?"

Woodrow blinked. "Why, they irritated me, Garner! One might go so far as to say they pissed me off. Apache burned one of my men about four years back. I found what was left of him hanging from a cottonwood. I was only returning the favor. Besides, they took out my two most recent companions. One, for certain. The second, I'm assuming."

He shrugged. "Stoic bastards, the Apache. Didn't make a peep until the end. I rather liked burning them, I must admit. I can see what they see in it. All that twisting and writhing and swinging. Takes a good amount of time before they tire, you know. However, I don't mind saying that if they hadn't died when they did, I might have taken mercy on them. I'd seen you coming, of course." He paused and smiled. "I saw someone, at any rate. How nice that it was you!"

Garner grunted.

"Talkative, as always, I see," Woodrow said with a smile. "As I recall, you didn't say a word that last night in camp, when I filleted that lovely Union boy." He closed his eyes and licked his lips. "Still fat. A recent inductee."

Garner growled, "Shut the hell up, Woodrow."

"We never saw you again, did we?" Woodrow asked. "Now, why was that?" When Garner didn't answer, he said, "Well, never mind. It's all water under the bridge. I've even forgiven Bloody Bill Anderson and the mighty Quantrill. Imagine, them mustering me out! And at gunpoint! Why, we both know that Bloody Bill did more than his share of butchery. He and his men carved off the parts they wanted, then just left the meat lay! Of course, these last few years, I fear I've let most of it lay, myself. . . ."

Now Garner was the one close to losing whatever remained of last night's supper. Back in '62, he'd been sickened by the men he'd fallen in with, and now it was all flooding back in on him. He'd thought war would be just another grand adventure. He hadn't thought he'd be thrown headlong into a pit filled with snarling animals.

He'd lasted just two weeks, then hied out in the middle of the night, dodging cannon fire and patrols until he'd ridden clear out of Missouri, clear through Louisiana and Texas, and back to the relative safety of New Mexico. And then, for good measure, held kept going all the way to Arizona. And along the way, he'd shot every man who looked at him cross-eyed.

He shouldn't have run. He should have shot Jackson that night, one bullet in the brain, and taken the consequences. Any way you looked at it, it would have saved a helluva lot of lives.

Too late. Everything was too late.

"But enough of the past," Woodrow said cheerfully. He'd let himself all the way down, and sat in the dirt, cross-legged. He pulled out his case and plucked out a cigar. "I can't tell you how delighted I was to discover not only you, my dear old friend, but none other than the famous Elliot Quincannon, himself!" He bit the end off his cigar. "I am constantly delighted by what a very small world this is!"

With difficulty, Quincannon said, "You mentioned me before . . . How do you know of me?"

Garner could still see that elbow twitching. Good Christ, had the knife maker even *walked* that blade past a whetting stone?

"Oh, I know all about you, my boy," Woodrow said. He lit the cigar. "Cuban," he mused. "The finest." He watched the smoke curl up, then go to tatters in the breeze. "I know that you are employed by the firm of Peabody and Strauss." He shook his head. "Not a very high-ranking employee, I must say."

Quincannon swallowed, and Garner saw his elbow hesitate.

"I—I do my job," Quincannon said in a very small voice.

"That you do, Elliot," said Woodrow. He stretched out on his side, propped on one elbow, and puffed at his cigar thoughtfully. "You were instructed to deliver a small crate to Tucson, into the hands of one Señor Antonio Vargas, am I correct?"

When Quincannon didn't reply, only stuttered incoherently, Woodrow continued, "You have already met Señor Vargas, I assume. He's out there, somewhere." He waved his cigar in the direction from which they had come. "Full of Apache arrows."

Quincannon had found his tongue again. "I don't understand," he whispered. "Both those men were white, anyway."

From the corner of his eye, Garner saw Quincannon's elbow begin to move again, just slightly, and realized that he'd been holding his breath.

"Not everyone with a 'señor' in front of his name is Mexican, I assure you," Woodrow said. "Mr. Vargas is Spanish on his father's side and French on his mother's. Or was, I should say. And the arms of Mr. Malcolm Peabody are long indeed, dear boy. Also, his fingers. Many pies, many pies. You see, I was hired to steal the crate—and that pretty cup—from you, and Mr. Vargas was hired to meet you in Tucson, where you would arrive empty-handed and very embarrassed. Mr. Vargas was going to give you quite a dressing-down, I can tell you! However, our dear Mr. Sanchez managed to muck the whole thing up."

Thinly, Quincannon said, "P-planned? It was all planned? I cannot believe that a gentleman such as Mr. Malcolm Peabody would stoop to—"

"Hush," said Woodrow with a wave of his cigar. "Whether you believe them or not, young Elliot, many things are true. Sanchez was not figured into the original agenda. No, no, he was a wild card. While he was holding up the stage, I was down in Tucson, preparing to ride north. I planned to take the Chalice from you a tad south of Picacho Peak. Naturally, when I heard about Sanchez, I was more than a little upset. You can understand that."

The boy was speechless, and Garner found himself feeling honestly sorry for him. It was a terrible thing to be killed, but it was almost a worse thing to find out that a man you admired had feet made from the thinnest clay. Jackson Woodrow was giving it to Quincannon with both barrels, and the stinking sonofabitch was enjoying it.

But Garner capped off his disgust. He had to keep Woodrow talking. He said, "So you rode north, and found out that Lazlo had already taken care of Sanchez for you."

"Bravo!" Woodrow sat up again, with his sword angled out behind him and one arm slung casually about his knees, as if he were sitting across the fire gabbing with comrades, not tapping a human head with his foot and toying with men he was about to butcher.

"You always were a clever man, Garner," he continued brightly. "Perhaps you'd like to tell us the rest of the story?"

Garner didn't answer, and Woodrow said, "Well, you were clever during our brief acquaintance, at any rate. But it wasn't so clever to let yourself be captured, now, was it? Did I tell you that the years haven't been very kind to you?"

"Been a real bitch to you, too, Jackson."

Woodrow laughed.

"How'd you find Lazlo?" Garner had to give the kid as much time as possible. Jesus, what was he using, a butter knife?

Woodrow fingered his cigar. "I should like to tell you that it was by clever subterfuge, Garner. But I find I can't lie to a man I'm about to gut and fricassee." He puffed twice. "Actually, it was quite by accident. I was looking for Sanchez."

"And you stumbled across Cherry Lazlo."

"And the cup. Of course, he didn't show it to me of his own accord." Woodrow shook his head. "An intellectual philistine, that Lazlo."

"But you paid him for it!" Quincannon said suddenly, and it was all Garner could do to keep from shouting, "Shut up and keep sawing!"

Woodrow stuck his nose up in the air. "I most certainly did not pay that common lout any money! The idea!"

Quincannon didn't know when to quit. "Well, you let him live."

"Professional courtesy," Woodrow sniffed. "Nothing more." He gazed upward, turning toward the sun. "My goodness. The day's getting on, isn't it? We're burning daylight, gentlemen. And soon," he said, putting one hand to the ground in preparation to rise, "we shall be burning something much more interesting."

"What brought you back, Jackson?" Garner said quickly. "You'd already done in those Apache. You could see there were three of us, but you sure as hell couldn't have made out our faces that far away."

It had the desired effect. Woodrow's arm went back around his knees. "That is certainly an appallingly fine red stud horse you have with you, Garner. I don't believe I've ever seen his equal."

"The horse?" Quincannon shouted so suddenly that both Woodrow and Garner jumped. "You came back for the *horse?*" He twisted against his ropes, jerking sharply toward Garner. "Are you happy now, Mr. Garner? Poor Mr. Pike's dead, I've got a broken shoulder, and we're both trussed and ready for market. Any minute this escaped mental patient is going to slice us up like so much bacon, and all because of your damned horse!"

Woodrow laughed. "I do believe he has his finger on the pulse of the situation, Garner, old chum! Except for that mental-patient allusion. I have never in my life seen the inside of such an institution, young man." He climbed to his feet and threw down his cigar. He slowly drew his sword and ran his thumb along the blade.

"Hold on, Woodrow," Garner said in desperation. "Why'd that Boston lawyer hire you to steal his jug in the first place?"

Woodrow didn't look at him. He turned the blade in the morning light, admiring it. "You're stalling, Garner. It's beneath you."

He pointed at Quincannon. "You first. Sliced first and cooked later, or vice versa? Your choice."

Quincannon looked up, and with a voice full of contempt, spat, "You, sir, are utterly, irredeemably mad."

Woodrow's face soured. He said, "That does it," and quickly stepped behind them.

Before Garner had a chance to shout, "Wait!"—for what little good it would have done—he heard a *whoosh* as Woodrow's blade sliced the air.

But Quincannon's head didn't fall. Instead, much to Garner's shock, he felt a quick pressure on his legs, and then their release as the saber sliced through his ropes. His hands were still snugly tied, but his feet were free. His muscles, bound too long, complained at the sudden slack, and he grunted as he fell over on his side.

"Don't dillydally," Woodrow said impatiently, and grabbed his arm. "Up on your feet, man."

Garner rose, his knees, his thighs, and calves aching.

Woodrow gave him a shove, and he stumbled forward, narrowly skirting Pike's head.

"Move," Woodrow ordered. "Toward my favorite ironwood. I think it would do our smart young friend a world of good to hear you scream."

19

As Quincannon watched, Jackson Woodrow forced a stumbling Mr. Garner toward the middle of the valley, toward that lightning-struck tree, at the point of his sword. Quincannon sawed at the rope double time. He'd nearly dropped the knife twice, now. The muscles in his right hand had all but seized up from making the same, short, repetitive motion for so long.

Additionally, he was certain he'd lost quite a bit of blood from the stab wound in his left wrist. He felt oddly lightheaded, and wet slicked the blade and its grip, making it slither in his grasp.

Please, he prayed as he sawed, *please let this rope be one that releases the others. Let that gun be loaded when I get to it. If I get to it.*

And then he thought, *If you can hear me, Mr. Pike, I would appreciate some assistance from you, too.*

Down by the ironwood, Woodrow had forced Garner to the ground. A coiled rope in his hand, he knelt at Garner's feet.

Quincannon's rope was nearly cut through. He'd made substantial headway when he'd lurched toward Garner. He hoped Garner didn't really think he was angry about the horse. He twisted again, pulling against the rope that tethered his hands to his feet. His shoulder screamed in complaint, but he felt a few more fibers pop. The blade went back to work.

Damn that Malcolm Peabody anyway! Why in God's name had he wanted his own relic stolen?

At the ironwood, Jackson Woodrow suddenly cried out, flew up into the air, and flipped onto his back in the brush. When he scrambled to his feet, his gun was drawn and pointed down into the weeds, where Garner lay. He was saying something. It was too low to hear at this distance, but Quincannon assumed that Garner kicked Woodrow over backward.

For just a moment he swelled with pride that a companion of his would be so brave in the face of such terrible odds!

But then Woodrow's gun barked, just once, and he shouted, "Hold still, dammit!"

Quincannon froze, as if the order had been directed at him.

Woodrow slowly twisted his head to look at Quincannon. "Don't you worry your pretty little head, boy," he called cheerfully. "Your friend Garner isn't dead. Heaven forfend! He's just ... more manageable now." And with that, he holstered his gun and knelt down in the pale weeds again.

Quincannon sawed with all his might.

Jackson Woodrow stood up, threw his rope over a stout branch, and began hauling Mr. Garner aloft, feet first. Garner twisted momentarily in Quincannon's direction, and he could see blood on his chest. Woodrow was singing some sea chanty Quincannon didn't know.

Once again, Quincannon jerked hard against the ropes and nearly passed out from the pain in his shoulder. Eyes closed, sweat running down his nose, he waited the agony out. When he felt the rope again with his finger, only a few blood-soaked fibers remained intact. With a mighty heave and a savage slice, he cut the rest of the way through.

He had the presence of mind not to swing his arm out immediately and take the pressure off his aching legs. A good thing, because just then Woodrow glanced his way.

"Don't look so anxious, young Elliot," he called. "I'll come for you soon enough." He turned and walked out through the brush, gathering kindling as he went. Garner swayed softly from the ironwood, head down, mute.

Quincannon shook the remaining ropes from his wrist. Whatever he had done had freed his right hand, but his useless left hand remained bound to his feet. This complicated things somewhat. It would take him substantially longer to get to the gun.

In addition, Woodrow had wandered far from the old ironwood in his quest for kindling. Quincannon had never shot at anything so distant. He'd never shot at anything half so far away as the ironwood, for that matter. If he missed, Jackson Woodrow could go down into the brush and sneak his way forward and shoot long before Quincannon, trussed as he was, could work his way to cover. Not only that, he could kill Mr. Garner outright.

Quincannon decided that he had to get the gun first: get the gun and return to his position, and wait for Woodrow to move closer. Perhaps lure him in.

When Woodrow began to walk yet farther away, Quincannon took his chance. Always watching Woodrow, crawling on his side, his feebly pumping feet yanking his shoulder until he thought he would scream or go mad, he made it to their heaped possessions and slipped the pistol into his hand. Then he painfully scrambled back to his former position. He sat up again, his breath coming in shallow pants.

The whole world went lopsided for a moment, but he fought against the almost irresistible urge to pass out, fought it as desperately as his forebears had fought for Irish soil. And at last the landscape came slowly back into focus.

Woodrow, still singing, was walking toward the ironwood with an armload of branches and sticks.

Belatedly, Quincannon remembered to check that Woodrow hadn't unloaded their weapons. This one, anyway. With difficulty, he thumbed out the cylinder, and gratefully felt five cartridges. *Always keep the sixth one empty and keep the hammer on it,* Pike had warned him. *Elsewise, someday you'll shoot your damn knee off.*

Dear Mr. Pike.

He curled his hand around the grip and took a deep but ragged breath. He was as ready as he was ever going to be.

Jackson Woodrow dropped his burden next to Garner's head with a clatter. He said something to Garner, then laughed.

Quincannon called, "Jackson Woodrow!" His voice broke. "Mr. Woodrow!" he shouted again.

Woodrow turned toward him, smiling. "You're a polite little dandy, aren't you?" he called. "Was there something of importance you had to impart, Mr. Quincannon?"

Quincannon was stumped. He hadn't even thought about what might lure Woodrow closer, and he would have kicked himself if held only had a leg free.

"My Chalice," he shouted. It was the first thing that popped into his mind. "Do you have it?"

Woodrow shook his head, as if he thought Quincannon was an idiot for having asked the question. "Well, certainly!"

"Might I see it? I mean, might I see it now? Before you . . ."

"Oh, there'll be plenty of time for that, young man," Woodrow called. "Plenty of time. I'll set it where you can see it while you burn." He bent down and started laying firewood beneath Garner's head.

Garner wasn't moving anymore. Maybe he was dead. And just for a fraction of a second, Quincannon felt relief that he could wait, that he had the luxury of time. He only felt this for a slice of a moment, though. No matter how much he wanted the time to coax Jackson Woodrow nearer, he wanted more than anything that Garner should still be alive. Someone worth his salt had to live through this ordeal, and Quincannon knew that someone was not himself.

Woodrow was busy with the firewood, and slowly, Quincannon brought the pistol up. It seemed heavier than it ever had before. It took every ounce of will he had to keep his hand from trembling.

This wasn't a brash, hotheaded action, like killing the bandit who'd shot bottles off his head. No, this would be cold-blooded murder. It didn't matter to the law that Jackson Woodrow was beneath contempt, it didn't matter what he had done in the past or planned to do in the future. Quincannon knew that much. And for the first time, he didn't care.

He also knew that if he couldn't manage to hold his hand steady, he was as liable to shoot Garner as Woodrow. Feeling cold despite the sweat that poured down his face, down his neck, and soaked his shirt, he at last steadied the pistol.

Give me strength and guide my aim, he silently prayed.

He squeezed the trigger.

It gave out a *click,* but nothing else. The empty chamber! Shocked beyond reason, Quincannon hesitated. And in that moment of hesitation, Jackson Woodrow looked up.

"What?" he roared, and went for his gun.

Quincannon pulled the trigger again.

Woodrow went part-way down and managed to get off a shot, but it went wide, into the brush. He sat there, swaying on his knees, and Quincannon, weeping hysterically by this time, fired a third time.

Jackson Woodrow toppled backward.

"God," Quincannon whispered. "God. God." And then he shouted, "Mr. Garner!"

There was no answer.

Once again, he slowly half crawled, half dragged him-

self to the pile of blankets, and wincing in pain, began to
go through them one-handed. At last he found Garner's
knife and, with a moan of relief, cut his left hand free. The
rope around his feet was next, and he stumbled toward the
ironwood on cramping legs.

"Mr. Garner?" he cried all the way there. "Mr. Garner?"

When he reached the ironwood, he kicked at Woodrow
savagely, feeling a certain satisfaction when he heard something *crunch*. Probably a rib. Then he remembered to kick
Woodrow's gun away. He wasn't breathing, but Quincannon wasn't about to take any chances. Then he turned to
Garner.

A stain was spreading slowly on Garner's chest, but if
Quincannon remembered his anatomy, the slug had missed
anything vital. He'd lost a great deal of blood, though.

"Mr. Garner?" he asked again, kneeling down. He pushed
aside the kindling.

Slowly, Garner opened his eyes. His breathing was labored. He whispered, "About goddamn time."

Quincannon felt his face stretch into a grin so wide he
thought it would burst his face. He didn't care. "You're
alive, Mr. Garner!"

Garner's eyes closed again. He growled, "Stop flappin'
your lips and cut me down."

"Oh! Oh yes! Certainly!" With difficulty, Quincannon
stood up. "I'm afraid you're going to take a tumble. You
see, I can't use my left—"

"Just do it, dammit!"

Quincannon went to work, and in short order, Garner
landed on his head. "Ouch," he groaned as the rest of him
slowly slid to the ground, down Quincannon's body. Once
he was down all the way, Quincannon cut his hands free.

Garner didn't sit up. He rubbed his wrists and looked
over at Woodrow. He looked terribly weak, but he said,
"That bastard all the way dead?"

"As near as I can tell."

"Shoot him again, just in case."

Quincannon complied without question.

Before the echo had a chance to die, Garner said, "What's wrong with your shoulder?"

"It's broken, I think. He kicked me."

Garner stared at him. "Did it make a sound?"

Quincannon nodded. He didn't see that there was any point to this. They ought to be getting to the horses and starting on their way before anybody else showed up.

"A crack or a pop?"

"I don't know. A pop, I guess. Do you think you can ride?"

"Help me up," Garner whispered, and with difficulty, Quincannon did. But when he tried to start Garner in the direction of the horses, Garner said, "No. Prop me up against the tree."

"But—"

"Just do it, boy!"

He walked Garner three steps to the trunk, then leaned him against it.

"Go round the other side," Garner said. His every word was labored. Quincannon humored him. Garner reached through the crotch of the tree and took hold of Quincannon's wrist, gripped it surprisingly hard. "This the one?"

"Yes, but—" Quincannon let out a bloodcurdling scream, because suddenly Garner yanked his left arm through the ironwood's crotch. His body slammed against the trunk at the same instant he felt a horrendous pain in his shoulder, and heard a *pop*.

At the same time he discovered that he could use his arm, he realized Garner was on the ground again. Even as Quincannon was rounding the ironwood to go to him, even as he realized that Garner was very near to passing out, Garner was giving him orders. As usual.

"First, get that hand bandaged," he breathed. He was panting from exertion, even though all he'd done was grab Quincannon's wrist, and then fall backward. "Next, bury

Pike. Say some words. We're not leavin' him for the buzzards, you got that? Then get . . . get . . ."

He passed out.

Quincannon worked as quickly as his sore shoulder and punctured wrist would allow. After he packed and bandaged Mr. Garner's wound, he gathered up poor Mr. Pike, dug a shallow pit for him, covered him with a cairn of rocks and, hat in his hands, spoke the Twenty-third Psalm.

"Thank you, Mr. Pike," he said softly when he was finished. "Thank you for everything. I guess you got your wish. You didn't die in a feather bed, anyway."

He had determined, as he worked, that his shoulder had been dislocated, not broken. That Garner had known it right away, even in his weakened condition, only added to Quincannon's respect for him. But now Garner lay unconscious beneath the ironwood. He'd never be able to ride out of this valley, let alone back to town.

Quincannon had, for some time, been a sporadic reader of *Harper's* magazine, and he remembered an illustration he'd seen in its pages. It was some sort of an arrangement of poles that a horse could drag, and a man could lie upon. An Indian travois, he believed it was called.

With nothing but the memory of that drawing to go on, he set to the business of trying to construct the contraption. He checked Garner again—there was no change—then gingerly pulled Woodrow's sword from its sheath and set off down the valley, looking for an appropriate tree. He'd tried the ironwood first. The sword didn't make a dent in it.

He found a stunted mesquite about a hundred yards down the valley. The branches, the ones thick enough to use, were far from straight, but they'd have to do. He chopped off two long, stout limbs, trimmed them hurriedly, then cut shorter lengths for crosspieces. He dragged them back to the horses and had it halfway put together before he remembered that the horses had had neither food nor water since the night before.

Mr. Garner would not approve.

Quickly, he fed and watered them, and discovered that Jackson Woodrow had tied his own string—a handsome black gelding and two Indian ponies—at the far end of the picket line. He fed and watered them, too, shoved a piece of jerky into his mouth, then got back to the business of travois building.

When he was finished, he slipped the halters off all the horses save Red and Faro, both of whom he'd already saddled. He figured that even if he and Garner lived to get back to town, Garner would surely kill him if he turned the red stud loose, and he couldn't lead more than Red, not without slowing himself down considerably. His mare, Rosie, moved gingerly away from the picket line, as if she couldn't believe she was free, and then she wandered off and began to graze.

"Good-bye, old girl. Take care of yourself," he whispered before he shooed the other horses off. And then, quite suddenly, he grinned. If Mr. Garner was so bloody set on pulling horseshoes, he could come out here later and do it.

Bone-tired, he stepped back to admire his work. All in all, he thought he'd managed to construct a fairly sturdy conveyance. The poles ran though Red's stirrups, and were secured snugly to his breast strap—and for good measure, the saddle horn. The body of the travois was well back from Red's heels, braced with more mesquite wood, and lashed together with ropes, which also formed the narrow bed of the thing.

He didn't spend a great deal of time congratulating himself, however. He covered the rope bed with blankets. He packed Faro with Garner and Pike's firearms and as much of their belongings as would fit, and enough food and water to get them back to Mormon Wells. And then, almost as an afterthought, he went to the pile of possessions that he'd stripped from Woodrow's gelding.

He didn't have to search very far. He found a flour sack, its top knotted. He peeked inside just long enough to see a glint of gold, then tied it up again and fastened it to Faro's saddle. He didn't want to look further, at least not right now. If it were up to him, he'd cast the blasted thing into a volcano.

He glanced up at the sun. Past noon.

He led both horses back to where Garner lay, and knelt to check his pulse. It was weak, but at least his heart was still beating.

He pulled down his canteen and held it to Garner's lips, as he had already done several times before.

As always, Garner swallowed, but didn't open his eyes more than a flutter's worth. He peeked beneath the bandage again, and found that his packing of it had succeeded—the bleeding had stopped, at least for now. He couldn't be sure what miles of bouncing on the travois would do.

At last, carefully, he inched Garner onto the travois and tied him into it. He picked up Woodrow's sword one last time, drove the blade into the hard soil as deeply as he could, and then, using all his strength, snapped the blade in two.

He mopped the sweat from his brow and said, to no one in particular, "All right, then."

He swung up into Faro's saddle.

20

The gently rolling hills, which had seemed so easy to climb when they were working their way toward the valley, suddenly became a nightmare to traverse. The travois caught on everything and nearly flipped over several times, which had even the heretofore calm Red hopping and white-eyed.

Additionally, Faro was so sensitive—and so well trained—that every shift of Quincannon's weight had him turning right or left or stopping altogether. But eventually, they emerged on the plain again.

In the far distance, Quincannon could see the deceptively soft rise of pale rocks that marked Indian Creek Canyon. He gave serious thought to riding around it. Cherry Lazlo would still be dangling beside the cliff dwelling, which would more than likely be already inhabited by another group of bandits. But he didn't know the way, and he feared that he'd get lost out here and wander aimlessly until Mr. Garner died. He had to take the quickest, surest route. He had to get Garner to a doctor.

He would take his chances. For the present, he just hoped he'd be able to find the entrance again. He'd worry about bandits later.

He set out across the plain, always keeping an eye to the eastern horizon. He hadn't forgotten about those Apache.

Stops to water the horses and rest were short and nervous. Garner was still unconscious most of the time, but Quincannon forced water down his throat, and repeatedly wet down his bandanna, which he placed loosely over Garner's face.

He grew accustomed to Faro's ways. "You'll make a horseman of me yet, won't you?" he said to the bay as he rode along.

He passed a swarm of feasting buzzards, cut them a wide berth, and continued along the trail they'd made the day before.

An hour later he spotted a long, low billow of dust behind him, to the southeast. Apprehensively, he dismounted and dug through his pack until he found Garner's spyglass. It didn't help much, just made the dust cloud bigger, but it confirmed his first observation.

Apaches, moving fast, were probably making that dust. And it wasn't coming in his direction. They were cutting across the plain, probably following the trail of those errant braves. They hadn't come to the first dead man. And they hadn't seen him yet.

Quickly, he put the spyglass back and mounted Faro again, fighting his instinct to make a run for it, and telling himself repeatedly to walk, go slow, don't raise any more dust than you have to.

If he were those Apaches, he'd follow the trail down into the valley. That would use up another two hours—all right, one, at their speed—but by that time he'd be safely inside the canyon, and it would be nearly sunset.

Of course, he wasn't those Apaches.

It was nearly dark when he at last slipped inside the yellow walls of Indian Creek Canyon.

It had been a good two hours since he'd seen any dust.

Of course, that didn't mean anything, he reminded himself. Garner had told him that Apache could turn themselves into wind when they wanted to.

The thought was chilling, and despite the clinging heat of the day and the sweat that soaked his shirt, he shivered.

His revolver drawn, he proceeded slowly into shadows of the canyon. The limestone walls rose up around him, cutting off what little remained of the day, and he listened keenly for any sound out of the ordinary. The saddle leather seemed to creak inordinately loudly, and the pole ends of Garner's travois seemed to hiss and skip through the dirt with uncommon noise, advertising his presence to bandits and badmen.

But when the canyon at last opened to reveal the cliff dwellings, lit eerily by the moon, all was quiet. No ruffians were poised for battle. There was only the wind, blowing a soft melody over the rims above. That, and Lazlo's corpse.

The birds had been picking at it, and it had separated into two pieces. Quincannon circled wide around the part that had fallen to the ground. He didn't need to see it. Smelling it was bad enough.

But the stink of death was everywhere. The bandit Garner had left behind had fled without burying anybody. So much for honor among thieves, Quincannon thought. He held a bandanna over his nose and rode on through without stopping.

At last he came out the other side of the canyon and, after searching a bit, found a sheltered place against the rocks. He pulled up the horses. It was as good a place to camp as any.

He saw to Garner first. He made a pallet for him, then walked Red up so that it was an easy matter—much easier, now that his shoulder wasn't so sore—for him to shift Garner from the travois to the ground. Once Garner was comfortable, he tended the animals.

He couldn't for the life of him figure out how he'd be able to get the travois back on Red once he'd gotten it off, so he just loosened Red's girth and left the saddle on him and the travois hitched. He supposed he probably should have read that article in *Harper's* instead of just looking at the pictures. Maybe there was a trick to it. Maybe he shouldn't have constructed it on the horse.

He wasn't going to complain, though. It had held up just fine.

He built a small fire, figuring the rocks would shield the light from any prying eyes, Apache or otherwise, and fixed a kettle of beans. After all, he'd watched Mr. Pike. The jerky was hard to chew, and Mr. Garner always spat it out, no matter how small he tore it up. He thought he might be able to get some mashed beans, thinned with water, down Garner's throat. He only wished he'd paid more attention when Mr. Pike had made the biscuits. He could use six or eight right about now.

He pulled the bandage away from his wrist, and found the puncture mark, as well as the flesh about it, angry and swollen. Wincing, he squeezed out a good amount of pus and clear fluid, then washed it and went looking for Mr. Pike's little pouch of medicines. Of course, he didn't know what any of them were, since Pike hadn't believed in labels. But he opened each tiny tin until he found the stuff Pike had given him for his blood blisters. He dabbed it on, then wrapped his pounding hand again before he gently rubbed some of the same concoction beneath the bandages covering Mr. Garner's chest wound. Garner didn't move.

He was worried about Garner. His breathing was regular, if shallow, but it didn't seem right that a man would be unconscious the whole day. It crossed Quincannon's mind that the bullet might be pressing on something important. Or worse, that he'd remembered his anatomy wrong—or the slug's trajectory wasn't what he'd thought—

and that it had pierced a lung. But he wasn't about to go digging around in Garner's chest, looking for it.

He was afraid he'd kill him.

Later Quincannon managed to force a little slurry bean soup down Garner's throat, and Garner actually woke up.

"Jesus Christ!" he groaned. "Ain't you ever heard of salt?"

It was all he said and he closed his eyes again directly, but Quincannon couldn't have been more delighted. If Mr. Garner was complaining about tonight's cooking, he had a good chance of making it to town tomorrow.

He found Pike's goody bag and salted the beans before he ate any, though. And he ate until he thought he would burst.

He was almost asleep before he remembered the Chalice.

His wrist hurt and pounded too much to allow sleep, anyway, so he sat up and reached for Woodrow's dirty flour sack. Now was as good a time as any to take a good look at this prize that had cost Mr. Pike his life, and very nearly cost Garner and Quincannon theirs. It seemed to him that it had taken out about half the outlaw population of the Territory, too.

Carefully, he drew it out. The gold gleamed bright in the firelight. The rubies glinted fire, the emeralds glowed with the color of moist glades, the diamonds sparkled, the pearls glistened warmly.

How many hands had held it? he wondered. How many hands, through the centuries, had turned it before an evening fire such as this one, had pondered its mysteries, had marveled at its beauty? How many people, since the twelfth century when it was crafted, had died for it, killed for it? With how much blood had it been washed?

Frowning, he dropped it to the ground. Filthy thing! He would have given ten such chalices to have Mr. Pike back and sitting here beside him, telling bad jokes and complaining and doing the cooking, and telling him that Garner was going to be fine.

The Chalice rolled against his boot.

He glanced down, then suddenly picked it up again. There was a long, fresh scratch in its gold. Whether he'd just done it or whether it had received this insult at Woodrow's hands or Lazlo's was of no importance. Because beneath that scratch, beneath the gold, silver metal showed through.

He ran his thumb over the scratch and looked again.

Plate! It was nothing but plate!

Quickly, he picked up a smooth, palm-sized rock. Diamonds were supposed to cut anything, weren't they? He rubbed the rock against a large diamond set into a cross, rubbed it hard, heard it grate. When he lifted the rock away, the "diamond" was reduced to powder.

Paste. Paste and plate.

"Son of a *bitch*!" he whispered. And then he launched into a veritable tirade of words, every curse word he'd ever been exposed to, every filthy colloquialism he'd ever heard Pike or Garner come up with, and it still wasn't enough.

Panting, he hurled the Chalice across the campsite.

Malcolm Peabody, that bastion of the law, that gleaming, upright, solid citizen, had sent him to the wilds of Arizona with a fake. And he'd known it was a fake, he'd known it from the start!

He'd hired an outlaw to pose as the injured recipient, and hired a worse outlaw to steal it. And he'd picked Quincannon, the youngest man in the office and the most naive, the only one without family, the only one poor enough that he had to attend law school at night—and the only one, therefore, who wouldn't be much missed by anyone at the firm, at least socially—to play his fool.

Quincannon rubbed fists against his eyes. "And I thought he trusted me," he muttered. "I thought it was an

onor! Lord, I am twice the idiot he thought I was, chas-
ng it all over Creation!"

How Peabody must have laughed behind his back! What
a joke, sending poor Quincannon two thousand miles, into
he arms of bandits!

And for what? The insurance money, of course, Quincannon realized with a start.

Just when the original Chalice had gone missing, been
melted down, or sold off was of no importance. The vital
information was that Malcolm Peabody knew he had a
fake, and had kept up the insurance premiums anyway. A
million dollars' worth.

Fraud. He'd been an unwitting party to an insurance
fraud.

"Not anymore, Malcolm Peabody, you sonofabitching
weasel's behind," he muttered as he reclaimed the Chalice and jammed it back in its flour sack. "I'll see you dis-
barred and in prison if it's the last thing I do!"

The next morning, Garner was somewhat improved. He
ate his mashed beans—seasoned, this time—and rolled in
and out of consciousness the whole day. He didn't seem
aware of where he was, though. Quincannon didn't tell
him about the cup.

Quincannon plodded grimly on. He saw no Indians, but
his wrist, which had been swollen to twice its normal size
by the morning, was hurting him more and more as the day
stretched on. By late afternoon, when he checked it again,
angry red streaks were running up his forearm. They might
have gone past his elbow, but he didn't look. He didn't want
to know.

He was dizzy and swaying in Faro's saddle when he
finally rode into Mormon Wells at just past dusk, with Red
and Garner in his wake. Fortunately, Faro had given up
responding to every weight shift, and steadily carried him
forward.

He rode straight down Main Street, or as straight as he

could manage. The buildings seemed to careen and pitch gently, like reeds seen underwater, and their lit and bobbing windows were hazy around the edges.

"Too bright," he muttered. "Too bright."

He made it as far as the hotel before Faro stopped. That was the last thing he remembered.

21

When Quincannon woke, it was in a sunny hotel room looking out over Main Street. This one was much nicer than the one he and Garner and Pike had shared previously. It didn't face the alley, for one thing, and there were three windows instead of one. Bleached lace curtains were tied back from the open windows, and across them, someone had hung white dish towels, wrung out in water. The effect, as the breeze wafted through them, was quite cooling.

He tried to push himself up, and stopped immediately, his eyes tearing at the sudden, stabbing pain in his hand and wrist. He'd forgotten all about his injury. It seemed terribly ironic, he thought, that after all he'd been through, the wound that finally brought him down had been self-inflicted.

He was blinking back the tears and lifting the edge of his bandage for a peek when the door opened.

"You're awake!" said Lisa Boudreau, grinning wide.

It took him a moment to recognize her, and the first thing that came out of his mouth was, "You're wearing a dress!"

Her grin mutated into a scowl. "Well, don't you think I could have a dress? I've got plenty, you know. Three, to be exact."

He thought it best not to comment on her hair, which was most attractively piled atop her head in loose, golden ringlets. In that pale green dress, she looked like a spring confection.

"Well, listen to me!" she said, softening. "You're a wounded hero, and here I am, yammering at you about a silly dress."

"It's not silly," he said. "It's beautiful."

He was almost shocked when she blushed, and he looked down, grinning lopsidedly at his bandaged hand.

"Thank you," she said at last, and dragged a chair to his bedside. When he looked up at her, she was smiling sweetly.

"Where's Mr. Garner?" he asked. "Is he all right?"

"Next room over," she replied. "You fellas kept shouting in your sleep and waking the other one up. Guess you deserved to shout a bit, after what you've been through."

After what he'd been through? Garner must be awake, then. Garner must have told them.

But Lisa Boudreau continued, "Doc Martin and me pieced the story together. Did you really have a run-in with Cherry Lazlo?" She leaned forward anxiously, hands clasped in her lap. "Did you really kill that fiend, Jackson Woodrow? And what about the Apache? Why, the fellas have been toasting you two boys in the saloons for the last two days!"

He blinked. "Two days? We've been here two days?"

"Be three this evening. Doc took one look at your arm and was convinced it had to come off, but I threw a hissy, so he said he'd try to treat it." She grinned. "He says you have 'remarkable natural healing powers.' That's a quote. 'Course, all the stuff he did to it probably helped some. Practically tons of silver nitrate. He opened it up again and poked silver nitrate in it until I thought I was gonna pass out, just watching!"

Quincannon shook his head. "I don't remember a thing."

"With all the opium we've been pouring down your gullet, I'm not surprised. But see?" She pointed at his arm, and it was only then that he realized his torso was naked. He was afraid to peek under the sheets. "Look at your red streaks."

He raised his arm and looked. The knotty, inflamed, red cords were nearly gone. Only faint, pink lines marked where they had been.

"Who stabbed you? Was it Woodrow? Did he really hang Garner upside down from a tree?"

"Lisa? Can you get me some writing paper? A lot of it."

She frowned prettily. "And just how are you going to write anything? You dictate, and I'll scribble."

"It's my left wrist that's bandaged, not my right," he said with a smile.

"Oh," she said, the corners of her mouth bowing up into a smile again. "Of course it is. Yes, I can get you paper and a pen. Anything else?"

"As a matter of fact, you can. I'll need a small crate built." He gave her the measurements, which she committed to memory, and then she brought him writing implements and helped him prop himself up on his pillows.

"I'll go to the undertakers," she said, standing in the open doorway. "Bill's always got plenty of scrap lumber. Wouldn't be surprised if he nailed it up free of charge, after what you men did out there. You're heroes!"

And then, almost as an afterthought, she marched back over to the bed and said, "There's something I've been wanting to do, Elliot Quincannon."

And she bent over and kissed him, kissed him square on the lips, so long and soft and warm that his arms went around her, and it was all he could do to keep from pulling her down right on top of him.

She pulled away, far too soon to suit Quincannon, and stood up, straightening her dress. She looked a little flustered, he was happy to note. "Well," she said, her cheeks nearly as pink as her lips. "Well."

And then she was gone, leaving Quincannon to compose himself, which took longer than expected, and then compose his letter.

He began the story in Boston, told it through the stage robbery, the death of Mr. Trimble, and the subsequent theft of the Chalice. He relayed most all of the story, even though parts of it were embarrassing to him. He told of finding Garner and Pike and chasing Ramon Sanchez, his saddle sores, and how he'd nearly perished from lack of water; of finding Sanchez and his men tortured and dead, then chasing Lazlo. He told about the poisoned water hole and the horrible storm they had endured, and how they had found Lazlo's companion dead in the desert.

He didn't mention Garner's temporary desertion, however, or the fact that he'd had to steal the man's horse to get him to come along. He only said that circumstances were so dire that it took quite a bit of convincing to persuade his companions to continue.

He told the rest of the tale, then. He spent two paragraphs just on the bravery and cruel death of Mr. Lemuel Pike, and another two on the steadfast and stalwart qualities Mr. Garner had displayed in the face of the gravest danger, and added that at this moment Mr. Garner lay near death in the room next to his.

He said he was enclosing the reason for all this carnage—a worthless fake, insured by his employer, Mr. Malcolm Peabody of Peabody & Strauss, Boston, with the firm of Lloyd's of London. A fake that Mr. Peabody had hired the twisted Jackson Woodrow to steal for him, most probably so that he could claim the insurance money.

If I were going back to Boston, he wrote, *I would surely whip Malcolm Peabody through the streets. However, since*

I have no intention of returning east, I leave this matter in your hands.

He reread the letter, and was signing it when Lisa Boudreau rapped on the door and stepped inside. The crate was under her arm.

"That was fast!" he said. He decided not to worry about whether she was going to kiss him again. Sooner or later one of them would get around to it, and the waiting was half the fun. He knew that now. He folded the pages and stuck them in an envelope, then sealed it.

"Bill put it together while I waited." She grinned. Was there ever a prettier smile? "No charge. Told you!"

He instructed her to fetch the flour sack, which he'd already spied sticking out from beneath his saddlebags, and when she lifted out the Chalice, she gasped. "Must be worth a fortune!" she said.

"About fifteen cents," he said. "Did Bill give me some excelsior, too?"

While she packed the Chalice, he addressed the letter, then had her stick it inside before she put on the lid. "Where's it going?" she asked.

"Address the crate to Lloyd's of London in London, England. You'd better put 'Attention, Fraud Division' on it, too. I don't know that they call it by that name, exactly, but it'll surely get someone's attention."

"Well, it's sure got mine," she said, before she repeated the address to make certain she had it right. She picked up the crate, her blue eyes sparkling. "I'll paint on the particulars when I take it back to have Bill nail it closed. You gonna tell me about this someday, Elliot?"

Elliot. His name never sounded sweeter than when she said it.

"Someday soon," he replied, as smiling, she left.

He sat there, staring after her for quite some time. She was the one. He knew it in his bones. He supposed he'd known it from the first moment he saw her, or at least, the first moment he'd heard her speak. Would have realized it, too, if he hadn't been so damned pigheaded. She had such verve, and beauty, too! He'd move the earth for her, if she'd only have him. After that kiss, he was pretty sure that she would.

While he was writing the letter to Lloyd's of London, he'd been thinking about his career. Going back to Boston to finish his law degree was out of the question. Regardless of who had been at fault, there would be a scandal. There probably already was one. But many men—great men, in fact—had practiced the law without a formal degree. They had become governors, senators, even presidents!

He could practice the law out here, in the west, although preferably someplace without bandits or scalpers or any kith or kin of Jackson Woodrow. On this point, he was most firm.

But things being what they were, he couldn't make a move just yet. Any plans he made for his future would have to concern Lisa Boudreau, and there was Miss Minion to consider. How did one begin to couch the dissolution of affections in so harsh a vehicle as a letter? He mustn't seem cruel, or brusque, or thoughtless. He would have to make it as easy on her tender feelings as was humanly possible.

He picked up the pen again, dipped it in the inkwell, and carefully, he began to write.

"You going to stay awake for more than three minutes this time?" the portly man beside the bed asked.

Garner waited for the room to swim back into focus again. "What's it to you?" he asked grumpily. His head felt like the inside of a clock. *Boom, boom, boom.*

"I'm your doctor, that's what," the man said. Crisp, white hair ringed his head, and his silver mustache was neatly trimmed. "Name's Martin. You'd better sit up and talk for a spell, or you're going to ruin my reputation."

"Your reputation as what?" Garner asked as gingerly, he pulled himself up. "A quack?"

"Very funny." Dr. Martin jammed an extra pillow behind Garner's back with scrubbed-pink fingers. "There."

"You been givin' me laudanum, haven't you, sawbones?" Garner growled. "Jesus, I hate that stuff."

"Then you'll be happy to hear that I'm not giving you any more of it," the doctor growled right back at him. "You'll do just fine on your own. 'Course, it'll be painful as hell, but that'll only serve to keep you alert."

Garner grunted at him, and took a quick look around. It was a nice room, but he and the doctor were the only ones in it. He was going to ask about Quincannon, but instead, he said, "Where's my horse?"

Sighing, the doctor shook his head. "For the third and final time, that red stallion you're so worried about is down at Boudreau's Livery getting fat. As is your bay."

Garner felt something inside him relax. He could breathe easier, suddenly. He said, "How's the kid?"

"Nice of you to ask, finally," replied the doctor. "He's in the next room. And he saved your hide, by the way. Did a nice job of stopping the flow of blood, and packed you into town on that travois as carefully as an egg."

Garner tucked his chin in disbelief. "He built a travois?"

"Yes. And after I worked so hard to dig that slug out of your shoulder—or I should say, your chest—I didn't want you moving around and opening yourself up again. Thus the laudanum. It was sitting right next to your heart. The slug, that is. Interesting trajectory. Another quarter inch, and that would have been it." He snapped his fingers.

"Thanks," Garner said.

"Oh, please," said the doctor sarcastically, waving his hand. "Don't carry on so." He leaned back in his chair and took a pipe from his pocket. "I must say, Mr. Garner, that never in my career have I come upon such an assortment of scar tissue as I found on your person. Fourteen bullet holes! And I stopped counting the miscellaneous scars when I got to twenty-five."

He tamped down the tobacco and lit it. "You seem to have quite a reputation, according to our Sheriff Spencer. I use the term 'sheriff' advisedly. He's already been up here half a dozen times to see if you were awake. Tell me, Mr. Garner, have you made it your habit to throw yourself into the path of every weapon you encounter?"

In spite of himself, and in spite of the mention of that horse's backside, Spencer, Garner grinned. "Didn't throw myself at 'em, Doc, but it seems like a few of 'em have surely found me. Guess I'm just a natural magnet for implements of destruction. You didn't say about the kid."

"Blood poisoning, but we got to it in time. Miss Boudreau—who, by the way, has played an exemplary nursemaid to both of you—tells me he's up and writing a letter. Said she was going to send Johann up from the café with some broth and toast for him. I told her to order some up for you, too."

"I'd rather he drew me a beer an' tossed a steak on the fire."

"I'm sure you would, but it's broth for now."

There was a rap at the door, and Quincannon entered shakily, without waiting for a reply. The doctor rose immediately and helped him into the chair he'd just vacated.

"Easy there, lad!" He roosted at the foot of Garner's bed. "You shouldn't be out of bed so soon! Did you dress yourself?"

Quincannon nodded. "Had to sit down three times, but I did it. I take it you're my physician? I should like to thank you from the bottom of my heart."

"You're quite welcome, my boy." The doctor sighed happily. "Respect, at last."

It seemed to Garner that Quincannon looked pale but fit, despite the bandage that all but covered his left hand and wrist. Just the tips of his fingers poked out. Garner had been surprised—all right, poleaxed—when he'd heard that the kid had thrown together a travois to drag him back to town. He didn't remember much of any of it after Woodrow had shot him.

He noticed the top of a white envelope sticking from the boy's breast pocket. The doc had said he was writing letters. Quincannon had turned out to be a real corker, but he was a little too damn literate if you asked Garner. Hell, Quincannon should have been kissing that gal of his instead of scribbling!

He asked, "How's that hand, kid?"

A smile flickered over Quincannon's face. "Been better. How's your—"

"Well, how do you like that?" said Lisa Boudreau, who had suddenly appeared in the doorway, arms folded. And he'd be damned if she didn't have a dress on! "Everybody's in here having a party, and you didn't invite me!" She dug into her skirt pocket and handed a folded envelope to Quincannon. "When I hauled your box to the postmistress, she had this for you. Just came in on the morning stage."

It seemed to Garner that Quincannon took the letter like she'd just offered him a rattlesnake. Quincannon glanced at the return address, gulped once, and said, "Excuse me, please." He rose and slipped from the room, closing the door behind him.

"What on earth?" said Lisa, staring after him.

"You give that boy a kiss yet?" asked Garner.

"Oh, shut up," she said.

Garner grinned. "You did, didn't you?"

In his room, Quincannon opened the letter with shaking fingers. Not because he feared any communication from Miss Minion, but because he was worried that she might have done something drastic, like boarding a train. She might be on her way to Mormon Wells right now!

But the letter, when he opened and smoothed it, contained no such information. Miss Minion, it seemed, had been greatly upset by his failure to deliver Mr. Peabody's package. Mr. Peters, from the second floor, had told her all about it. Mr. Peters had confided that Quincannon would be sacked upon his return, if indeed, he had the courage to do so. He'd told her that Mr. Malcolm Peabody was most upset at this betrayal of trust.

He'd told her this and much more during their frequent walks upon the Common and their dinners at DelFlorio's.

At least he isn't taking her to our *restaurant,* Quincannon thought as he turned the page.

Miss Minion was sorry, but she thought it best to cease any further communication with Quincannon. It went without saying that their "arrangement" was a thing of the past. She was sorry, she said, but she was certain he would understand that she couldn't let the least hint of scandal fall upon her name or her reputation, or that of her family's. She didn't know what she would have done during this trying time if it were not for Mr. Peters. Mr. Peters, it seemed, was being very kind to her during her ordeal.

"I'll just bet he is," Quincannon murmured with a smile as he crumpled Miss Minion's missive and dropped it to the floor. "She's all yours, Mr. Peters," he whispered. "Take her with my compliments and my blessing!"

And then he merrily plucked the letter from his pocket, the letter he'd so laboriously written to Miss Minion, and tore it into tiny pieces that gaily fluttered to the floor like so much confetti. Miss Minion had bade him good-bye and Lisa Boudreau had kissed him, he'd hammered the last proverbial nail into Malcolm Peabody's coffin, and discovered that not only was he alive, but Garner was, too, and all in the same day! Plus, he had just remembered that they still had Lazlo's money. He could set himself up in business quite handily, and Mr. Garner could have his ranch. Things couldn't get much better.

When minutes later, a weak-of-limb—but light-of-heart—Quincannon made his way back to Garner's room, the door was open and loud voices were coming from inside. Garner was arguing with someone, and Lisa and the doctor were getting in some vocal jabs, too.

Quincannon leaned against the door frame, took in the situation, then shouted, "Stop it!"

They all turned toward him.

The short man who'd been arguing with Garner, and who was wearing a badge, demanded, "You Quincannon?" Without giving Quincannon the chance to reply, he said, "If you're hangin' around with this trash, you're bad news, too. I don't care what you say you done out there, and I don't believe for a slap second that you two no-accounts did in Jackson Woodrow. Better people than you been tryin' to kill him for the last ten years or so, and ain't nobody done it yet. Garner's awake, and as far as I can see, he's fit to travel. I want the both of you out of Mormon Wells inside an hour, you got that?"

Quincannon was unmoved. Still leaning against the door frame, he stared flatly at the dull-eyed little man, and said, "And what might your name be, Sheriff?"

"Spencer, Ed Spencer," the sheriff fumed. "And I expect the two of you gone, or there'll be the devil to pay! A man with Garner's reputation has got no place among decent folk!"

"I see," Quincannon said calmly. "Sheriff, would you mind stepping out in the hall for a moment?"

Spencer looked at him as if he were mad, but he came out. Quincannon partially closed the door behind him, then leaned his weary body against the wall, bracing his good hand against the hall's chair rail.

"Sheriff Spencer," he began, "my name is, indeed, Elliot Quincannon and I am an attorney-at-law, late of the Boston firm of Peabody and Strauss. I tell you this, because you should know with whom you're dealing. To the best of my knowledge, neither Mr. Garner nor myself has committed any crimes, grand or petty, within the confines of your jurisdiction or any other. You therefore have no grounds upon which to base your complaint. If you persist in this senseless harassment, I will bring the full force of the law, both criminal and civil, to bear. You will be, at the very least, stripped of your office and your source of income. I will personally see to it that you will not be able to find employment anywhere in the whole of this territory. Furthermore, I shall press civil charges and you will find yourself divested of all your possessions, both personal and jointly held, right down to your horse and your pocket watch, and everything but the clothes you are wearing. Do you understand me?"

All the cockiness had gone right out of Sheriff Spencer. He stood there, looking smaller than ever, and blinking rapidly.

Quincannon had kept his voice low and conversational throughout his speech, more to conserve his rapidly vanishing energy than anything else, and he added, "I asked if you understood, Sheriff."

Spencer opened his mouth, then closed it. He turned, and walked slowly down the steps, still blinking and looking very confused.

Through the partially open door, Quincannon heard the doctor chuckle while Garner muttered, "Well, I'll be a ring-tailed monkey!"

Dreamily, Lisa Boudreau purred, "I believe I'll keep that boy."

"You'd better," said Garner.

In the hall, Quincannon slid slowly to the floor, grinning like an idiot all the while.

Life was good.

Turn the page for a special preview of
Gunning for Regret,
available from Berkley Books in March 2001!

Dix Granger had yet to hit fifty, but just at that moment, with the storm-muted afternoon sun slanting across his craggy features, he looked like he was pushing sixty. Arizona did that to a man, Yancy Wade thought as he and Dix ambled slowly through the low, scrabbly, wind-blown growth on the canyon floor, looking for a trail that Yancy was solid sure they weren't going to find.

That picture of Dix hadn't been just a trick of the light. To Yancy, Dix looked old at night and in the morning, too. He looked, in fact, like he'd been tunneling for ore and using his face for the shovel and pick. His dark hair was only marginally shot through with gray, but wrinkles bracketed his mouth and his deep blue eyes, and cut furrows into the tanned leather hide of his neck and cheeks.

He didn't see so well, either, and he refused to wear glasses. That griped Yancy no end, for he knew Dix figured wearing specs would be admitting not a flaw so much as a weakness. Just plain silly, if you asked Yancy, but that was Dix. Silly, and mule-stubborn. As it was, Dix had squinted for so many years that when he slept and the wrin-

kles relaxed, white lines of secret flesh spun out from hi
eyes like spider webs.

Yancy figured that he'd go all spidery in the eyes, too.
if he waited around long enough. Too much beating sun
scorching his body, too many heat-shimmers in the distance. Too many dry howlers, like the ongoing storm that
had quieted some during the day, but which was gathering
again, gearing up to beat more gravel and grit into his face.
It made a fellow dizzy. It could kill him, in fact.

And that was before a man started tallying up the stickup
artists and bandidos and thimbleriggers and shootists and
back-stabbers that were around practically every rock.
Sooner or later, the worst ones headed for the wild places,
and that meant Arizona Territory.

Yancy supposed that when you were in the law business, the scare factor alone could put years on you.

Dix was the town sheriff twenty-some miles north, up
in Gushing Rain, Arizona Territory. Gushing Rain was south
of the Gila in the Estrella Mountains, and it was a place
Yancy figured had to have been christened by either a certified optimist or a certified lunatic, because it by-God sure
wasn't rainy, gushing or otherwise. It was a sleepy little
silver mining town—no big strikes, just slow and steady
dusty production—where not much ever happened.

Well, that wasn't exactly true. Yancy, who at twenty-
seven was more than two decades younger than Dix, and
who had signed on as Dix's deputy two years earlier, had
been shot exactly three times since Dix swore him in: once
in the arm, once in the shoulder, and once in a place he'd
rather not think about.

He'd also been beaten up twice, although one of those
beatings—by far, the lighter of the two—had come from
Dix himself.

He supposed he'd deserved it, after that stupid stunt he'd
pulled. He'd never pop up in Dix's line of fire again, that
was for sure! Dix had shot him square in the backside, and

hen, when he'd realized his deputy wasn't dead, Dix had
punched him in the jaw for pulling such a jackass stunt.

Yancy wasn't sure which was worse—the .44 slug in
his sitting parts or the broken jaw. He hadn't let it happen
again, though, no sir, and the two of them had brought in
Frank Wheeler.

Well, actually, Dix had brought in the both of them,
slung over their saddles like a couple of feed sacks with
legs. But where Frank Wheeler went straight to the undertaker's and into a pine box, Yancy spent the next few
days flat on his stomach, and the two weeks after that
sitting on a pillow.

It had been embarrassing as hell. Frustrating, too, par-
ticularly so because Doc Fedderson had wired his dad-
blasted teeth shut on account of the busted jaw, and he
couldn't even talk back to the wags that teased him, let
alone chew solid food.

Talking back and eating were Yancy's strong suits.

Dix, who was currently about forty feet out and searching the ground off Yancy's right shoulder, whoaed up his
horse and leaned down toward a hummock of brush.

Yancy stopped, too. "Got somethin' over there, Dix?"
he asked over the low whine of the wind.

Dix sat up straight in the saddle again. "Looks like."

That was all he said, and as usual Yancy had to prod
him for details. "Well, what is it?" he asked.

Dix didn't answer, just leaned over again and stared at
the ground. He shook his head.

"Line of Injun ponies pass through?" Yancy asked conversationally, shifting his weight in the saddle. He figured
somebody should talk, and he was the only one willing.
"Shod horses, Dix? Circus wagon? Mex bandits? Antelope?
Elephant? Quail track? Dove shit?"

"You're a card, Yancy," Dix said dryly, and he got down
off his horse. He bent over and lifted a branch. It came
away in his hand easily, with no sound other than a little
swish and crackle of leaves against leaves, barely heard

over the wind. Now that Yancy looked closer, he could tell
that the leaves were browning on their thorny stems. Somebody had cut that brush and piled it up.

"Aw, crud," he said under his breath, and he reined his
bay toward Dix's sorrel. "What is it?"

Dix stood up. "Malone's horse, I reckon."

The brush explained why they hadn't seen any buzzards.
"It dead?"

Dix swung back up into the saddle. "No, it just laid
down for a nap and decided to tuck itself in with hopseed
and creosote," he said dryly. He took out his spyglass and
began to scout the canyon's perimeter.

"Funny," said Yancy, who'd just been trying to make
conversation.

"Didn't mean to be," said Dix.

Cash Malone was on foot now, and he could be just
about anyplace. He'd robbed the bank in Gushing Rain the
day before, and Dix and Yancy had tracked him just fine
up until last night.

But then the wind had come up, and it blew and it blew,
adding another year to Dix's features and forcing grit and
grime into every crevice in Yancy's body. And any trace
of Cash Malone's trail had been blown south, to Mexico.

This morning, Yancy had been ready to head back to
town. There was no trail to follow after all, and they could
have been back in Gushing Rain in time for supper. He
could practically smell the beefsteak and fried onions at
Kendall's Café. Mrs. Kendall could char a slab of beef like
nobody else. Maybe she would've made a few dried-apple
pies, too. His mouth suddenly gushed saliva, and he swallowed.

But Dix? Not Dix. He wouldn't have any of it. The
peckerwood never took the easy—or sensible—way out of
anything. Which was why they were still out here, still
headed in the opposite direction from town, going farther
and farther south while Yancy got farther and farther away
from that steak and dried-apple pie.

"What you tryin' to do?" he muttered too softly for Dix to hear. "Give me the rickets?"

The wind had been soft and fairly steady all day, just enough to erase all but the most sheltered track, but now it was picking up again, getting ready for another mean blow. Clouds the color of dirty nickel had moved in to blanket the skies. A wind-blown piece of brush stung Yancy's cheek, and he swore under his breath. Now he was going to have to spend another night huddled in his blanket and cowering behind a rock, listening to a dry storm howl and bitch and thunder.

His head jerked when Dix said, "Got him," and collapsed his spyglass with a heavy *click*

Leave it to Dix to find a gol-darned needle in the hayloft.

"I'll be damned," Yancy muttered.

If Dix heard him, he gave no sign, only urged his gelding into a slow lope down the canyon. Yancy followed, the wind pushing at his back.

Now, frankly, he didn't expect Cash Malone to offer much resistance. He was just a kid, after all, and a piss-poor excuse for an outlaw if ever there was one. He'd struck the bank on exactly the wrong day, when the silver shipment had just gone out and the time lock on the safe had secured most of the town's money. He'd only made off with fifty some dollars from the teller's cash drawer, which was why Dix and Yancy were not exactly overwhelmed with posse.

In fact, nobody in town had been real upset. Yancy supposed the folks just figured Cash could have the money. He'd had hard times lately, and most everybody liked him. Everybody except Old Man Peterson, that was, and Old Man Peterson owned the bank.

They hadn't ridden far before Yancy began to make out what he supposed was Cash Malone. He went from a distant red speck to a running man in a red-checkered shirt pretty fast, though, and he didn't stop until Dix rode up beside him, leaned over, and grabbed a fistful of shirt.

Yancy stopped, too, but stayed back about ten paces. He had his Peacemaker out and leveled. Cash Malone was just a kid, and he was well-liked in town, as had been his ma and pa and baby sister before the smallpox took them. Cash probably wouldn't hurt a fly—at least, he hadn't hurt anybody at the bank and had said, "Thank you, Mr. Peabody" to the teller, real polite—but a man couldn't be too careful. At least, that's what Dix kept hammering into Yancy.

"Quit it, Cash!" Dix was shouting over the wind. It had come up a good bit in just the last few minutes. "You're caught! Just hold still!"

"Dang it, anyhow, Sheriff Granger!" Cash panted. He was played out, but still trying. "Dang it! I got no luck at all!"

"Quit jerkin' around!" said Dix. The boy was flopping like a catfish on the line.

"Aw, let him go, Dix," offered Yancy. "He's about to fall down, anyhow."

Dix let loose of the boy's collar, and Cash staggered back a couple feet before the wind pushed him over sideways into a weary sit. He stayed where he plopped, his chest heaving.

"Hands on top of your head, boy," Dix said over the blow, and stepped down. The wind was flipping his hat brim every which way, and he was holding it on with one hand as was Cash. Yancy supposed the order had been more habit than anything else, but Cash brought his other hand up anyway and planted it atop his hat.

Dix relieved him of an old Smith & Wesson pistol while Yancy watched, and then he pulled the boy to his feet and dragged him over to his horse. He looped his rope around Cash's waist.

Neither Cash nor Dix spoke. Yancy was full of questions, though, like what the hell were they going to do now with this wind whipping up mean like a bag full of badgers? But he kept his lips pressed tight together and his questions to himself, mostly to avoid taking in a mouth full of dust and grit.

When Dix remounted and motioned the prisoner out ahead of him at a march, Yancy tugged his bandanna up over his mouth and nose and silently followed.

Dix was going south again, farther away from Gushing Rain. Well, maybe Dix knew a place they could hole up, Yancy thought. In all of the time he'd deputied for Dix, he hadn't been down this way. Well, he'd been south of town, all right, but never this far. And this canyon was a new one for him. But Dix knew this part of the country like the back of his hand, and he probably knew a nice, snug cave.

Yancy closed the distance and rode off Dix's near side, one hand on his reins, one hand clamping his hat to his head, hoping for the best.

But within fifteen minutes, the sky had gone such a dirty yellow and so dark—and the air was so full of stinging dirt and gravel and blowing brush—that he could barely see fifteen feet in front of himself. And poor Cash was on foot, up ahead on Dix's tether, trying to fight the wind. He was bobbing and weaving so much that he looked for all the world like a cork float with a great big fish teasing at it.

Yancy brought his horse closer to Dix's flank, and shouted, "Cash Malone might have stole fifty dollars, but it don't seem to me that he deserves to get blown to hell and gone for it, and take two officers of the law along for company!"

Dix looked over and mouthed "What?" at him.

Yancy tried yelling louder. "You got a destination in mind?"

They both pulled up, for Cash had fallen. While he struggled against the wind to regain his feet, Dix shouted, "Give over your guns!"

It was Yancy's turn to shout "What?" He couldn't have heard Dix right.

But Dix slapped his holster and shouted, "Guns!" again and motioned to Cash, and Yancy finally figured out what he wanted.

Yancy handed over his Peacemaker and his rifle. Then, the wind howling in his ears, he eased his horse a few feet ahead. He leaned over toward Cash Malone and shouted through his bandanna, "Take your rope off!"

Cash looked at him quizzically, and Yancy jabbed a finger toward the rope. "Off!" he yelled again. "Take it off and climb up!"

Cash worked the knot free. Behind them, Dix reeled in his rope while Cash shoved a foot in Yancy's stirrup and climbed aboard.

"See what a mess you got us into?" Yancy called over his shoulder. "Nice kid like you, sticking up Old Man Peterson's bank! You're barely eighteen! Got your whole life ahead!"

Cash made no answer.

"Just don't go tryin' nothin' funny," Yancy continued. He could hardly hear himself for the wind. It milked tears from his eyes, filled them with dust, then blew them away. "Dix is watchin', and he's armed enough for three men!"

"Where we goin', Deputy Wade?" Cash shouted back at him as they began to move once more through an afternoon that had become as black as night, an impossible afternoon full of the howl of harsh, roaring wind and pelting grit and gravel and twigs.

"A place Dix knows," Yancy called back. At least, he hoped Dix knew where in tarnation he was leading them.

It looked to Yancy like they were going straight into the mouth of hell.

No one knows the American West better.

JACK BALLAS

☐ *THE HARD LAND*

0-425-15519-6/$5.99

☐ *BANDIDO CABALLERO*

0-425-15956-6/$5.99

☐ *GRANGER'S CLAIM*

0-425-16453-5/$5.99

The Old West in all its raw glory.